I'VE LOVED THESE DAYS

The Abigail Phelps Series
Book One

D1523912

BETHANY TURNER

http://www.abbyphelps.com

The Abigail Phelps Series
(*I've Loved These Days, Scenes From Highland Falls, Two Thousand Years*)
is a work of fiction. The characters and events portrayed in this book are, in many
cases, *not* fictitious.
Any similarity to real persons, living or dead, is anything but a coincidence, and is most
likely completely intended by the author. But only if their name is printed.
The author is not sneaky about it.

Anything apart from the absolute facts, which can be researched through any internet
search engine (Because the internet only produces facts, right?), originates from the
imagination of the author.
The author has developed this work of fiction based on preconceived ideas in the
public consciousness.

But it is fiction nonetheless.

Reality is in the eye of the beholder.

Abigail Phelps Series Website: www.abbyphelps.com
Bethany Turner Author Website: www.seebethanywrite.com

Turner, Bethany, 1979-
I've Loved These Days: a novel / by Bethany Turner. - 2nd ed.

ISBN-10: 1500504920
ISBN-13: 978-1500504922

For <u>my</u> First Three - Kelly, Ethan, and Noah.

With special thanks to my muse, Billy Joel.

CONTENTS

March 17, 1994

Dear Mrs. Onassis,

It was such a lovely gift to receive your letter. I did receive some advance notice that it was on its way, of course, but I can't tell you how touched I was when it showed up in my mailbox. I'm so very sorry that your health is as it is and, as is often the case in life, I wish we didn't wait for dire circumstances to force us into conversations which should have taken place years ago. And I want to apologize for my share of that blame.

The twelve years since you and I last spoke have not been without their challenges, have they? I'm not certain, however, that I can agree with your assertion that all of the difficulties between John and myself stem from that day. Truthfully, they go back further, and I shoulder the responsibility. Be that as it may, he and I are in a good place now, and I can't ask for more than the friendship we have developed. It's the most important of my life.

And then there are your other assertions, which I wish I could deny. I wish I could laugh about how far off-track you are, but of course I can't. You're absolutely right. He knows it and I know it, though I really had no idea that you knew it as well. I shouldn't be surprised, I suppose. He always said you knew from the very first day – which is why you gave him the ring. That very first time you met me you knew that he would never be the same again, didn't you?

For the record, I was never the same again either. And while times have changed and opportunities have been lost, I still know in my heart of hearts that I never will be. But we can't go back, and we can't undo. What's more, I don't really want to. While my life is not perfect, it is uniquely, ridiculously mine, and I would not trade it.

So, put away the regret. I have. It didn't take me long to discover that it didn't do me any good, and it didn't do him any good. But thank you. Thank you for acknowledging that you wish it had gone a different way – there's nothing wrong with that, is there? And while I don't regret, I'm not too proud to admit that yes, I wish some things had gone a different way as well.

Please take care of yourself. Relish these days, surrounded by your friends and your family and your books, and the people and things that you love. And please know that my affection for you remains strong. You never said an unkind word to me, and I thank you for that.

And yes, don't worry - I promise to take care of him for you.

With sincere affection,
Abby Phelps

FROM THE DESK OF DR. ALEC B. REDMOND
Cedar Springs Hospital
Colorado Springs, CO

When I first laid eyes on Abigail Phelps, she was being restrained by two large orderlies on the day of her admission to Cedar Springs Hospital in Colorado Springs, Colorado. I'm not sure I know just what it was that stood out for me. It might have been her tears, which were laced with fear and anger, but were made up predominately of sadness, or it may have been her frustrated insistence that Senator Edward Kennedy was to blame for all that was wrong with her life.

As of that day in early 2002, I had been a consulting psychiatrist at Cedar Springs for more than fifteen years. My position at the hospital, a state-funded psychiatric facility, is such that I can choose the cases and the patients which interest me, and delegate every other case to a doctor with less seniority. Abigail was an easy diagnosis. The notes on her chart stated severe bipolar disorder, but after two minutes of watching her struggle before being sedated, I knew she was actually suffering from mixed type delusional disorder. She felt threatened, which could have been a symptom of any number of disorders, were it not for the fact that she believed the threatening force to be the senior U.S. Senator from Massachusetts.

I looked over her chart, and I looked into her eyes, and I knew she was my patient. Any third-year resident could have handled the case, but for whatever reason, I felt instantly protective of her and I wanted to see the case through. I began meeting with her the following morning, and we met regularly after that. We broke through the delusions of grandeur and fear and abandonment in record time as she allowed me to peel away the layers and discover the real Abigail underneath.

It didn't take much time at all to realize that Abigail didn't need round-the-clock care. She was a danger to no one, not even herself, and she was a fully functional, independent woman. She needed therapy, and lots of it. That much was clear. She did not, however, need to be locked away in a facility for acute mental and behavioral conditions. So why was she there? She had been admitted against her will – that would have been obvious without access to her chart – but in our daily sessions she made it very clear to me that she had no family, very few friends.

Our breakthrough came about when I told her, point blank, that I knew Senator Kennedy was not responsible for her situation, and that deep inside she knew it too. I told her that I knew she didn't want to be there, and that I could help her, but she would have to start telling me the truth about her life. Our work together had to be based on trust.

That reached her, and she began to allow me access to her real life. She was alone in the world, she confessed. Her parents died years ago, she was an only child, and she never married, or even had a serious relationship. There are thousands of technical terms I could use to explain to you Abigail's diagnosis, or rather the root of her disorder, but it basically came down to two things which I believed to be true: Abigail Phelps was bored and she was lonely.

The initial delusions revolved around the Senator, but as she and I formed a stronger connection of trust, and as more and more of the real Abigail came out in our sessions, she confided additional delusions. In each story she told, she had an exciting career, famous friends, plenty of wealth, and always love. Love is more often than not the common thread of delusional disorders, so that came as no surprise.

After a couple of weeks meeting with her daily at

Cedar Springs, where she was still under continual surveillance, I ordered her discharge. She would return home, return to her life, but still meet with me regularly – at least once a week, sometimes more often. I sent her with homework, if you will, which I wanted her to have ready for me the next time we saw each other. My treatment plan for Abigail centered on my belief that the key was not to make her delusions go away, but to help her realize that they were simply figments of her imagination. I encouraged her to write the delusions down in story form, and then she could visit them when she chose, but they would be disassociated from her own life. They would be as meaningful to her as any other work of fiction she enjoyed. This is a device I have used with dozens of patients, and the results have been overwhelmingly successful. She was to start slowly, and by our first session, I wanted her to have an outline of one story she had previously chosen to view as reality.

I have been Abigail's therapist for more than seven years now, and for seven years we have dealt with the delusions as fiction, and we have discussed them as if we were members of a private book club. In the meantime, Abigail has lived her life. Though I should never confess this, Abigail Phelps is my favorite patient. She is intelligent and kind and understanding of my methods, and she is always a willing participant in whichever course of treatment I choose. I look forward to our sessions, as does she, I believe. Nevertheless, after years of regular therapy, Abigail had progressed to the extent that I was beginning to feel her weekly sessions were no longer a necessity.

The very session during which I intended to convey that determination to Abigail, she informed me that she had put her isolated stories of delusion together into a book. I opened my mouth to commend her for taking the exercise a step further and for being healthy enough to take on such a task when she dropped the bombshell. Not only had she pieced the stories together into a cohesive work of literature, she had sought and attained publication, she said.

I asked to read her book, and she consented. Inside

the sanctuary of our sessions, the delusions had been transformed into generic stories of someone, somewhere, living an extraordinarily fascinating life. Suddenly, in Abigail's latest literary exercise, the delusions seemed to have become delusions once more. She wrote in first person of love and loss and adventure and fame and heartache. Abigail Phelps had written her delusional memoirs.

That evening, I read a good portion of what she had written. I read in sadness and disappointment, and I didn't want to put the book down because I kept hoping that on the next page, or the next, or the next, some sign that she knew it was all madness would come shining through. But I also read in fascination. I had heard many of Abigail's tales before, but I was amazed that she had somehow pieced them all together into the story of one extraordinary life. The characters were as rich as you could hope for in any novel, and yet most of them were real people - celebrities - known to us all. As I read, I initially fact-checked everything, easy enough to do with any internet search engine, and I made notes of the many - countless perhaps - distortions of the truth Abigail included. But the more I read, the less fact-checking I did, simply because I got caught up in the story.

When Abigail and I met again the following week at our scheduled time, I set about getting to the bottom of the question of publication. She was extremely forthcoming, as she had always been with me, and she even gave me the name and contact information of the woman she said was her publisher.

Her name was J. Avery Brennan, and I called her immediately after my session with Abigail, with Abigail's permission. With a signed confidentiality waiver from my patient in my hand, I arranged to meet with Ms. Brennan at her New York City office the following day. I wanted to protect Abigail, and I wanted to make sure that her disorder was not being exploited for someone else's gain.

Any questions I had were multiplied as I arrived at the address I had been given, and I discovered that Ms. Brennan's office was not at a publishing house, or even a private office suite, but in the faculty offices at the Graduate Center of the City University of New York, well known as CUNY. I quickly set about my business of making sure that Ms. Brennan was not taking advantage of Abigail, but I was surprised to discover that Ms. Brennan agreed to meet with me that day so that she could put to rest her own fears for Abigail, or Abby as she called her. In the process, Avery Brennan and I formed an alliance of sorts, centered on the protection, and I suppose liberation, of Abigail Phelps.

What I learned that day, or rather what I began to learn that day, not only shook me to my core, it changed my life. What I had known to be fact was, in some cases, revealed to be nothing more than an intricate web of lies, and things which couldn't possibly possess an ounce of truth actually held the keys to the world's best kept secrets. But I will say no more of it now. Instead, I will direct you to Abigail's story and invite you, as Avery invited me, to go along on the journey. Some notes I wrote as I first read what was written, including initial fact-checking, have been added for clarification and, occasionally, to help keep you grounded. Or perhaps I was just attempting to keep myself grounded.

When the fact-checking ends, rest assured that does not imply that facts aren't out there and readily available, or that what you are reading has any real truth to it at all. Although, as you'll soon discover, you don't really know what is true and what isn't. I encourage you to do the fact-checking yourself if you care to, and you will most likely be intrigued and amazed, as I was, that the line between reality and delusion is quite often blurry, at best. Of course, you may get to a point, as I did, when you will make the conscious decision to disregard the facts and instead get lost in Abigail's interpretation of the facts. It is a journey, and I hope you will approach it that way. Get absorbed in the characters and the situations, the love and the loss. Above all, keep in mind the lesson which Abigail taught me: reality is in the eye of the beholder.

Kind regards and best wishes,
Dr. Alec B. Redmond

1. MY LIFE

This book is primarily about relationships. It's no secret that I have been in some fairly high-profile romantic relationships, and those will certainly be discussed, much to the relief and satisfaction of many of you, I'm guessing. But it's not just the romantic relationships...it's the friendships. Truth be told, I think my greatest friendships are what make my life interesting to all of you. My "inner circle," which has been the subject of many a tabloid headline ("Really? Just Friends?", "George and Abby Go Ring Shopping!", and my personal favorite: "Abby and the Boys Joined Together In Five-Way Commitment Ceremony") is made up of a few very rich, very attractive, and very famous men. That fact has led people to believe that I am a gold-digging, fame-seeking nymphomaniac. Sadly, no. If only that were true...instant bestseller!

The truth is, like so many other things in my life - though for some reason people refuse to believe it - simple. I am not a gold digger. I have had more financial success in my life than I ever could have imagined, but it's never really meant much to me. I live a comfortable life, but not one of excess. I am not a fame-seeker. I have more fame than I know what to do with, and while there have certainly been perks to the fame at times, it is not without its challenges. And I am not a nymphomaniac. Just keep reading for proof on that front.

The truth is my life is one of fame. How do you meet your friends? At work? Well, quite often so do I. I just happen to work with people who are maybe a little more well-known than your friends. That's just the way it is.

Much has been made of my First Three, as I call them - the three guys who have made up my most famous friendships. I met the First Three before I was much of a celebrity at all, more than thirty years ago - and I met them at a party, at an airport, and tripping over tree roots, respectively. Nothing glamorous about that.

Okay, so you may wonder why they are all men. Well, I don't know! I didn't plan it. Again, that's just the way it is. I guess I communicate a little more easily with men, but don't ask me why. That's a question for my therapist, I suppose.

[FROM THE DESK OF DR. ALEC B. REDMOND Well, what do you know? I made an appearance. In all seriousness, Abigail does seem to relate better to men. I noticed this on her second day at Cedar Springs. It's not that she has issues with women, she just doesn't seem to know how to be as natural with them. I noted this to be true in the way she related to patients as well as doctors and staff. For some time, I held the belief that there may have been some abuse or neglect which resulted in the tendency, but none was ever uncovered.]

I have been through things with my guys which have bonded us for life. And yes, some of those friendships began as a romantic relationship – or at least many of them were romantic relationships at some point. That's no big secret, though. For instance, everyone knows that Tom Hanks and I went out on one less-than-stellar blind date in early 1988. He was cute, and a rising star on the verge of taking over Hollywood, but I wasn't attracted to him. He would later say the same about me. Actually, what he said was, "She was cute as a button, sweet, funny…and I couldn't wait for the date to end." In all fairness (to me!), Tom had just gotten divorced, and his head wasn't really in the dating game. And I was madly in love with someone else. There was no romantic chemistry whatsoever, which has made our on-screen chemistry, which we apparently have in spades, quite the mystery.

But without that disastrous date, about which I'll

probably go into more detail later, Tom and I wouldn't be the great friends we are today. I definitely have carried some great friendships out of failed romantic encounters, Tom being just one of several. Without a doubt, though, there is one friendship which seems to interest people the most. I never used to understand why people were so intrigued, but I think I finally figured it out.

My best guess is that no one can believe we have never slept together. Well, it's true. George Clooney and I have never been romantically involved. At all. Not even a little. Through rough patches and dry spells, I've had Clooney by my side, closer to me than anyone, and yet we've never even given a serious thought to being more than the closest of friends. He's been married and divorced, he's dated, and dated, and dated...and I am the constant. I've been married and married...engaged a couple of times in there...and he is the constant. No one seems to understand that. But to George and me, there's nothing to understand.

I grew up and attended high school in Florence, Kentucky, just across the Ohio River from Cincinnati, Ohio. Just forty-five miles away in Augusta, Kentucky lived a future Sexiest Man Alive - but I assure you, the word "sexy" did not come to mind when I first laid eyes on him. It was April of 1978. I had just turned seventeen years old in March; George was sixteen until May. I had begun to have a fair amount of success as an amateur figure skater on the junior circuit. In fact, I was just transitioning to the senior level, preparing to compete in the U.S. Figure Skating Championships for the first time in 1979. As you can imagine, I was fairly big news in Northern Kentucky.

[FROM THE DESK OF DR. ALEC B. REDMOND Here Abigail has introduced one new theme and one recurring one. Kentucky is new. Never in our many years of meeting together has she ever mentioned being from Kentucky, or ever visiting, or even having a desire to. She grew up in Colorado Springs, where she still resides. In fact, I don't believe she has ever been far from home. However, figure skating is a regular theme. Many of her delusions have cast her as a figure skater, or in love with a figure skater. I once asked her what it was about figure skating which fascinated her so much, and she said,

"To be that much in control of your body and your muscles and your brain, and yet know that you aren't really in control at all...isn't that what life is all about?"]

I was chosen to be one of the honorees at Cincinnati's 1978 Athletes of the Year event. That was a huge deal for me. There I was with Pete Rose, Johnny Bench, and other now-legendary members of the Cincinnati Reds. I'm sure there were other athletes being honored as well, but I don't remember them. I just remember Pete and Johnny. I wasn't (and I'm still not) much of a Reds fan, which of course made me an outcast in the days of the Big Red Machine. But I was, and am, a baseball fan, and those guys were famous all over the world - just imagine if you lived in the Greater Cincinnati area. The master of ceremonies for the evening was Cincinnati's most famous newsman, Nick Clooney. Nick had always been on the television in my home growing up. He was the journalist my parents trusted - the Walter Cronkite of our little part of the world.

[FROM THE DESK OF DR. ALEC B. REDMOND Abigail has done her research, and has interestingly blended fantasy and reality. The level of iconic superstardom which accompanies Pete, Johnny, and the Big Red Machine is of course completely accurate. The Clooneys are from Northern Kentucky, and Nick Clooney was in fact a legendary newsman in the area. What's more, Abigail is an avid baseball fan. The subject of baseball was one of the first through which she and I connected. I am originally from Chicago, and a lifelong Cubs devotee. For some reason, Abigail insists on complete, unabashed loyalty to the New York Mets. Be that as it may, I can find no indication that any such Athletes of the Year event took place, and it goes without saying that if it did, Ms. Phelps was not an honoree.]

My mother went with me to the awards that evening, mostly hoping to meet Nick Clooney's wife, Nina. Nina is a former Miss Kentucky and, as my mother said, "always made herself up like she cared." I think that was a subtle encouragement for me to learn something from Mrs. Clooney. I never wore makeup, and I dressed in what was comfortable. Meanwhile, Nina always looked like Miss Kentucky. She still does! My mother may have been hoping that we would meet Nina, and that Nina would take me under her wing and turn me into the beautiful swan my mother knew I could be, but Nick Clooney's companion for the evening was not at all what we had expected.

Young George Clooney accompanied his dad to the event that evening simply to meet the Reds. He spent the entire evening hanging on every word that one or the other of them said. I noticed him immediately and constantly - he was the goofiest boy I had ever seen. He had too much hair, his eyes were too big for his head, and he was just a skinny thing, but what really caught my attention was how he seemed like he belonged there. He possessed a confidence I couldn't even dream of having at that age. He was meeting his heroes (the heroes of every Kentucky boy in 1978) and he didn't seem out of place at all. I, on the other hand, had no idea what I was doing. I was ready to go home from the moment we walked through the door. That must have been obvious. George glanced my way as he was laughing at a story Ken Griffey was telling, and he smiled. It wasn't a flirty smile, or a snide or insulting smile like many teenage boys would have given an uncomfortable teenage girl. It was a smile which said, "Relax. You belong here just as much as I do." I saw all of that in that smile, and I was able to relax - a bit.

Whenever I could do so without being spotted, I watched George for the rest of the evening. I wasn't interested in him as a boyfriend. I had no time for dating anyway - I trained eight hours every day and I was finishing high school. I wasn't allowed to home-school because my parents believed that if I trained so much that I didn't have time for school, then I trained too much. So unlike almost every other serious skater in the world, I attended classes at my local public high school.

But George fascinated me. I knew that I wanted to be more like that awkward, gangly son of Nick and Nina Clooney. With all the courage I could muster, I went to him and said hello.

"Hi. You're Nick Clooney's son, right?"

"And you're Abigail Phelps."

"You know who I am?" I asked in disbelief.

"Sure I do. Part of the reason I came was to meet you."

I laughed loudly. "Are you kidding me? I've been watching you all night. You came to meet Johnny Bench and Pete Rose."

He smiled that smile again and I have to admit it was pretty irresistible, even then. "I like figure skating. Well," he clarified, "I like *your* figure skating. I like when you jump." And then I realized he was trying not to laugh.

"What's so funny?" I suddenly felt like he was making fun of me, and I could feel my cheeks getting warm. "Are you putting down figure skating? Oh, let me guess," I said as I crossed my arms. "You don't think it's a real sport. You think that what I do is easy and not athletic at all, just because I do it to music while wearing a skirt. Right?" I shot him an icy stare which I hoped said, "Don't mess with me."

George continued to smile, but he looked a little less confident. "No, that's not it at all. It looks really hard. I just like when you jump because when you jump you look happy. Sometimes when you are moving around on the ice and stuff, you look like you are concentrating really hard, but it's weird because you look like you relax and really start having fun right before you jump. I never understand that. To me, it looks like that would be the part you need to be worried about."

George held my eye contact, daring me to stay mad, challenging me to keep my guard up - and I couldn't.

"That's the only thing I'm good at," I muttered.

"What?" George was leaning in closer to hear me.

"Jumping. That's the only thing I'm good at. I do feel happy when I jump. When I jump, I'm in charge. When I jump, I'm the best skater in the world." I realized immediately how ridiculous and conceited that sounded, but I meant it.

George told me later that was the moment he knew we would be friends. He kept staring at me - at the time I had no idea why. I began to feel incredibly self-conscious and I just wanted to go away, and yet I didn't. But I did have to break through the silence.

"So are you going to answer my question? Are you Nick Clooney's kid or aren't you?"

George smiled at me. "I am. I'm George. And you *are* Abigail Phelps, right?" After the conversation we had just had, the question was hilarious.

I laughed. "I am. But please call me Abby. I'm only Abigail in grown-up situations."

"Well then," George said just loudly enough for me to hear, smiling as he winked at me, "that settles it. You'll always be Abby to me."

George and I hung out together for the rest of the evening - telling each other everything there was to know, and laughing like crazy. The event became much more enjoyable, and time began to fly. Before I knew it, it was over. We said our goodbyes, exchanged phone numbers, and promised to stay in touch. And stay in touch we did. The first time George called was less than twelve hours later. I was the one to answer the phone when it rang, since I was the only one awake.

"Hello?" I answered incredulously, wondering who in the world would be calling at 5:00 in the morning.

"What are you doing up?"

I knew instantly that it was George, and I smiled as warm memories from the previous evening flooded in. "Well, I had to get up to answer the phone."

"I know that's not true. You were already up. You have to be at the ice rink at 5:45. But nice try."

I was impressed that he had been paying attention. "All right then, what are *you* doing up?"

"Well, I woke up feeling like I was forgetting something, and then I remembered what it was, and I wanted to catch you before you left your house."

He had my attention. "What did you forget?"

"My prom is tonight."

I started laughing. "I don't know what's more ridiculous - the fact that you forgot about your prom, or the fact that you called me at 5:00 a.m. to tell me that you had remembered. Seriously, George, you don't just forget your prom. People put a lot of thought and planning into it."

I could hear the smile in his voice. "Well, you see, the problem is…I don't have a date. I was going to just go by myself, with a buddy of mine, actually, but then he went and got a date, and it would be weird to go totally by myself, so I was wondering if you would go with me. I could pick you up really early, if you could get out of school early, and skip a little bit of skating time tonight, and we could grab a bite to eat in Cincinnati and then head back here, and then my mom said you could stay in my sister Ada's room tonight - she's away at college - and then I could take you home in the morning. Will you please?"

Still to this day, when George asks for a favor, he tends to speak in long sentences without taking a breath.

I didn't ask him if it was a date or if we were just going as friends. I didn't have to ask. George and I have never had any uncertainty as to what our relationship is. Even then, the day after we met, it was clear and easy.

"Sure, I'll go. But you have to do a favor for me, too."

"Name it."

"You'll have to go with me to *my* prom. I just remembered mine is next weekend."

We laughed so hard about us both forgetting our proms, and from then on, we laughed hard about everything.

[FROM THE DESK OF DR. ALEC B. REDMOND As strange as it may sound, the Phelps/Clooney friendship somehow makes sense to me. Of course there is no truth to it, but as I read the chapter, I saw much of Abigail's actual sense of humor shine through. Her true sense of humor seems to mirror, at the very least, the public perception of George Clooney's sense of humor - dry, sarcastic, goofy, never taking himself too seriously, and yet extremely intelligent. The question I'm interested in exploring with Abigail is whether Clooney was selected because she identifies with his personality, or if she has adopted her sense of humor to mirror that of her fictional best friend.]

2. A MINOR VARIATION

About seven months after my two proms, in November of 1978, I received a phone call which was even more unexpected than the one from George.

"Good afternoon, Miss Phelps. This is Franklin Jensen with the United States Figure Skating Association. May I have a moment of your time?"

This was it. I knew it was the moment when I would get thrown out of figure skating. Doggone…just when I was starting to get the hang of it, too. "Yes, sir. Of course."

Mr. Jensen got right to the point. "You're going to get a call in just a few moments from Sven Bengtsson. Mr. Bengtsson is the president-elect of the International Skating Union. He's going to ask you to do something that, frankly, will seem like something you shouldn't be allowed to do. He wants you to team up with an ice dancer from Great Britain. You can keep competing for the U.S. in singles skating, if you like, but I know that may create a ridiculous amount of work for you. So if you don't want to, that's fine too. You've done well and you should be proud of yourself. You don't have to accept his offer, of course, but I can't see any reason why you would want to pass on this opportunity, can you?"

I'm sorry…WHAT? "Umm…I don't know…" I stammered.

"President-Elect Bengtsson will be calling soon, so you should probably have your answer ready."

"Mr. Jensen, can I ask you a question?" There were countless questions running through my mind, but he didn't seem like the kind of man who would be patient enough to answer them all, so I would have to settle on one. How would this work? Would we compete for the United States or Great Britain? Actually, would we be able to compete at all? Of course not - this had to just be some exhibition thing. So I would be expected to give up everything I had worked so hard for, give up the dream of the Olympics, so that I could put on a show with some British guy?

Mr. Jensen sighed and, as sweetly as he could muster, said, "Of course, dear."

I asked the question which mattered most of all: "Why me?"

"Well, you are a young skater who shows a lot of promise. You're very entertaining, and getting better all the time. President-Elect Bengtsson wants to begin his term with a real international symbol of solidarity. He asked which American up-and-coming skater I would recommend, and I thought instantly of you." My head was about to explode with pride. I really was headed somewhere, I allowed myself to think for the briefest of moments. But Mr. Jensen continued, "You're talented, but you've probably gone as far as you can go. We don't really have anything invested in you, so we can indulge the president-elect in his experiment, at no real cost to the USFSA. It's a win-win."

"I see," I replied, the wind knocked out of me. The United States Figure Skating Association was writing me off. They were looking at this as a silly endeavor, and if they had to contribute a skater to it, they wanted it to be one who wasn't going to advance anyway. And that skater was me.

I think we said goodbye and hung up the phone after that. I couldn't really tell you with certainty, as I was in a daze, but I came to again with the shrill ring of the rotary phone.

Mr. Bengtsson was very pleasant. His thick Swedish dialect would have been charming had I not just had all of my hopes and dreams pulled out from under me. I tried to listen to all he said with an open mind, but ice dancing? All I knew about ice dancing was that ice dancers don't jump.

The words I had said to George came back and hit me like a ton of bricks. "Jumping. That's the only thing I'm good at. I do feel happy when I jump. When I jump, I'm in charge. When I jump, I'm the best skater in the world." Gone.

"Mr. Bengtsson, this is really important to you, isn't it?"

"Why, yes. It will be very good for figure skating. Maybe very good for the world!" I thought he was getting a little ahead of himself with that one.

"If I say no, do you have anyone else lined up?"

"Well, no, actually. The USFSA hasn't found anyone else with…" He paused, no doubt trying to decide how to say it tactfully. "The right amount of talent." The right amount, meaning not enough. Yes, very tactful indeed.

"Okay then, I will do it. Under one condition." What did I have to lose?

"If it is mine to grant, then any request will be honored."

"I want to have the option to compete. I don't care if it's for the United States or for Great Britain." The way my own country had just done away with me, I was leaning towards Great Britain. "If this guy and I are any good, we can compete just like everyone else. That's what I want. If you want me to do it, that's what you'll have to give me." I have no idea where my courage came from in that moment, and it didn't escape me that if he said no, I had most likely thrown away any future in figure skating.

"That would be very difficult to do, Miss Phelps. You are a citizen of the United States, your partner will be a citizen of Great Britain. Nothing like this has ever been done."

"Well, Mr. Bengtsson," I challenged, "isn't that the point?"

There was a long pause. Much longer than I was

comfortable with.

Finally, he spoke. "The odds of you being good enough to compete at any serious level..."

"Astronomical, I know. This is almost certainly going to be a moot point anyway, but I want to know that the option is there." I could tell I didn't quite have him convinced, and I was going to have to do better than that. "You see, sir...since the chances are so slim, you really have nothing to lose. But think of how interesting it would be to people. Think of the advantages."

"Advantages?" he asked, his tone betraying the fact that his interest was piqued.

"Oh yes. I'm fairly well-liked, you know - with my limited talent." I swallowed my pride, but it sure didn't go down smoothly. "I make the perfect underdog. And now, with all of this added to it: trying to learn how to ice dance, trying to get along with a partner who, as of now, I've never met, dealing with the inevitable challenges and limited time training together... You know I don't have a chance of making it. I know that as well. But the people, well, they love cheering for the underdog, don't they?" I went in for the kill. "I just can't help but think of all the wonderful attention that it would bring to your fantastic diplomatic initiative."

Sven sighed. "Would you consider a dual citizenship?"

"Absolutely." I spoke impulsively, having not the faintest idea what that involved.

Another excruciating pause.

"Yes, yes. You obtain dual citizenship, and you train to the point of being good enough to compete by International Skating Union standards, and you do all of this before you are too old to compete - let's face it, Miss Phelps, you are rather advanced in years to be starting anew in a discipline, with a partner for the first time - then, yes. I will see to it that you are eligible to compete. I give you my word." He sounded exasperated, and yet I knew that as far as he was concerned, he had given away nothing. He was completely confident that he would never have to deal with my pesky little request.

I, on the other hand, felt the growing fire within me - the flame which had been all but extinguished just a few moments prior. It was suddenly back with a vengeance.

"Well then, you have yourself a deal."

The next three months were spent taking care of business. Thankfully, I didn't have to go through with the dual citizenship. My friend Sven found another way. He named 1979 the International Skating Union's "Year of Peace" and opened a limited window in which any eligible skater from any ISU nation could file an application to skate with any eligible skater from any other ISU nation. He announced the opportunity on January 1, 1979. Applications had to be received by 12:00 p.m. GMT on January 3rd. Needless to say, I was the only skater with an application ready to go, and a partner picked out and prepared to join me in my intercontinental endeavor.

His name: Christopher Dean. We had yet to speak, or even see a photo of each other. We did each write one letter, introducing ourselves and saying how much we were looking forward to working together. I couldn't help but wonder if he was lying as much as I was.

[FROM THE DESK OF DR. ALEC B. REDMOND This is the first instance in which Abigail basically puts herself in someone else's shoes. Christopher Dean is an actual ice dancer from Great Britain, and a rather legendary one at that. In the late 1970's he was competing as an amateur ice dancer, but his partner was not, obviously, Abigail Phelps. Jayne Torvill filled that role. Torvill and Dean are still considered to be the greatest ice dancers of all time. Sorry, Jayne Torvill - in Abigail's version of history, I suppose you never existed. I am extremely curious as to what any of this represents. There have been several red flags upon which I have zeroed in - being forced into a life for which she has no affinity, feelings of unworthiness, being made to see herself as a disappointment... There is something there.]

The other business I took care of in those three months was training harder than I ever had before. I got stronger, my jumps got higher, and my spins got faster. Occasionally George would show up to watch me practice. I think he knew that it would be the only time we would have together. I was determined to show them all. My confidence had taken such a beating, and I didn't know if I would ever truly recover.

I was certain that I would never be a top competitive skater, but if I could just make a respectable run for it, the USFSA and the ISU would have to admit I had exceeded their expectations. I would settle for that. When the time came for Chris and me to finally meet, I was a fierce machine of a skater - more mature, less carefree, and maybe a bit too jaded.

We were to make our debut at the 1979 World Figure Skating Championships in Vienna. We wouldn't be competing, of course - that was a dream that I had said goodbye to, and I had tried to come to terms with that goodbye in the three months prior. No one should have to say goodbye to their dreams at seventeen years old.

My parents accompanied me to Austria, and George insisted on driving us to the airport. When we got there, my parents headed to the ticket counter to give me a moment to say goodbye to my best friend.

"So what are you going to do while you're there?" He began nonchalantly, giving no indication of the lecture which had been building up inside of him for weeks and was about to break free.

"Meet Christopher, of course. And find a rink to work in."

"No," he replied sharply.

"What? No, what?"

He was obviously frustrated with me but I didn't understand why. "You're going to Vienna, Abby. How many times do you get a chance to do something like this, especially with someone else footing the bill? Why don't you and your folks tour the city? Eat fattening food. Strudel, right? Isn't that what they have there? Seriously, you never eat enough. Go for it. And get some sleep. Do what you need to do with the British guy, and then just have some fun and get some rest."

I laughed, certain he was joking. "George, you know I can't do that. I can't afford to lose that much training time. And I certainly can't afford to gain weight!"

"I'm worried about you." He was convinced I had

19

an eating disorder, I think. I didn't. I ate - maybe not quite enough some days, but only because I was busy. Besides, a skater's weight always has to be maintained - more than ever now that I would have a partner lifting me.

"Well, you shouldn't be. I'm fine." I stared at him as if willing him to believe it, but I didn't believe it - why would he? I didn't have an eating disorder, but I wasn't fine. George and I had gotten so close in the eleven months since we met and we knew everything about each other. We were closer to each other than to anyone else in the world. What made me think I could keep anything from him? I realized I couldn't, and I lost it.

I began to cry, and then I began to sob - big, heaving sobs. All of the tension, stress, sadness, and hurt that I had been keeping inside, and that I only released in the form of salchows and loops and axels on the ice, all bubbled over. George didn't seem surprised. In fact, I think it was exactly what he wanted to happen. He pulled me into his arms and stroked my hair and just let me get it all out.

"I wish I could go with you. I'd make sure you have a good time."

I blubbered out my reply, "It's hard to imagine ever having a good time again. I hate this."

"I know you do," he said sweetly, "but I don't understand why."

I pulled away from him and looked at him as if I'd never seen him before, or at least I wondered if he had ever seen me before. "How can you not understand? This has ruined my life. Everything I have worked so hard for, they just threw it out the window. Don't you see that? I should have been competing at this World Championship, not going to meet my mail order partner. And now I don't ever get to experience my dream. Ice dancing? Seriously? Do you know what ice dancing is, George? It's dancing on the ice. Really, that's it. How stupid is that!?"

George reached over and wiped the tears from my cheeks, then leaned in and tenderly kissed me on the forehead. "You're going to hate me for saying this, but you need to hear it. If it wasn't for this whole stupid ice dancing thing, you wouldn't be going to these World Championships at all, and you know it. It's easy now to look back and say you were destined for greatness, and it was just around the corner, and the only thing standing in your way was high school. But you only liked to jump. And I loved to watch you jump, don't get me wrong. But, from what I know, just jumping isn't really enough to take you to the top."

I was crushed again.

"Go to hell, George."

With that, I picked up my suitcases and stormed off to meet my parents at the gate. George didn't follow me. I'm sure he knew it wouldn't do any good, and he had said his piece. But he did yell after me, "I'm your biggest fan, Abby Phelps. You know that."

I didn't reply, I didn't turn, I didn't stop.

3. YOU LOOK SO GOOD TO ME

I cried myself to sleep on the plane to Vienna. How dare he? He was supposed to be my best friend, and yet I felt that he had been so cold and unfeeling to me. He didn't think I was good enough to make it on my own? Whether that was true or not, I certainly didn't feel that it was right for him to say it.

But *was* it true?

Right about the time that thought entered my mind was when I dozed off. I must have been awake when we changed planes in New York, but I have no real recollection of it. My next clear memory is of landing in Vienna. I must have been exhausted, which of course made me involuntarily consider if George was correct when he insisted I should sleep. No - don't give him any credit for being right about anything, I told myself. I was still so mad. The long flight hadn't changed that.

I was supposed to meet up with Christopher for lunch, but first we had to get to our hotel, and I didn't have any idea how we were supposed to do that. None of us spoke any language apart from English.

"Don't worry," my mom said, reading my mind. "The ISU said they would send someone to pick us up."

And just then I saw the handmade sign: "ABIGAIL PHELPS AND GUESTS"

And holding the sign was the most adorable guy I had ever seen - an Austrian roughly my age, with hair so blonde it was almost white. I glanced at my mom with uncertainty. As pathetic as it sounds, I wasn't used to being attracted to anyone - I was always too busy to notice. So I wasn't sure why my cheeks were getting warm looking at this cute blonde boy who was here to drive us to our hotel.

My mom winked at me and said, "Maybe we'll get lucky and he'll only speak German. That could be fun!" I wasn't sure what she meant, but as soon as she said that I began hoping against hope that he spoke English. I wanted to get to know this guy.

We walked over to him, my cheeks getting warmer with each step. When he saw us, he began to look nervous. He started shuffling his feet and clearing his throat. Was Cute Blonde Boy shy? It just made him even more adorable.

My dad began the introductions. "I'm David Phelps, and this is my wife Marsha." He was enunciating very clearly, uncertain which language Cute Blonde Boy spoke. "And this is my daughter Abigail."

I nervously put out my hand to shake the hand of this beautiful specimen, while mentally crossing my fingers that he was going to be our driver for the entire trip. And then came the words which would set my life on a different path from any I had ever imagined, and those words came out in perfect Nottingham English.

"Abigail, it is so wonderful to finally meet you. I'm Christopher Dean."

THANK YOU, SVEN BENGTSSON!! My good pal Sven had delivered to me the cutest ice dancer that had ever lived on the face of the planet, and I was amazed that I had even noticed, much less been delighted.

"Abigail..." My mother nudged me with her elbow. Oh no, I was staring. Possibly drooling? I don't know. I was so into him, right away. He looked young and innocent, though at twenty he was three years older than I, and he had just enough of a mischievous gleam in his eye that I doubted he was as innocent as he appeared. More than thirty years later, I still remember exactly how he looked, what he was wearing, how he smelled. His hair was such a light blonde, it was almost translucent. I loved his hair.

Finally, I pulled my thoughts together, and away from the unbelievable attraction I was feeling, enough to speak. "Christopher. What a surprise." What a surprise, indeed. "It's just…phenomenal…really great…so happy to meet you." Okay, maybe I hadn't pulled my thoughts together quite as much as I had thought. I was completely lost in his eyes.

"Um, come along David, let's go gather the luggage and let these two get to know each other." Oh no, my mother knew.

Thankfully, Chris didn't seem nearly as out of sorts as I, although there was no denying that there was a shyness there which surprised me.

"Do you prefer to go by Abigail or Abby? You signed your letter 'Abby.'"

"What do you prefer?" What? Did I really just say that? I was instantly horrified and opened my mouth to try to find a way to erase that embarrassing moment, but he beat me to it.

"Hmm." His eyes studied me closely, taking my ridiculous question very seriously. "I think you're an Abigail trying very hard to be an Abby. Or maybe it's the other way around. You prefer Abby?"

"Typically, yes. My friends all call me Abby."

"Then do you mind if I call you Abigail?"

Oh my. Was he flirting with me? Was I brave enough to flirt back? Did I even know *how* to flirt? That question entered my mind, and immediately I knew the answer: Yes. I could flirt with Christopher Dean. I'd been waiting my entire life to flirt with Christopher Dean.

I smiled at him with a confidence I wasn't used to feeling. "Why? You don't want to be my friend?"

He blushed and smiled back, then looked down at his feet, the bashfulness overtaking him momentarily. "On the contrary," he said softly, still looking down. "I just don't want to be just another one of your friends." He brought his eyes back up to meet mine, and I mentally begged my knees not to fail me. "Abigail is such a beautiful name, and I like the idea of always being the person who calls you Abigail, while everyone else calls you Abby."

Oh. Wow. "Well, what does everyone call you?"

He chuckled. "Probably equal parts Christopher and Chris, so take your pick."

"What's your middle name?"

"Colin. What's yours?"

"Katherine. Does anyone call you Colin?" I obviously wasn't a natural at flirtatious banter, and I was beginning to have a difficult time remembering what I was even trying to accomplish.

And that seemed to amuse Mr. Dean a great deal. "No. Colin is my dad's name. Does anyone call you Katherine?"

"No."

I had nothing.

"Okay, it's settled then. I'm just going to have to call you Cute Blonde Boy."

And there it was. I had taken him by surprise and delighted him. *That's* what I was trying to accomplish. He laughed so loudly that he had to cover his mouth with his hand to contain his slightly embarrassed laughter as passersby turned to see what was so funny, and saw nothing. It was the first of countless times we got lost in a world all our own.

"You're not at all what I expected, Abigail Phelps," he managed to force out while trying to catch his breath.

"And you aren't at all what I expected, Cute Blonde Boy."

His fantastic laughter started again, and my heart leapt. Ice dancing was going to be fun.

We went to lunch at a delightful little café Chris had selected ahead of time. I nibbled at my food, and it was delicious, but I was horrified to think of how fattening it all was. I was even more horrified thinking about how much Chris would have to touch my body when we began skating together. There was no way I was going to allow myself to put on even a pound.

Chris noticed.

"Do you not like the apfelstrudel, Abigail? I can order you something else."

"No, no…it's delicious, thanks. I'm just not very

hungry." Chris squinted his eyes at me, appearing concerned. Oh no, not another George, always worried I'm not eating enough.

George. It was the first time I had thought about George since meeting Chris. I didn't welcome his return to my thoughts.

My mother interrupted my brooding, once again making an exit. "Well, thank you for lunch, Christopher. It was just delicious. Now, if you'll excuse us, we're going to tour the city a bit before the jet lag sets in too much. You two have a nice time, but don't forget: big day tomorrow. And the jet lag is really going to take you by surprise, Abby. Be back to the hotel in time to get some good sleep, okay?"

"Sure, Mom. Actually, maybe I'll just go back with you now and go to the hotel gym for a while…" I stood to leave with them.

"No, no, no. You and Christopher need to get to know one another. Have fun. Unless of course you have other plans, Christopher?"

"No, Mrs. Phelps. Not at all. All of my plans for the next few days revolve around your daughter, actually." He smiled at me, and I felt myself blushing again. There was absolutely nothing wrong with what he had said, and yet I was embarrassed that he had said it in front of my parents.

"You be careful." My dad kissed me on the cheek. "Christopher." He put out his hand to shake Chris's.

"Mr. Phelps. Thank you. I'll take good care of her. I promise."

My dad patted him on the back. "We're counting on that. From now on."

[FROM THE DESK OF DR. ALEC B. REDMOND As I stated, Abigail's parents died many years ago, when she was very young. She was raised by relatives, and based on everything Abigail told me, she lived a relatively normal, happy childhood. Her family was not wealthy, but her parents did leave behind enough to provide for a solid education for their only child. Abigail took full advantage of the opportunities which came along, she worked hard, and she did the best she could with the cards she had been dealt. She has always seemed to be at peace about it all, and any pain or feelings of abandonment which she may have had concerning the death of her parents seemed to have been put to rest long before I met her. And yet, the parents she created for herself are loving, supportive, and very much present.]

We walked around Vienna for hours, lost in conversation and the beauty of the city. It was almost two hours from the time we left the café before skating was even mentioned. For my part, I can honestly say that I didn't even think about it until Chris broached the subject as we crossed the Danube.

"Why do you skate?"

I was taken aback. Why do I skate? I don't think anyone had ever asked me that before. I know that I hadn't ever really thought about it.

"I don't know. I like it, I guess. I've invested a lot of time and energy, and my parents have too, not to mention a lot of money. I don't know what I would do if I didn't skate. Why do *you* skate?"

Chris didn't pause for even a moment. "It's all I've ever wanted to do. I got a pair of skates as a birthday gift when I was a child, and from the first time I laced them, and stepped on the ice, I couldn't imagine doing anything else. I tried hockey for a little while, but it just wasn't for me. I quickly discovered I could move very quickly, and I hardly ever fell, but then they started trying to teach me jumps, and I just didn't enjoy it. I never did."

"Are you kidding me? Jumps are the only reason to skate, as far as I am concerned. The freedom of being in the air, no ground or ice needed… I don't understand how you didn't get into that."

Chris stopped. We were on a foot bridge, still crossing the Danube, and I wasn't sure if I enjoyed the view of Vienna or Christopher Dean more. I looked at him, not sure why we had stopped, but not minding a bit. When we were stopped, I didn't have to waste time worrying about pesky little things like watching where I was going - I could just focus on Chris. But once I was focusing on him, I noticed he didn't look as thrilled with me as I was with him.

"Jumping is the only reason to skate? Then why in

the world do you want to be an ice dancer?" He looked hurt, or confused - I didn't know him well enough to read him yet.

"Well, I don't really *want* to be an ice dancer, but what else can I do? The USFSA and the ISU pretty much decided that I'm not good enough to do anything else." Against my will, tears welled up, threatening to expose the vulnerability which I worked so hard to conceal.

Chris didn't appear to feel at all sympathetic. "Look, if you aren't in this 100%, can you please just tell me now? I for one am absolutely not settling for being their sideshow - skating's goodwill ambassadors to the world, or whatever. When I was told that you had demanded competition eligibility, I thought you felt the same way, and I thought we might do really well together. If you aren't going to give this your all -"

"No, I will! Really!" I was so frustrated. No one understood me at all. I just wanted someone, anyone, to say they understood why I was so sad, and that I had every right to be, and that they'd be angry too, if they were in my shoes. No one ever did that, and I was getting really tired of it. I began yelling at Chris. Poor Chris. He didn't deserve it. There, along the Danube, he just happened to be in the wrong place at the wrong time.

"Who do you think you are? You know nothing about me. Nothing! I've spent my entire life skating, working, working, working! No friends, no dates - did I even have a friend before George?" I asked of myself, in my fury. "I don't think so. Not since, what…third grade? And I don't really have a friend now, do I? Even George turned on me! 'Go to Vienna and eat and sleep, Abby.' Why is everyone always telling me to eat and sleep? Man…and to think, I *liked* you. From the moment I saw your little sign and thought you were our Austrian driver, I started to think maybe this wasn't going to be the worst thing in my life after all. But you're just like the rest. Why can't anyone just say, 'Yeah, you're right, Abby. This is a bad situation you were put in. And you look really nice, by the way. You look well-rested, and well-fed, and it's just too bad this happened because you were going to be the next Dorothy Hamill. Sorry those ISU bastards ruined your life.' That's all I want. Well? Say something!" I shouted at him before even giving him a moment in which he could respond.

Chris didn't say anything. He turned his back to me and began walking in the direction we had already been.

"What the hell? What do you think you're doing?" I stormed after him.

He turned suddenly with fire in his eyes. "Okay, Abigail. I'll tell you what you want to hear. You're right. It's not fair what the ISU has done to you."

Finally. "Thank you. It's just so hard -"

Chris stopped me. "I'm not done yet. It's not fair what the ISU has done to you, or even what they've done to me. You've worked hard, yes, and I have too. Just like hundreds of other skaters who are probably just as good as we are, or better. Yet, in spite of that, a Dorothy Hamill comes along how often? Not very. And you and I were probably on the fast track to coaching at our local skating clubs in a few years, but for whatever reason - maybe because we're just not quite good enough - we were selected. We were singled out from those hundreds of others who are working hard every single day, and we were given an opportunity that no one else has ever gotten before. You're right. That's not fair. Maybe in a lot of ways we're starting over, but we've been thrust into an international spotlight to do it. Tomorrow, you and I will be introduced, center rink, at the World Figure Skating Championships. And the best part about all of this is no one expects us to amount to anything. That's not a bad thing, Abigail. You need to quit looking at it like it's a bad thing. Without this," he gestured to indicate the two of us, "we might have made it. Eventually. Who knows? After I tried out partner after partner, and you went it alone, maybe we'd have had a lucky break after another two thousand years of hard work, but maybe not. I've never been to Kentucky, and you've never been to Nottingham, but I do know one thing: they're both a very long way from Vienna. It's up to you to decide if you want to go back to Kentucky and return to the status quo, or if you would rather skate to center rink tomorrow and begin taking the world by storm."

I stared at him in shock. I was stunned to discover that Cute Blonde Boy, with his cherubic flushed cheeks and his proper British accent and his chivalrous manners, could actually give as good as he got. And I was stunned because he was right. He was absolutely right. None of that had truly clicked for me until that moment, and I felt like a fool.

"Two thousand years *does* seem like an awfully long time to have to keep competing at the junior level," I said with a half-smile, hoping that he would interpret my use of his well-placed exaggeration as what I meant for it to be: an apology and a commitment.

His slightly smug, but undeniably pleased, smile told me he understood perfectly, and as I realized just how well he understood me, already, I was somehow able to sense, though I wouldn't have known how to put it into words then, that Christopher Dean and I would always be partners. Of course, even if I had known how to express that then, or had a care to, I never would have imagined that meant anything more than a long career together.

"It does rather, doesn't it? On the other hand, something about the idea of spending the next two thousand years getting to know you doesn't sound quite as unbearable," he said, arms crossed, trying to maintain the tough guy image he had displayed with such success just seconds prior, but it just wasn't working right then when he was saying sweet things like that. And he knew it, so with a laugh he uncrossed his arms and smiled at me as he said, "Let's do this."

I signed our symbolic partnership agreement with a nod and a smile.

"And one more thing," he continued, the smile leaving his face. "You don't look well-fed, and you don't look well-rested. If anyone does actually say that to you, you be sure to let me know, so I can kick their ass. You need to eat. You need to sleep. You think you have worked hard up until now, but you haven't even *begun* to work yet. The work that you and I have in store for us is going to be unlike anything either of us has ever experienced. The Lake Placid Olympics are next year, so we can't possibly qualify in time, but I plan to be ready by Sarajevo. I need for you to be as strong as you can be."

Sarajevo? He was planning on the Sarajevo Olympics in 1984? Excitement flowed through my veins and, for a moment, I disregarded everything else he had said. But then the fierce skating machine took a backseat to the insecure little girl. The tears silently rolled down my cheeks, and I made no attempt to contain them.

"Why does everyone say I need to eat more? I do eat, and I sleep, but I have to make sure you can lift me. No one has ever had to lift me before."

Chris sighed involuntarily and reached over and grabbed my hands in his. "Oh, sweet girl. My main reason for saying you need to eat more is I don't want to hurt you. I guarantee we'll be burning off enough calories in training. If you don't eat, you'll get too skinny, and if you get too skinny I'll hurt you in holds and lifts, and I don't want to do that. So, it's for me really. I promise that the day I can no longer lift you, I will - with great care and sensitivity, of course - let you know that you need to double down on the lettuce or something." We both laughed and he removed one of his hands from mine and wiped away my falling tears, but his other hand kept holding on. "Until then, Abigail: please eat the damn strudel!"

We both erupted in laughter again, and then, still hand-in-hand, we continued across the Danube. Everything had shifted. For the rest of our time together that day, we talked of nothing *but* skating, and we reveled in the possibility of things to come. He walked me to my hotel and we said good night, and I went immediately to bed - for the first time truly excited about what was in store the next day.

[FROM THE DESK OF DR. ALEC B. REDMOND On the fact-checking front, the 1979 World Figure Skating Championships were indeed held in Vienna, Austria, but I can find no truth to any of the rest of it. This chapter did, however, bring forward a theme which has been present in many, if not most, of Abigail's delusions - the idea of love at first sight, or at the very least, instantaneous attraction. I'm concerned about the body image issues. That just doesn't compute in my mind as to how it relates to the real Abigail. Abigail Phelps may be many things, and she may have many insecurities in relation to her life and her situations, but not as they relate to herself and who she is. I don't know that I have ever met a woman who is as comfortable in her own skin as the Abigail Phelps I know.]

4. GETTING CLOSER

The next day, Chris and I were introduced to the world, center rink. We both thought we were prepared for that, but the feeling was unlike anything we could have ever expected. In the middle of the ice, on international television, with thousands of people cheering for us. We were young and fresh-faced, and we both blushed a lot. On top of that, we represented something unique and new and groundbreaking - and we were the ultimate underdogs. They loved us. We soaked in their love and left that day ready to get to work.

We signed up for some rink time at the official training facility, and what fun that was! The condition of the ice was better than anything either of us had ever skated on. We warmed up, and then skated around a bit, each of us showing the other what we had. We raced each other across the ice, we pulled out some fancy footwork, and I jumped a bit - just because I could.

Then, our new reality began. "Okay," Chris began nonchalantly. "Let's get used to going out there together." And he took my hand.

We skated around the ice together. Chris had only been an ice dancer, but of course I was not used to the feeling of being tethered to another person. I looked down at my skates the entire time, certain I would lose my footing if I didn't. It felt unnatural and uncomfortable. We came to a halt, and he reached over and with one finger raised my chin, forcing me to look him in the eyes. He held his hand there, while his other hand pulled the hand of mine he was holding, and we started moving across the ice again. This time it was smooth and fluid and natural and comfortable, and my eyes were locked with Chris's the entire time.

Chris stopped in the center of the ice and pulled me to him for an ecstatic hug. "Did you feel that? That was so natural! *That* was how it should be!" He was giddy.

I, on the other hand, knew that it felt natural, and it was certainly improvement, but I really didn't know what made it so special in Chris's eyes. And as far as what I felt…all I felt was an insane attraction to Chris. What did *he* feel?

"Yes, that seemed better," I said uncertainly, trying to act as if I understood what it was that had him so excited. I was so uneducated and naïve regarding the whole concept of skating with a partner. "I know this is probably a stupid question, but why was that anything special? We just skated across the rink. I don't understand."

Chris answered me immediately, with comical flourish. "Chemistry! That extra little component which sets apart the great from the legendary. Do you know how many girls I have skated with?" I shook my head no, and he laughed. "Neither do I! I've lost count. And not once, with any of them, did I ever feel what I just felt."

Then he kissed me.

It was just that sudden. I didn't have any idea it was coming, and I didn't feel any tension building up to it - no awkward moment, no shallow breathing or flushed face. The kiss just suddenly was, and just as suddenly, I responded. He had one arm around my waist and his other hand in my hair. As I recall, my arms were just dangling there, lifeless, but my lips were very much engaged.

It was my first kiss, and I can't imagine a better one. It was quite simply perfect - sweet, tender, and yet ridiculously sexy and passionate.

Chris finally pulled away and, as much as I didn't want it to end, it was probably a good thing that he did. I'm not sure that I ever would have. We stayed in the same position for quite a while, his arm still around my waist, neither of us speaking, both faces very flushed.

Finally Chris spoke, still a little bit out of breath. "You've never kissed anyone before, have you?"

Oh no! "Was it that obvious?"

He looked horrified when he realized how I had interpreted his inquiry. "No! I'm sorry, that's not what I meant at all. You told me yesterday that you hadn't dated anyone, and I know how busy you have always been, training, so I am assuming... And, I was just going to say I'm sorry. That shouldn't have been your first kiss. I was just so caught up in the way this feels, but I had no right to steal your first kiss from you, without your permission or anything. I was just caught up in *you*, I suppose."

Oh my. "Please don't apologize," I whispered, blushing. "It was perfect." I was working up the nerve to initiate a second kiss when Chris stepped back a little, grabbed my hand, and very casually asked if I wanted to start working on some compulsory moves or break for lunch first. For me, it was a no-brainer. I was delighted by the idea of spending non-skating time with him - although skating time had already showcased its advantages as well.

We returned to the café to which he had taken my parents and me the previous day, but this time I was starving and determined to not let another strudel go to waste, which seemed to please him. As we sat with our food, I thought about how to launch a conversation about the kiss: what did it mean to him, did he regret it, how did he feel about me, was he dating anyone in England, and so on. As it turned out, I didn't have to worry about initiating the conversation. He took care of that pretty quickly.

"Abigail, it's just unreal to me the chemistry that we have between us. And I need you to know, since I didn't do a very good job of making it clear a little while ago, I thoroughly enjoyed kissing you. Without a doubt, that was in the top ten kisses of my life."

My stomach dropped to the floor. "Top ten? Wow. How many have there been?" Did he kiss every girl he skated with, or every girl he met, maybe, searching for that mysterious chemistry?

"Kisses? Well, I can't count all of them, obviously,

but there haven't been that many girls. Fifteen. Twenty, maybe." Calm and cool, he took a bite of his wiener schnitzel.

I wanted to be furious, but I knew even then that I had no right to be, so I tried to let it roll off my back. I doubt I was very convincing. "Well, then I guess I should be honored to be in the top ten." I felt the sting in my eyes as tears threatened to develop, but I held my chin high, determined not to let them.

Chris rubbed my arm up and down. "Hey, I'm joking!" He was obviously in such a good mood, and it was completely contagious, so I couldn't be mad, but I also couldn't help but be relieved.

I laughed a little, still worried about just how much more experienced he was compared to me. "No fifteen to twenty then?"

He smiled widely. "No. Actually, three. And without a doubt your kiss was number one. I swear. That was the hottest thing I have ever experienced and frankly I'm surprised we didn't melt the ice back there, Miss Phelps." His hand was suddenly in my hair, his fingers twisting my curls around and around.

"Whew!" I exhaled and laughed. "I'm so glad to hear you say that. I mean, I thought it was good, but what do I know?" Looking back, I'm amazed by just how vulnerable I allowed myself to be with him, right from the very beginning.

"See, that's the great thing about chemistry - which is something you and I apparently have in spades." He winked at me. "It's usually not explainable, and there's no real formula for it, but when it's there it is abundantly clear. Any time you form a new partnership, you just have to wait and see. And you can be a really good team even without the connection, but you will probably never go to that next level. This partnership definitely passed that test. But now, you see, we have a new problem."

A new problem? He was teasing me again, right? "What problem could we possibly have?"

He sat back in his chair and sighed. "We can't date, Abigail. I've always sworn that I would never date a skating partner. What if we broke up - worse, what if we broke up bitterly? Then the partnership ends too. I never expected that to be a problem, but it is."

I knew it was indeed a problem for me, although until that moment I hadn't even realized that I wanted to date him. Or rather, I hadn't been able to regain my composure and see things clearly enough to put my desire to date him into concrete terms in my mind. The moment he said it wasn't possible, I was beyond disappointed. Was he actually feeling the same way about me, or was he just letting me down gently?

"So, um, that's a problem, is it?" I asked him, trying to play it cool, but fully aware that my voice was shaking and my palms were sweating.

"Well, it's a problem as far as I'm concerned. I've had decent - passable at best - chemistry with a couple of partners, but this sort of issue never came up because I didn't have any interest in dating them. I have extreme interest in dating you."

Hooray! My heart did triple axels, and then I remembered our problem. "But you can't or won't date me, because then you couldn't skate with me?"

"Right." He looked very sad. Just like I felt.

"What if that's the wrong choice? What if we shouldn't be partners, because then we couldn't date?" I couldn't argue with his logic about not doing both, but at that moment I felt confident that I would sacrifice the opportunity to be Phelps and Dean so that we could be Abigail and Chris instead.

It had been one day. One. I wasn't deceiving myself that I was in love with him already, or that he was the man I was destined to be with. I was much too level-headed for any of that nonsense, even as immature and naïve as I was. But I did know that I had never been attracted to any man like I was attracted to him. I knew that I was interested in seeing where our relationship could go if we were allowed to explore the possibilities.

He opened his mouth to shoot down my bold question, and then his mouth closed again without a word being uttered. Then again: he opened his mouth to speak, and closed it before he said anything at all.

I interpreted his hesitancy and inability to speak to mean he was considering what I had said. I knew how optimistic he was about our possibilities on the ice, so if he was even thinking about giving that up so that he could have a relationship with me, I knew that he had to be as interested in me as I was in him.

"Chris, how about this: we're in Vienna for four more days, and tomorrow's my birthday, so -"

"Is it? I didn't realize…"

"Yes. So, what if we don't decide anything right now? Let's do something fun for my birthday, let's enjoy Vienna, let's test out this new partnership on the ice -"

"And off?" He reached in and grabbed my hand again.

I blushed and smiled. "Yes. And off. And then before we each head home, we'll decide how to move forward."

"Oh Abigail, I love that idea. Really I do. But at the end of four days we will have to say goodbye to one aspect of the relationship or the other, and it's going to be much more difficult to do that then than it would be now."

He was right. Of course he was right. I stared at him and thought as hard as I could, trying to think of a way we could make it all work, and I came up with something. I just knew it would take a lot of patience. If we could stand to work together, and not let the attraction get in the way of our working relationship, then we only had to wait five years. We had to get through the 1984 Olympics, and then we could focus on the personal stuff. I would be twenty-two, he would be twenty-five. It's not as if our best years would be behind us. I was certainly willing to say goodbye to ice dancing, but I couldn't ask him to do that. Yes, waiting was our best option.

He was staring right back at me, and I guessed that he was doing what I was: trying to find a way to make it work. Surprisingly, he arrived at a different proposal than I.

"Oh, to hell with it," he muttered under his breath as he pulled my chair, with me in it, closer to him, cradled my face in his hands, pulled me close - his fingers getting tangled in my hair - and kissed me again. And I'll be damned if it wasn't even sexier than the first time. It certainly lasted longer. Minutes, hours, I'm not sure.

While Chris was kissing me, it certainly was difficult to maintain my resolve to be patient for five years, but I wasn't about to pull away from him any sooner than I had to. He did ultimately separate from me, once again, since I wasn't about to be the one who did it. He leaned his forehead against mine and we both, once again, tried to catch our breath. When he spoke, his voice was low and raspy which, combined with the already very sexy British accent, made me want him even more.

"I really can't believe I am saying it," he said, "but let's do this. I will contact the ISU in the morning and withdraw our partnership application."

He leaned in to kiss me again, and I almost let him. If I had, my life - not to mention figure skating history - might have turned out quite differently.

"No, wait." He stopped an inch from my lips, and as surprised as he was, I think I was even more so. "Let's think about this, Chris. Do you really think we might have a chance? I mean, on the ice? Because, if so, maybe we should focus on that first. We wouldn't have to choose skating over whatever relationship might develop here, we just have to choose skating now, and the other later. That will be tough, but it's the only way I can think of that we might actually get to have it all."

Chris stayed close to me, and we were practically whispering to each other. It was so private and intimate – and comfortable and natural. "I don't know. Five years?"

"Well, maybe. Here's another possibility: maybe we'll not be attracted to each other anymore after we work together a little while."

"Not likely," Chris laughed.

"Agreed. Okay, maybe we'll get to a point where we figure out that we can do both, because maybe we will get to a point where breaking up wouldn't be an option." I was hoping that point would come soon.

At that, Chris sat back in his chair. "Maybe."

We stared at each other, weighing the options, very seriously considering the years we had both put into figure skating, and the dreams and aspirations associated with all of that hard work - all of which suddenly seemed a little less significant.

"Okay, we'll wait," he finally said, and I tried to force down my disappointment by reminding myself it had been my stupid idea.

5. VIENNA

On my eighteenth birthday I awoke in a luxurious hotel suite in Vienna after a night full of dreams of Christopher Dean. My parents had a fantastic Viennese breakfast waiting for me, and just as we finished eating, the doorbell rang. They told me that my birthday gift from them was on the other side of the door, so I should go open it. The day couldn't have started out any better.

I was silly with excitement, but in no way prepared for what I found in the hallway. For my birthday, my parents had flown George Clooney to Austria.

"Happy birthday, Abby. I hope it's okay that I'm here. We had this arranged before our fight and I didn't want to tell your parents -" I cut him off with a hug, and I began to cry. I was so happy to see him.

"This is seriously the best birthday gift ever," I whispered.

He held me tightly. "Hey, are you okay? What's wrong?"

"Nothing's wrong. Nothing. But so much has happened since we got here and I'm so happy to see you, and I'm so sorry that I was so mean to you at the airport. You were right. Everything you said was right, and I just didn't know it. I'm so sorry."

We just held each other, no words being spoken, until my parents came in. I broke away from George and ran over to my parents and hugged them and thanked them for the perfect gift.

It was then 8:00 a.m. and I had to meet Chris at the rink at 9:00, so I had to get George up-to-date on everything very quickly. We walked from the hotel to the training facility, talking all the way.

"But you just met the guy!" George was having difficulty understanding the dynamic between Chris and me.

"I know. Trust me, I know. But, it's intense. I can't explain it. We just connected on so many levels. And even though we have agreed to just focus on the skating for now, I know it's going to be tough. He was really ready to give it a go, and just find another partner."

"That must be flattering." George held the door open for me as we walked into the training facility.

"Oh, yeah. Completely flattering. But it does worry me a bit. I was ready to drop the skating and be with him, but since we're not going that direction, we just really need to focus on the skating now. I hope he's able to do that, and get his head in the game."

I needn't have worried. When George and I walked into the arena, Chris was already on the ice, looking quite warmed up and settled in. He skated across the rink and stopped in front of George and me. He seemed to assess George, and then turned to me and said, "You're late."

I looked at my watch. "Sorry. Only five minutes…"

Chris did not appear to be in the fabulous, sexy mood I had so enjoyed the day before.

"Yes, only five minutes, but right now, Abigail, we are actually in the same city, on the same continent, and I feel we should take advantage of that. Don't you?"

Was he mad at me for not agreeing that we should withdraw our application? "Of course. I'm sorry. Um, I'd like to introduce you to my best friend, George Clooney. George, this is Christopher Dean."

They shook hands, though neither gentleman seemed too enthused.

"Nice to meet you," Chris said, then he turned back to me and asked through gritted teeth, "Can we please get to work now?"

I was shocked by how rude he was being. "No, we can't. I want to talk to you first."

"Well, I don't want to talk to you. I want to skate. Can we *please* do that? Get your skates on and meet me on the ice in ten minutes. I'm going to take a little breather, and then I want to work." He stepped off the ice and put on his blade guards, then he walked away as if he couldn't stand to be in the same room with me.

I looked at George helplessly. He had backed away, obviously not feeling incredibly comfortable being in the middle of all the fun.

"Should I go talk to him?"

"Actually, if I were you, I think I would just get the skates on and meet him on the ice, ready to work. He doesn't seem like he's in a mood to be messed with. But I can definitely see that chemistry you were talking about," he said sarcastically.

Being the stubborn-headed person I have always been, I ignored George's very sensible advice and ran after Chris. I found him outside leaning forward over a railing, looking at city lights in the distance. He hadn't put on his coat, and it was beginning to snow heavily. He didn't seem to notice.

"Chris?" I spoke softly, but I could tell he heard me by the way his shoulders involuntarily tensed. "Chris, are you mad at me? Can't we please talk about whatever is bothering you? If I did something to upset you, I'm sorry. But I don't know what it was."

He turned around and spoke through his teeth once again. "Can't we just get to work? Please?"

I was taken aback by what I interpreted as his hostility. Tears sprung to my eyes, and I willed them - begged them - to stay put, but the traitors rolled down my cheeks anyway. "Okay, of course. I'm sorry. I'll meet you on the ice."

I turned to walk back to the rink, but didn't travel more than a few feet before Chris had his hand on my shoulder. "Wait. I'm sorry. This isn't your fault."

I turned to him, in full-blown tearful mode, hating myself for being so weak that I couldn't keep a few tears from running wild. "I don't understand what's going on, Chris. *Are* you mad at me?"

"No. Not at all. I'm mad at myself. I've never let personal issues get in the way before, and I can't believe that I did this time. But regardless, if we're going to move forward, I've just got to stay focused on the work."

"Does that mean you will always be this mean to me?"

He blinked repeatedly. "Was I mean? I'm sorry. No, I'm not trying to be mean. But you should know that I work hard, and several of my previous partnerships ended because I 'took it too seriously' for them. I always leave it all on the ice, and that's why I don't quite know how to handle this situation between the two of us. I've never felt the pull off the ice before. And if I am going to skate at my best and be the best partner to you that I know how to be, I've got to leave it all on the ice."

"Oh." That was all I knew to say.

"But I am ready to give this my all with you, Abigail. And yes, I expect you to be on time."

I sighed. "That's fair. Sorry. I usually am on time. This morning didn't go as planned, with my parents flying George here for my birthday and all."

Chris inhaled sharply. "Your birthday. Happy birthday - what a birthday morning I've given you. Sorry."

"It's fine. After all that happened, I couldn't really expect you to remember, Chris."

He began shaking his head. "No, I didn't forget. Well, momentarily, I suppose I did. But, actually, I have a gift for you."

When had he had time to shop? "You do? What is it?" Would the surprises never stop coming?

"Well, it's nothing I can wrap. It's a song, actually. A routine to be more precise." He must have seen the blank expression on my face and realized that nothing was computing. "I choreographed something for us."

There were a million things I wanted to say and ask, but all that came out was, "When?"

He laughed, just a little, and it was a relief. "Well, last night. This morning. I didn't exactly sleep much."

"I'm so sorry. Are you feeling…I don't know, do you regret, or…" I didn't know how to say what I was trying to say, but I knew that I didn't want him to feel bad about anything that had happened between us.

"No. I don't regret anything. I just couldn't stop thinking about you, but I knew that I *had* to stop thinking about you, so I came out here and put this together. It didn't help me to stop thinking about you at all, of course, but at least I could focus it all on the ice." He paused, took a deep breath, and then proceeded. "I can do this. *We* can do this. But it has to be one or the other for me, okay? I can't stand on the edge or walk the line. I'm hoping that we can have a romantic relationship down the road, but I can't plan for it and I can't expect it, or I won't be able to remember that there is anything else in the world that I want."

He was baring his emotions completely, and it was so touching, and it made me care for him so much more than I had anticipated – beyond the attraction and beyond the skating.

I couldn't bear to think about my feelings for him, so I diverted by asking, "So, what is this song that I get for my birthday?"

He smiled. "I thought you'd never ask."

We walked back to the ice, side by side but not touching. As we walked, Chris explained his choice to me. "I think that the key to us being a success will be to, first of all, surprise them all. Not just with how good we are, but by our choices. For instance, Vivaldi is big this season. Vivaldi is big *every* season. Let's go far away from Vivaldi. When we start legitimately competing, we'll have to figure out some classical, of course, but for now, we just need to get through a few exhibitions. And they're going to expect us to play it safe. They're going to expect Vivaldi, so we give them modern and popular. They're going to expect compulsory moves – one pattern into the next into the next. So let's give them stories and characters for them to get into and understand. They're going to expect a lot of platonic, sibling-type of stuff on the ice. That's what ice dancing is. It's formal and safe and fun for the whole family. But that's not us." He stopped and turned me to face him. "Let's make them feel the connection we feel every time we look at each other."

I didn't understand the power he had over my internal organs, and the way he could just turn everything to mush. "I'm in," I breathed. Panted? "What do you have in mind?"

He once again smiled that adorable smile. "What else? Look where we are. Vienna!"

"You want to waltz?" That didn't sound like much of a break from the traditional.

"No, the song 'Vienna' by Billy Joel." He looked pleased with himself.

I knew and liked the song. There weren't many people in the world who didn't own the LP of *The Stranger* in 1979, but I couldn't picture it on the ice.

But then we skated. He masterfully led me through the choreography, and it was like the joy which comes from dancing with a truly exquisite dancer leading you. It didn't matter that I didn't know the moves. I knew exactly what to do.

I was blown away by his creativity. I, for one, had never choreographed any of my own routines, so the fact that he not only choreographed it but skated it, and was ready to teach it to me all within eighteen hours or so, amazed me. And the routine itself was fantastic.

We opened with a fifteen-second segment which was all formality and antiquity. He asked for my hand for a dance, I consented, we skated together onto the "dance floor." It was very Elizabeth Bennett/Mr. Darcy at the Netherfield Ball, which of course I would come to know very well later in life. Then, the modern verse began, in complete contrast to what had already occurred on the ice.

Chris's choreography was fluid, but less and less ballroom with each stanza. It was the story of a girl who didn't know who she was, or where she belonged - she wasn't comfortable in her own skin. Though incredibly driven, and outwardly buoyant, she was always putting on a brave front. She strove to be the life of the party, all the while lacking self-confidence and being filled with self-doubt.

Chris portrayed a man who understood and loved her, and wanted her for who she actually was, not who she tried so hard to be. He had limited time to make her understand that. The formal society in which they lived wouldn't allow him more than a dance, so he threw all his love and caring for her into that one dance.

He held her just a little more closely than he really should have, and he never took his eyes away from her face - even when the intensity was too much for her to stand and she had to look away.

From the first moment we touched, five seconds into the routine, until the moment we separated, five seconds from the end of the routine, Chris was touching me every single moment. It not only added to the emotion and longing you could feel between the characters, it also made the choreography exponentially more difficult. When his hand was not at my waist or holding my hand, his leg was against mine or his fingers brushed against my back. At a glance, there was nothing inappropriate - neither by ice dancing standards nor by standards of the period of history we were attempting to emulate. However, just like with Darcy and Elizabeth, if you looked just a little more closely, just under the surface, it was actually borderline erotica.

The modern lyrics would almost make you forget the time period in which Chris's story was set, but at the end the formal Austen-era ambiance returned with Billy Joel's final fifteen instrumental seconds, and Chris's desperation as he bid adieu to his would-be love with a bow and a kiss on the hand. They part, and he is left only to hope that she understood.

I absolutely adored skating with Christopher Dean. I knew that then and there. He was an artist, creating the most wonderful pictures on the ice, and I felt unworthy to share the rink with him. Tears came to my eyes as I realized that, unworthy though I may be, he was my partner, and I got to experience his creative genius from then on.

He held me in our final pose, and we stared at each other, the reality of the last twenty-four hours setting in.

And then another reality hit me.

"Chris, I didn't jump. Not once did I so much as leave the ice, and that was the most fun I have ever had skating. Ever." He released me from our stance and I continued rambling on, feeling exuberant and in love with ice dancing. "That routine was brilliant. Seriously brilliant. Every woman who watches that is going to fall in love with you."

"Well, that's certainly not a bad thing," he laughed. "But make no mistake," he said, suddenly very serious, but with a heart-capturing smile on his face. "'Vienna' is not for *every* woman."

I forgot to breathe for a moment. I had forgotten that it was my birthday gift, and I began to wonder what I was missing. I thought about our on-ice storyline and it became very clear: Chris understood me, perhaps better than I understood myself. Chris knew I would love ice dancing. Chris knew I had worked so hard at skating for so long that I never took the time to enjoy skating. I didn't do it because of any great passion for it, I did it because I had done it for so long, I didn't know what else to do. Chris knew all of that and he had set out to change it, and somehow, with a little help from Billy Joel, he had.

And I suddenly knew one more thing that Chris had told me through "Vienna." He was in love with me.

"Pretty great song, isn't it?" Chris asked me.

I swallowed the threatening tears, and also tried to swallow what felt like my heart, beating in my throat. "Yes. Thank you."

He looked into my eyes, and I could tell that he knew I was thanking him for more than just creating a beautiful routine for us to dance to. I felt as if the intensity in his eyes would burn a hole in my soul, but unlike my character on the ice, I couldn't look away.

He broke the spell. "Well, that's enough for today. Your friend looks bored." He gestured to George. Oh, George! I'd forgotten he was there.

As much as I loved the idea of hanging out with George for the rest of the day, I wasn't ready to say goodbye to my time with Chris just yet. "Are you sure? We were scheduled to go for another hour..."

"Are you kidding? It's your birthday. We got a lot of good work in today, so we'll just pick up tomorrow." He smiled, and I smiled back, and I got lost in his eyes once more, and then the rest of the world disappeared and I wasn't sure I would be able to move if I tried.

In that moment, I felt as if I could ask Chris to spend the evening with me, maybe even the night, and he would. I was so uneducated about these things, but I thought maybe he was telling me more than I was able to understand. Then again, maybe he was just telling me to go celebrate my birthday and not think about work for the rest of the day. Regardless, he had said he couldn't walk the line, so I knew I shouldn't blur it any further.

I decided to play it safe, and as much as it pained me, I forced myself to break the spell between us. "Thank you for the wonderful birthday present. It really meant more to me than you'll ever know. I'll see you in the morning?"

"Absolutely," Chris nodded. He, like I, was ignoring the elephant in the room and deciding to play it safe.

"Okay, see you then." I skated to the edge of the rink and then walked off the ice towards George.

"Oh, and Abigail," Chris called to me with a smile in his voice. "Try being on time tomorrow, okay?"

[FROM THE DESK OF DR. ALEC B. REDMOND I have no idea what the Billy Joel connection is. That's not one that ever came up in my conversations with Abigail. I just listened to "Vienna" for the first time - what does it have to do with her? Too much ambition? I don't know. Everything she has told me leads me to believe the only thing standing in the way of her leading a more full and successful life than the one she leads is her struggle with reality. I believed, of course, that she had that under control, but she was in her forties by the time she and I met at Cedar Springs. I encouraged her to chase some dreams, but her response was always, "Dreams are for the young and naïve." There may have been a great deal of ambition on her part when she was younger. She is well-educated, though she refused to ever tell me which college or university she attended. With many patients, I would take that to mean no school had been attended at all, but I don't believe that to be true in Abigail's case. When I would ask her why she refused to tell me, she would say, "Alec, I'm telling you tons of stuff here. Let there be some little secret which only the past and I share."]

6.   THIS IS THE TIME

Things continued on. My friendship with George grew continually stronger, always platonic, no blurry lines at all. Chris and I were continually blurry, but we learned to handle it better. We were passionate in every aspect of our relationship - on the ice, in our attraction to each other, and when we fought. Boy, could we fight.

Chris pushed hard. Once I fell in love with ice dancing, I had fun every time I was on the ice. He had fun too, but his fun was more serious. He didn't like to mess around or waste time. He was a perfectionist and a workaholic, and it would have been unbearable at times if he wasn't so insanely talented and always making us better.

We had limited time together, of course, so we did have to work ridiculously hard to make the most of our training opportunities. We decided to declare our eligibility for Great Britain so, according to ISU rules, we had to train at least 60% of the time on Chris's home turf. I spent a lot of time in Nottingham with him, staying at his parents' home when I was there. The remaining 40% of the time, we trained in Simsbury, Connecticut at the International Skating Center. I relocated to Simsbury in 1980, simply so we could get more training time together. It was much easier to fly from London to New York or New York to London than it was to fly into or out of anywhere in Kentucky. I would drive the hour or two into Manhattan to catch a flight, or to pick Chris up from the airport, then we would drive back to Simsbury and spend all of our time on the ice.

George moved to L.A. to start focusing on his acting career, and the rare times I got to go home to visit my parents, Kentucky just felt lonely without him. I did all right in Simsbury - all I really did was train. Oh, and I had to go to school. My parents - the same parents who decided I had to attend public school - also decided that I had to go to college. They wanted me to have something to fall back on in case the whole skating thing didn't work out, and I actually managed to get a full scholarship to Brown University. Somehow, in spite of my insane schedule, I had managed to be a really great student in high school. I guess I knew that if my grades slipped I would be forced to give up skating, so I worked very hard to make sure that was never an option on the table.

Brown is in Providence, Rhode Island, about two hours from Simsbury. Thankfully, I got to go to school on an extremely reduced schedule. Usually I could manage it to where I went one day a week, and one full week a month. When Chris was in town, we worked every moment that I was not at school and when I was in England, I took schoolwork with me.

My partner, meanwhile, was working as a cop in Nottingham. When I was with him there, I worked on schoolwork while he covered his beat as a bobby, and then we trained the rest of the time. We were both completely exhausted.

We hoped that it would all be worth it, but we really had no idea. We had a couple of routines in our repertoire, and we were pretty proud of them, but we weren't sure we would be ready for the 1980 British Figure Skating Championships in November.

Our first public performance together was at ISU President Bengtsson's birthday bash, which he threw for himself in Stockholm in the spring of 1980. Chris and I were invited to perform as the headlining act - he wanted to show off his little project - and we performed "Vienna." I was very nervous beforehand, mostly due to my uncertainty that the audience would really get it. The routine was incredibly personal to Chris and me, and I held it so close to my heart that I didn't think I would be able to bear it if there were so much as one bit of criticism against it.

I was worried for nothing. You couldn't hear anyone so much as breathe or adjust in their seat. We ended with the formal bow and curtsey to each other, he kissed my hand, and then we went our separate ways. And finally, there was some noise. As we skated back to each other for our bows to the crowd, the audience of 10,000 erupted. Chris and I looked at each other in shock - I think we had been hoping for them to be mildly entertained, but we weren't prepared for the reaction we received.

Right there, in the center of the rink in front of all of those people, in front of figure skating royalty, Chris and I could do nothing but laugh. I think it was mostly relief, but also a little bit of jet lag and a lot of exhaustion and sleep deprivation. He put his arm around me as we shared our private giggle, in a very public arena, and we skated off the ice together.

We were bombarded with praise from everyone we saw once we left the ice. Our skating heroes came up to us and told us they loved our routine, and people in very high positions within the ISU governing body told us they looked forward to seeing what we came up with next. We had officially arrived on the scene.

Chris and I went to dinner after the gala, almost giddy in the afterglow. And then something very curious began to happen. Random strangers began to ask us for our autographs. We began noticing camera flashes, but when we turned to look in the direction of the flash, no one was there. And, the questions began.

"When are you getting married?"

"Christopher, was it love at first sight?"

"Abigail, when did you know he was the one?"

What? Each time we heard one of these questions, we answered the same way: "No, we're just good friends."

No one seemed to believe us. Stockholm, it seemed, had fallen in love with Phelps and Dean, and we couldn't have been more pleased. Yes, it was a very limited fan base, we knew, but it was a start!

The next morning we took a cab to the airport together, said our goodbyes - like we did so often at airports - and he flew to London, I flew to New York. We had a week on our separate continents, then Chris would be flying to the States to train with me for two weeks.

A very long flight later, I stepped off the plane in New York, and as I entered the terminal, I immediately began to wonder what celebrity had been on the plane in first class without my noticing. I always traveled coach, of course, so I hadn't noticed anyone, but there were so many reporters, photographers, and fans waiting at the terminal that someone had to be behind me. I turned around to look, but I couldn't see anyone. Then I heard it:

"Abby! Abby! Over here!"

"Abigail! Just a photo, Abigail!"

"Abby, is Christopher with you?"

Once again…what? This was all for me? Everyone was respectful and gave me my space, but they were certainly interested. I couldn't believe it.

I stopped at a payphone in a secluded area after I managed to escape from the followers and made a long distance call to George. I probably should have called my parents, or maybe even Chris, but for whatever reason I needed to hear George's voice.

He answered on the second ring.

"I sure am glad to hear your voice," I said through the emotion caught in my throat.

"Abby, are you okay? Are you back?"

"Yes, I just landed. I'm still at the airport. You'll never believe what was waiting for me when I got off the plane. You'll just never believe it!"

"Photographers and reporters?"

"Yes! And fans. How did you know that?"

George laughed. "Because, you're everywhere! Even here in L.A., you're everywhere! You're in the papers, on the news…if I turned on the television right now, I'd probably see you at the airport! You're a total star, Abby."

It was all so confusing. "But why? All we did was skate, and I thought only people in Stockholm noticed us. This is crazy, George."

"Oh, come on…it makes for a great story." He started laying it on thick. "Brought together to represent peace and unity between nations, forced to balance training with career, education, and frequent intercontinental flights, these two unrealistically attractive young people represent everything for which the Olympic Games stand."

I laughed. "Well, that was just beautiful, George."

"Oh no, that wasn't me. That was a direct quote from this morning's *New York Times*."

I couldn't breathe. "You're kidding me."

"Nope. Not kidding. And it goes on to say, 'But will this fairy tale have a storybook ending? Miss Phelps and Mr. Dean have already mastered the art of being coy. Will they marry before the 1984 Sarajevo Olympic Games or will they wait until they are medalists to get their perfect ending? That remains to be seen. Only one thing is certain: like Vienna, figure skating glory waits for them.'"

"Okay, that's it!" For some reason, I was ignoring the gratuitous praise in the article and instead focusing on one minor detail which made no sense to me. "Why do they think Chris and I are together? And getting *married*? Where is everyone getting that?"

"Well, that one isn't hard to figure out, Abby. Now that they've seen you together on the ice, how could they believe anything other than the idea that you are madly in love with each other? The chemistry has been there since the very beginning. You know that. They see it too."

"Well, that's no good."

George laughed once more. "Isn't it? You wanted people to notice the two of you for being different from everyone else in ice dancing, right? Well, I think you got your wish."

My week until Chris got to the States to train was spent focusing on school. I spent four entire days on the campus of Brown getting caught up, and ultimately a little bit ahead. I usually loved my time on campus - I would go to classes, drink coffee in the student union building, study under the shade of a tree. More than anything, when I was on campus, I got to relax. Yes, I was studying at a prestigious university, and having to study more than I ever had in my life, but I was able to relax, pretending that I was just like every other student on campus. For that, I was very grateful to my parents and their college requirement.

But those four days on campus were very different. Photographers were everywhere. I had never experienced anything like it - so much for studying under a tree. It took all I had just to get to class on time, squeezing past reporters, politely answering some of their questions, and insisting, time after time, that Chris and I were just good friends.

On Friday of that week I was rushing across campus, desperate to make it to my Sociology class, but certain I was going to be late due to the reporters and photographers along the way. I was almost there, and only three minutes late. More impressively, I had lost my constant companions in the press. It was all going so well, and then I tripped over a bundle of tree roots laying just above ground. I went flying, my books went flying, and my confidence went flying.

"Whoa, are you okay?" A male voice sounded genuinely concerned and was getting closer, and then was quickly close enough to reach out a hand to try and help me up.

"Yeah, I'm okay. Just an idiot." I put my hand in his, accepting his offer of help – I certainly needed it - as I looked up for the first time to see the face of the man coming to my rescue.

I certainly wasn't expecting to see the most famous face on Brown's, or any, campus, but there he was: John F. Kennedy Jr.

[FROM THE DESK OF DR. ALEC B. REDMOND Okay, hold on a minute. A Kennedy has appeared. I don't believe any of Abigail's delusions ever featured JFK Jr. previously, though of course Ted Kennedy once had a starring role. What is her fascination with the Kennedys? Also, I'm curious about Brown University. I've never had a difficult time believing she received a college education, but I've never had any reason to suspect it was Ivy League. However, John Kennedy Jr. was in fact attending Brown University at the precise time about which Abigail has written.]

Obviously I knew he attended Brown - everyone in the world knew that - but it wasn't something I ever thought about. I had never seen him in person before that grand, humiliating moment.

"Where are you headed in such a hurry, anyway?" Once I was on my feet, John set about the task of helping me pick up my scattered books and papers.

"Oh, I'm late for Sociology 260. This is going to sound really stupid, but I had to run to get away from reporters." I was so embarrassed I could hardly stand it.

John handed me the last of my papers and smiled. "Really? You think that will sound stupid to *me*?"

Then the true embarrassment hit. "Oh, of course. Sorry. It must be like that for you all of the time. Or probably much, much worse. I'm Abby, by the way. Thanks for your help." I put my hand out and he shook it.

"I'm John." Well, obviously!

I smiled. "Of course I know who you are, John. It's nice to meet you." I found it very surprising and refreshing that he introduced himself.

"It's nice to meet you too, Abby. And, of course, I know who *you* are too."

"You do not." Without thinking I pushed him in the chest - gut reaction.

He laughed. "Sure I do. It's been refreshing this week. Thanks to you, the press has pretty much ignored me."

Was this my life? Was I really having a conversation with JFK Jr. in which he was telling me that the media was more interested in me than him, even for a moment? I had half a mind to pinch myself, but my biggest fear was that it *was* real, and I would just look really stupid for pinching myself. Okay. If this was my life, what was the harm in at least enjoying a conversation with the most famous college student in the world?

"Well," I said in a very cool I-can-hold-my-own-with-famous-people sort of way, "I'm so glad to be able to help. Whenever you need a break, you just let me know and I'll hold a press conference at the Phi Beta Kappa house or something."

He held his hand in front of his mouth as an imaginary microphone and spoke in his most serious reporter voice. "Abigail, three questions: Why haven't you gotten married yet? Are you getting married this year? And when are you getting married?"

"You joke, but that's pretty much what it's like!" I laughed.

"Oh, I know. I was standing a few feet away when they had you surrounded yesterday. I heard it. Actually, it was kind of funny - my friend dared me to see how close I could get without them noticing me, and I got pretty close. My goal was to get right in the pack and ask you a question."

"Oh really? What would you have asked?"

"I had a few different ideas, but I think it would have been, 'I'm not sure if someone already asked this, but are you married yet?'"

I involuntarily did a spit take, and then I just doubled over in laughter. "Oh, I wish you had gotten in there!"

He was laughing too. "I was pretty close. I'll get it next time."

As we stood there talking and laughing, I wasn't thinking about who he was, who his family was, or what his legacy was. I wasn't even thinking about how handsome he was, although it was certainly something I realized. Photos didn't do him justice.

Actually, what I was thinking was, "I'm going to marry this guy someday."

You hear of people who think that, or say that, and they have these gloriously successful happily-ever-after endings. John and I weren't destined for that, obviously. Nevertheless, on that chaotic, sunny spring day in Rhode Island, I met the love of my life. And John F. Kennedy Jr. met the love of his life, as well.

7. C'ETAIT TOI (YOU WERE THE ONE)

George and I had an instant connection - mostly comical. Chris and I had an instant connection - mostly physical. The instant connection which John and I had was both comical and physical, but more than that it was instinctual. I felt like I had known him all my life.

It probably won't surprise anyone to learn that I skipped Sociology 260 that day. It was the first time I had ever skipped a class for anything other than skating, but I just didn't want to stop talking to him. We sat under the tree with the roots which had led us to each other, and we fell in love.

I had never been in love before, but not only that, I had never really wanted to be. I had wanted to be with Chris. In fact, I had wanted to be with Chris up until that very day. But I wasn't searching for love. Chris was my first crush. John was my first love. I didn't really realize it immediately, though I certainly felt the connection. And yes, I felt strongly that I would marry John someday, but I didn't realize then that I was already in love with him. Looking back, I know it without a doubt.

John later told me that he was very sure of his feelings for me right then and there. He also told me years later that, while he was very much enjoying our time talking under the tree, he was also a bit stressed, trying to figure out how he was going to break the news to his girlfriend. At the time, his girlfriend was never mentioned in the conversation, so I got to be blissfully unaware.

We sat under that beech tree, mostly hidden from view and certainly not sticking out in a crowd, until the sun began to set. It had been a perfect afternoon, and I didn't want it to end. Thankfully, neither did John.

"Will you go to dinner with me tonight?" he asked as he held my hand to help me stand.

Unfortunately, I had to turn down my first real date request. "I would love to but I can't. Chris is flying in on a red eye tonight. I actually need to get on the road. I have to pick him up in New York."

John's face lit up. "I was going to drive to Manhattan in the morning anyway. Let me drive you. Which airport is he flying into?"

I was giddy thinking about the additional time we would have together. "Kennedy."

I'd taken his celebrity completely in stride - it just didn't matter. But that was a very surreal moment. John F. Kennedy Jr. was about to give me a lift to the airport named after his father.

[FROM THE DESK OF DR. ALEC B. REDMOND As I read this last paragraph, something suddenly felt very familiar to me. So I just spent the last two hours combing through Abigail's files, and I discovered that I was mistaken. She did once include JFK Jr. in a delusion, and she told me this very story. It was the second day we met together - her third at Cedar Springs. We were talking about moments, and I was trying to get her to separate the real from the delusional. I asked her a series of questions regarding moments - What was your happiest moment? What was your funniest moment? What was the first moment you remember considering yourself an adult? What was your most surreal moment? Well, her answer to that question was, "It doesn't get much more surreal than getting a ride to JFK Airport from JFK Jr., does it?" My reply: "I imagine that would feel very surreal, but that didn't actually happen, did it, Abigail?" "No," she said. "It was a delusion. I see that now." I don't believe JFK Jr. was ever mentioned in our sessions again.]

"Kennedy it is! I just need to stop off at my apartment and we can go. Sound good?"

I smiled at him. "Sounds great."

It wasn't until we were about an hour into the drive that I realized I had overlooked one crucial detail when I left my car at Brown.

"Oh no! How are we going to get to Simsbury?"

John didn't seem too worried. "Oh, don't worry about that. We'll work it out. What I want to know is when do you sleep? How do you keep up this crazy schedule?"

With ridiculous timing, I involuntarily yawned. "Oh, it's not so bad. This part of the schedule, for instance - I guarantee Chris is asleep on his flight right now, and then he always drives us to Simsbury in my car while I catch a nap. He drops me off at my apartment, I sleep for about three more hours while he goes to the rink and gets to work right away - mostly to avoid the jet lag. Then he picks me up, we grab some breakfast, and we're on the ice by 6:30."

He laughed. "Not so bad, huh?"

"It's worth it," I said sincerely.

That was followed by the most comfortable two minutes of silence, which was then broken by, "So, what's the real deal with you and Chris? *Are* you together? Sorry - I probably should have asked that sooner."

I hadn't spoken openly about my relationship with Chris with anyone besides George, but I didn't feel any hesitancy in telling John whatever he wanted to know. "No. We're not together."

"But it's not as simple as that either, is it?"

"No."

We sat in silence again - not quite as comfortably as before, but I think that was only because I was taking a realistic look at my relationship with Chris. I had wanted to be with him. Though he and I didn't discuss our future, I think we had both assumed we had one. Suddenly I wanted a future with John, and while I wasn't at all apprehensive when it came to telling John about my feelings for Chris, I was extremely nervous when I thought of telling Chris about my feelings for John.

"I guess I should give you fair warning," I said, trying to keep it light. "Chris and I tend to be sort of intense."

"In what way?"

"In *every* way," I chuckled. "When we fight, we really fight. We work hard on the ice, we work hard off the ice, and we do really care about each other. But no, we're not together."

John exhaled in what I think was relief.

I couldn't leave it at that, though. I felt compelled to tell him everything. "But we almost were. He was willing to give up skating with me so we could be in a relationship, and we kissed a couple of times. And we kind of decided we would skate together through the 1984 Olympics, and then be together."

He cleared his throat. "Well, that complicates things a bit, doesn't it?"

I turned toward him. "Does it? Not for me. That's how I felt, but it's not how I feel." I broke every rule in the book and on day one I laid it all on the line. "I don't know how you feel - and in case you don't feel the way I do, I probably shouldn't say this halfway through a long car trip - but I want to be with *you*, not Chris. I have never felt this way before. I don't know anything about how any of this works, and I probably look really stupid right now, but I don't care. And if you don't feel the same way, I'll deal with that, but I really don't want it to not work out because you think my relationship with Chris complicates things. It doesn't. Not at all. It couldn't be simpler."

John stayed facing forward - which was a good thing, since he was driving - and didn't mutter a sound. I knew I had messed up. I wanted to take it back, and yet I was so relieved it was out there. I waited for him to say anything, hoping it would be "I love you" but fearing it would be "Get out of my car, you psycho." What he did finally say was more frightening than the latter and somehow more exhilarating than the former.

"I want you to meet my mother."

That would be a frightening prospect no matter who the guy, no matter who the mother. But John's mother was the most famous woman on the planet.

John continued, "Do you think I could pick you up tomorrow afternoon and you could come to Manhattan for dinner?" He paused and then muttered, "Chris could come too, of course."

Now I just couldn't see *that* happening.

There was nothing I wanted more than to go with John to meet his mother, but I couldn't. "I can't, John. Chris and I get so little time as it is. I'm sorry. Another time?"

He was obviously disappointed. "Oh, of course. Sorry. I should have thought of that. Yeah, another time. And Abby, I think I should tell you something."

And then he told me about Christina Haag. His girlfriend. His steady, serious girlfriend. They had been dating for a year or two and were practically living together. She had been in his apartment when he ran in to grab a few things before we left Brown. No surprise: he hadn't mentioned that I was waiting in his car.

I tried to remain calm. "John, I don't want to be the other woman. I'm sorry. I had no idea you were in a relationship." I felt like I should tell him I would completely understand if he dropped me off at the airport and that was the end of it, but I couldn't bring myself to say it.

For the first time since we left Brown, he pulled off the interstate, taking an exit to a little gas station. He stopped the car and turned to me.

"I don't want you to be the other woman, either." For several seconds, neither of us said anything. We just sat there, trying to figure out how to proceed. Every moment of silence felt like a death sentence for the hope and anticipation which had been so consuming for most of the day. But then John put me out of my misery. "Is it okay if I kiss you?"

I was speechless, and breathless, so I just nodded.

Then he kissed me for the first time, softly and gently. It was nothing like the heated, passionate kisses Chris and I had shared. When Chris kissed me, it felt like a kiss straight out of a movie - hot and steamy and somewhat exhausting, but in a wonderful way, of course. John's kiss was the type of kiss I wanted to experience every day for the rest of my life.

He pulled away from my lips and pulled me to rest my head on his chest, and he held me tightly. "I sure didn't see you coming. I'm sorry that I'm not handling this the right way. Not that I know what the right way would be."

"It feels pretty right to me."

He pulled me even closer. "It does, doesn't it? Unfortunately I can think of a couple of people who may not see it that way."

If only there were just a couple…

8.   ANGRY YOUNG MAN

John and I spent a few more minutes at that gas station, then we got back on the road. The remainder of our drive to Kennedy Airport was spent holding hands and carefully planning how to break the news of our relationship to Chris and Christina.

When we arrived at Chris's terminal, I walked in alone to meet him at the gate, while John waited in the car. When I saw him, I was genuinely delighted to have him back in the States. I cared about him deeply - there was no doubt about that.

It was fairly obvious he was happy to see me too. He ran to me, scooped me up in his arms, and swung me around.

"How are you, kid? I've missed you," he said with a smile.

"I've missed you too. Have you had a good week?"

"The best. I have another program ready to go for us. I think you'll love it. I can hardly wait to get you on the ice."

He was in such a great mood, and I wasn't thrilled that I was about to ruin it, but I had no choice. We were just one baggage claim away from Chris finding out that JFK Jr. was his chauffeur for the evening.

"Hey, I need to talk to you for a minute." I pulled him aside to a bench, close enough to see his luggage when it came out.

"Sure. Everything okay?" He looked concerned

and held my hand as we sat down.

"Yeah. Everything's great. I just need to let you know about something really important that happened." I took a deep breath. "I met someone. I think we're dating."

Chris let go of my hand and looked down at his own. "You think?"

"Well, it's all very new, but yeah, I'm sure we're going to be together now. We really connected, we just haven't put a definition on it yet." As I said it I knew that no words could do justice to the depth of the feelings between John and me.

Chris looked back up and met my eyes with his. "You 'connected,' huh?" He paused, carefully measuring his words. "Like you and I connected?"

He was hurt, and that made me feel like a creep, but I had to be honest with him. He was going to be around, and I was pretty sure John was going to be around, so there was no point in sugarcoating anything. Especially since I knew he would see for himself soon enough.

"Not exactly. Differently." I braced myself. "More deeply."

I could tell that had stung. "I see. Okay, well thank you for telling me."

"That's all?" I don't know what I had been expecting.

"Yes, that's all. I couldn't very well expect you to sit around waiting for me for the next five years, could I? If you're happy, I'm happy. Now let's go get my bags and get to the car so you can get some sleep." He was obviously not as okay as he wanted me to believe, but I appreciated the effort. And then I remembered the two very important details I hadn't yet mentioned.

"Actually, you don't need to drive tonight. He actually drove me here, and he's going to give us a ride to Simsbury." In retrospect, that hadn't been a very tactful move, I realized.

He noticeably tensed, but he controlled himself. "Okay. As long as you sleep, I don't care. But you have to sleep."

"Okay, I'll sleep. And one more thing…" It was so

awkward and uncomfortable.

"More? I don't know if I can stand more!" He ran his hand through his hair, and attempted a laugh, but it didn't sound as relaxed as I think he meant for it to.

"It's John Kennedy Jr., not that that matters. I just didn't want you to be surprised when we get to the car."

He looked shocked. Then he spoke in a sarcastic, bitter tone. "Now, now - don't you worry about me, Abigail. Come on. I see my suitcase." And he stormed off toward baggage claim.

When we got to the car, John was all kindness and effort, and Chris was not. I needed to sleep, but I didn't want to leave them alone. After a while, in the dark and the silence, I couldn't help but doze.

«« ◊ »»

John gently rubbed my arm to wake me when we got to Simsbury. "Abby, sorry, I don't know where I'm going. Where do you live?"

Chris spoke up from the back seat. "You didn't have to wake her. I know where she lives."

"Sorry, I didn't realize you and I were on speaking terms," John sighed.

I whispered to John, "Did I miss something?"

"I'll fill you in later."

"Oh, don't act like any horrible thing happened. Can you please just drop me off at the rink first? I have work to do." I couldn't believe the level of hostility from Chris.

I knew I had to try to fix this before it got completely out of hand. "Chris, I'm actually feeling pretty rested. Why don't I go to the rink with you now?"

"Actually, I'd rather you didn't. Don't think I could stand to be around you right now, frankly."

"Hey, that's not really necessary, is it?" John said, coming to my aid.

Chris's voice was tense and loud. "Please, I *beg* you to stay out of this."

John's voice was getting pretty tense and loud as well. "I absolutely will *not* stay out of this."

"Stop it! Both of you, stop it! John, turn left up

here." I directed him to the training center.

When the car came to a stop Chris got out immediately. Actually, I think he got out a little before the car fully stopped. I opened my door to follow him.

John grabbed my hand. "Are you sure you want to do that? He's pretty angry. Maybe you should just leave him alone."

"I can't, John. He's my partner. I'll be fine."

He sighed, understanding me already. "Okay. I'll wait here."

I shook my head. "No. Don't. You still have to drive back to Manhattan. It's so late as it is. I'm going to stay here - we'll sort this out and then we'll get to work. I'll call you tomorrow, okay?" I looked at my watch and smiled. "Or today, I suppose."

John didn't look happy about it, but I think he knew I would not be swayed. "Be careful."

"I'm fine. It's just Chris." I said those words as lightly as I could, but I was truthfully a bit worried. I wasn't worried Chris would actually *do* anything to me, of course, though that may have been what John was afraid of. But I knew it was going to be much chillier than it normally was on the ice.

I leaned in closer to John. "You're going to get some rest tonight, wake up, and realize you don't want anything to do with me after all of this."

He smiled. "Not a chance." He gave me a quick kiss and reluctantly let me go.

When I got inside Chris was already on the ice, warming up. I laced up as quickly as I could and got out there with him. Or as "with him" as I could anyway. He wouldn't let me skate anywhere near him.

I'd had enough. "Would you please stop for just a minute so we can talk?"

He shouted at me from the other side of the rink, which thankfully was abandoned at 3:00 in the morning. "Talk? Really, what is there to talk about, Abigail?"

I started shouting too, more than anything angry with him that he was ruining what otherwise would have been one of the happiest days of my life. "Well, we could start with the obvious: Why are you so mad at me?"

"Are you serious? Do I really have to explain this to you?"

"I guess you do. I met someone. I'm *dating* someone - for the first time in my life, I should add. You and I were not dating, and if you recall, you are the one who said it had to be one or the other for us. We chose the other. So what's the problem, Chris?"

He skated over to me, and the yelling stopped. "You have every right to date someone, Abigail. Of course you do. And *I* have every right to date someone. But it wasn't until tonight that I realized the difference between us."

I prepared myself for whatever he had to say, because I instantly knew that it wasn't going to be pretty. "Which is?"

I wasn't prepared enough. "I'm an adult who understands serious grown-up emotions, while you're just a little girl going through her slutty stage."

I felt as if I had been slapped in the face. "I'm sorry. My slutty stage?"

"At least I hope it's a stage. First me and now him. Actually, George too."

"What? What are you talking about? You know George and I are just friends."

"Well, so are you and I, right? But you were bonded for life to George the very first day you met. Now this guy. You met him yesterday, and only *technically* yesterday. And day one when you and I met you were considering giving up everything you have ever worked for so that we could be together."

"Yes, well, so were you!"

"I know, but again it all comes down to the difference between the two of us."

I wasn't sure if it was the lack of sleep or if he had suddenly started speaking Greek, but I didn't understand what he was saying.

"What are you talking about?"

"You connected to John more deeply?"

"Yes," I said bluntly. After his "slutty stage"

comment, I was a lot less worried about hurting him.

"That's where I see the difference, and you don't have any idea. This isn't some infatuation for me, Abigail. I'm in love with you."

I probably should have seen that coming, but I didn't. I had felt like Chris was telling me he loved me through Vienna, so I suppose on some level I knew, but to hear him say it to me was completely different.

But it didn't change a thing.

And what was more, I was furious. He had called me a slut. Me! I didn't know anyone less slutty than I was. I admit things had progressed pretty quickly with John. And Chris. And George in a very different way. I can't explain the immediate connections I had with those three men, the First Three, and I really don't care if anyone understands. At that moment, I certainly didn't care if Chris understood. My feelings for him had been real - but I had also never deceived myself, or him, as to the depth of them. I cared for him a great deal, and he was certainly one of the most important people in my life. And yes, I felt an intense attraction to him, and I would continue to feel that intense attraction for years. Who am I kidding? I still feel it. But I was certain that I was not in love with Christopher Dean.

I wanted to lash out at him, but I didn't even know where to begin. Instead, I spoke calmly and deliberately, choosing each word for its ultimate value.

"I'm sorry that you love me, but it's not my fault that you do. And you know me too well to really believe I am going through a 'slutty stage' which means those words were only chosen to hurt and offend me, and you succeeded. But that's all I'm going to say about it. I don't owe you an explanation. How I feel about someone is frankly no concern of yours. If you would like to continue skating with me, I will continue to be your partner. But you are not my boyfriend, and you never will be. And from this moment on, you are not my friend either. I'm just punching the clock from now on."

Without another word I skated off the ice, doubtful I would have a job to clock in for by sunrise.

9. BABY GRAND

I walked to my apartment, which was only about a mile from the rink. I sat and fumed until 7:00 a.m., and then called John at his mother's number in New York. I was sure he was probably sleeping, after I kept him out all night, but I just couldn't take it any longer. I had to talk to him about everything that had happened.

I was really hoping that his mother wasn't the one to answer the phone. I was sure if she knew anything of what had happened, I had already made a pretty unfavorable first impression. To call just a couple hours later would look pathetic.

Thankfully John answered, on the first ring, sounding much more alert than he had any right to.

"Hello?"

"Hi John, this is Abby. Sorry to call so early..."

"Abby, thank God. Is everything okay? Are *you* okay?"

I immediately realized he hadn't slept, and that he had been sitting by the phone waiting for me to call.

I just broke down crying, and tried to sound composed through my tears. "I'm fine. I'm tired, but I'm fine. Are you okay? You must be exhausted."

The concern in his voice was thick, but laced with what I sensed was disgust for Chris. "No, I'm fine. So, what happened after I left?"

I told him everything, word for word. I had gone over it in my mind so many times already, and I still remember it today so clearly. I don't think I even knew then just how hurt I was.

I got to the part which hurt the most. "So, then he said that he was in love with me and that I was just going through a 'slutty stage.'"

There was complete silence on the other end of the line for long enough that I began to wonder if John had fallen asleep.

And then, "He said what?" He was livid.

The slut part bothered me the most, but I was sure that what would bother John the most was the fact that Chris had said he was in love with me. I was wrong.

"He called you that?"

"He said it just like that - that I was going through a 'slutty stage' because I moved into a relationship with you so quickly, after he and I had the initial connection we had. And I hope you're not upset that he said he's in love with me. I'm not sure that he even is, honestly. And I know that I'm not in love with him."

"I know that, Abby. And I know that he's in love with you. While you were sleeping in the car, he just kept trying to talk about this incredible bond that the two of you have, and how he was fine with me dating you, because he knew that you'd end up with him someday. He just kept pushing and pushing, and I tried to ignore him, but then I'd finally had enough. So I told him."

I hadn't realized I had been that deeply asleep.

"Told him what?"

John didn't hesitate - he was so full of self-confidence, and I had such admiration for that. "I told him that just moments after I met you, I was filled with an overwhelming feeling that I am going to marry you someday, so if he was going to continue skating with you, he needed to get used to having me around. After that, he told me he thought it was best if we didn't talk anymore. So we didn't." He sounded like he was smiling at the memory.

I didn't say anything. I couldn't. I was in shock - wonderful, euphoric shock. I wanted to tell him that I had felt the same way, that I'd had the exact same feeling: that

I was going to marry him someday. But I couldn't form the words. My heart felt like it would explode, and every bad thought and memory - in fact every thought that wasn't "John" - was erased from my mind. I had known him fewer than twenty-four hours, and I knew he was the great love of my life, no matter what else happened.

"Abby, sorry...I hope it didn't freak you out to hear that. Coming on kind of strong, aren't I? The point is, his feelings for you don't come as any big surprise to me. But I'm definitely going to have to talk to him about talking to you the way he did." The anger was back.

And with his anger returned my sadness. "I wouldn't bother if I were you. I think Phelps and Dean are history."

"Well then, you're free for lunch, aren't you?"

I laughed a bit in spite of myself, and in spite of everything. "Yes, I suppose I am."

"Great! I'll pick you up and you can meet my mother after all."

"Hold it. Have you slept at all?"

"No, but I'm fine."

"I don't think so. Get a few hours of sleep, and I could probably use a bit myself, and then I'll go for dinner instead. How about that?"

"I'll take it."

«« ◊ »»

John knocked on my door seven hours later, and greeted me with a kiss I know we had both been anxiously awaiting.

"Are you ready to go?" he asked.

"Should I try to find Chris and let him know where I am?"

The look on John's face gave me his answer, but I decided to leave a note on my door anyway - just in case.

Chris,

If you want to talk, I'll be back in the morning. Feel free to stay here. You know where the key is.

Abby

"You're being too nice," John said, looking over my shoulder as I taped the note to the door.

And part of me knew that I probably was being a bit too nice, but another part of me had realized, after getting some sleep, that Chris had acted out emotionally because he really was in love with me. And maybe he hadn't handled things the best possible way, but I knew I hadn't either. I did still want to be Chris's partner, and I still wanted to be his friend. It would take some work to get through it all, but I was willing to make it work if he was.

Something you need to know about me, if you haven't figured it out already: at that time in my life I was incredibly idealistic and naïve. I really did believe it would all work out, and I couldn't really imagine any reason why it wouldn't. Yes, Chris and I were going through a rough patch, but we cared about each other and I knew that we would continue skating together. And we would be great friends forever, and someday we would look back on all of it and laugh. What's more, I knew that John and I would get married, and Chris would marry some great girl, and in ten years we'd all get together for family picnics and let our kids play together while John and Chris and I filled Chris's wife in on our ridiculous backstory.

Yes. I was naïve.

Of course, the reality of how it all ended up happening had its elements of perfection beyond anything I could have created in my naïve, teenage brain, but we'll get to that soon enough. For now, on to dinner with Jacqueline Kennedy Onassis.

«««§»»»

As we took the elevator up to Mrs. Onassis's beautiful apartment overlooking Central Park, I was struck by the absurdity of my emotions. I was very nervous, but not because I was about to meet the most famous woman in the world, a former First Lady. I was nervous because I was about to meet John's mother, and that realization actually helped me to relax. We were a normal young couple, and he was taking me to meet his mother for the first time. It just didn't get more normal than that.

I had just convinced myself of that when we stepped out of the elevator and into the most enormous, beautiful foyer I had ever seen. And I began to hyperventilate a little. We weren't like any other couple at all! I was a famous figure skater, I had just met this guy yesterday, and his mother was going to hate me. Maybe I *was* a slut, I thought. I'd barely slept and I wasn't sure if I would even be able to put intelligent sentences together - and this was the woman who had charmed heads of state and foreign diplomats and legends of every art form known to man. The enormity of the situation truly dawned on me for the very first time. I was in love with John-John!

I shrieked a little. "I have to go, John-John."

John looked shocked, and then he began to laugh, and he continued to laugh until he was struggling to catch his breath.

"Did you just call me John-John?" He was still laughing.

Had I? Oh no.

I was completely mortified and I wanted to die.

"I'm so sorry. I really do have to go. I can't do this." I turned to go back into the elevator.

John blocked my path, and he was no longer laughing.

"Hey, what's going on?"

"I just called you John-John! I'm an idiot and I am not cut out for this."

"Really, Abby, it's not that big a deal. I think it was hilarious. Why are you freaking out on me?" He looked a bit freaked out himself, like he didn't know what to make of me.

I think I was just so tired - physically, mentally, and emotionally exhausted. I knew I was being irrational, but I also couldn't control it.

"I'm sorry. Can we do this another day? I just have so much on my mind."

Before I could get completely absorbed in my pity party, I heard a very familiar, breathy, elegant voice from another room.

"John, is that you?"

I looked at John with eyes which must have been the size of golf balls.

He quickly and quietly pulled me into his arms and whispered into my hair, "You can do this. The *idea* of meeting my mother is much more horrifying than actually meeting her, I promise. You're going to love her, and she's going to love you. This is just my mom, Abby, and you are beautiful and sweet and hilarious and smart and perfect, and I can't wait for her to meet you. Please stay."

I looked up into his beautiful brown eyes and knew that there was nowhere else I would rather be.

"Do I call her Mrs. Kennedy or Mrs. Onassis?"

John smiled the beautiful smile I already treasured. "Mrs. Onassis will be fine. Let's go." He gave me a quick peck on the lips, then looked at me mischievously and said, "I'm sure Truman Capote and Katharine Hepburn are finishing up their brandy in the parlor, so she'll be waiting for us." I thought I was going to hyperventilate again, but thankfully John called off the ruse quickly. "I'm kidding!" he chuckled. He put his arm around my waist and pulled me close, then called out to his mother, "Yes, it's me. And Abby's here."

Around the corner came the exquisite woman I had pretended to be while playing with my Kennedy Family paper dolls as a little girl.

"Abby. It's wonderful to meet you. Won't you please come in?" She shook my hand with a grip which was both delicate and surprisingly firm before leading us into a sitting room.

"Mrs. Onassis, it's wonderful to meet you. Thank you so much for inviting me into your lovely home."

"Of course, dear. I'm so glad you are able to join us for dinner. Now, if you will just excuse me a moment, I will go and check on a couple of things for us. John, why don't you show Abby around?"

"Yes, ma'am." John was always so respectful of his mother, and not just because of the good manners she had instilled in him. He genuinely loved and respected her, and she was his role model in so many ways.

As Mrs. Onassis exited into the dining area, John took my hand and pulled me to him. With his arms wrapped around me, it did all feel very normal once again.

"How much does she know about me?" I asked quietly. "I know you haven't had much time to talk to her since we met."

"She doesn't know much, actually. She knows who you are, of course - she follows figure skating to some extent. But all I had a chance to tell her was that you and I met and I really like you a lot."

I smiled. "You like me a lot? That's a little seventh grade, isn't it?"

He smiled back, still holding me close. "Trust me, since we just met yesterday, she will take me liking you a lot better than, 'So, this is the girl I love and we're getting married someday.' But that will come soon enough."

My breath caught in my throat. "The girl you love?"

His smile melted away, and the expression which replaced it was breathtaking. "Absolutely. I know it's crazy, and that everything is moving so fast, but I really do love you."

I had no qualms about saying to John what I couldn't say to Chris. "I love you, too."

"This is the start of forever. For as long as I live, you will be my heart." He kissed me again, and when he pulled away, the smile had returned. "Now come on, let me show you around."

Dinner was fantastic, and of course John was right: I loved his mother. And she seemed to like me, though I assumed she was probably that kind, generous, and polite with everyone. Regardless, it was a lovely day. The conversation was always easy and natural. Only once did it get slightly uncomfortable, when Mrs. Onassis asked John how Christina was enjoying her semester.

I don't believe it was a faux pas on the part of our hostess, and I also don't believe it was meant to be a snide commentary on our somewhat messy state of affairs. While not pretending to be something we weren't, John and I had also been intentionally nonchalant about things and of course completely appropriate in the presence of his mother. I think on some level we assumed that the feelings we had for each other would be obvious to the world.

Whether they were or not I can't say for certain, but what *was* certain was that technically Christina was still John's girlfriend, and I was not.

I felt guilty at the thought of the girl whose heart was going to be broken soon, and that feeling of guilt led me to thinking about Chris. I was still angry with him, and though I certainly could have handled some things better, I did not feel that I had done anything wrong. The worst thing I could be accused of was not realizing the depth of his feelings for me but - again - I reassured myself I had made no commitment to him. It was all very unfortunate, but I was not cheating on him.

John *was* cheating on Christina Haag.

He looked uncomfortable at his mother's mention of his girlfriend's name. I knew that all he needed to do was answer the simple question honestly and succinctly, and then we could change the subject. He went a different route.

"I think so. Actually, this is as good a time as any to let you know that Christina and I won't be seeing each other anymore." He continued to eat his Beef Wellington.

Mrs. Onassis seemed taken aback by the information, and after a brief moment of absorbing the news, she glanced at me. I unintentionally caught her eye and smiled a polite smile which I immediately hoped didn't come across as smug. I wasn't feeling smug at all. She returned the smile - guarded, but kind.

She instinctively knew how to diffuse the awkwardness of the situation, and did so by exhibiting the class for which she was so well known.

"I see. Well, she's a sweet girl and I'm sure she'll do very well. Speaking of doing very well: Abby, I would very much enjoy getting to see you skate some time."

And with that, the awkward subject was gone and I was talking to Mrs. Onassis about ice dancing.

I stayed the night in one of the guest rooms, and the next morning, after many thanks for the lovely day and the hospitality, and promises to visit again soon, I left Mrs. Onassis's beautiful home and was driven by John back to Simsbury. As we got closer to town, I began to get nervous

78

that Chris would be at my apartment waiting for me - and even more nervous that he wouldn't. John sensed my tension as we drove the last few miles, and he just silently held my hand, which was exactly what I needed.

He broke the silence as we rounded the last corner to home. "Don't worry. He'll be there."

"Do you really think so?" I paused. "And do I really *want* him to be?"

"Yes. And yes. You both just need to focus on the bigger prize and it will be fine." John seemed confident, and he was very reassuring, but I could tell that he would be happier if he never had to see Christopher Dean again.

That dream wasn't destined to last for long. Chris was sitting on the front stoop of my building when we pulled up and parked in front of it.

John sighed. "Okay, no matter what happens, just know that I'll be around. Okay? You're stuck with me now, so do what you need to do, and it won't affect a thing with me. Got that? Skate with him or don't - I don't care. I'm sticking around for you, and if I have to put up with him, that's what I'll do."

My eyes filled with tears. I was already so in love with the man.

Always the naïve peacemaker, I said, "He's actually a really great guy -"

John cut me off. "Don't do that, Abby. I don't like him and I will *never* like him. And he'll never like me."

I lowered my head, not thrilled that two people who were so important to me were destined to be lifelong enemies.

John put one finger under my chin and lifted my head until I was looking in his eyes. "But, like it or not, we both love you. So we'll make it work."

I kissed him goodbye, telling myself I didn't care if Chris was looking, but hoping that he wasn't. Then I got out of John's car, and he drove away. We had made plans for him to drive me back to Brown the following week, and I didn't want to think about how much I was going to miss him by then.

10. EVERYBODY LOVES YOU NOW

I hesitantly walked across the yard to Chris. I didn't know if I would be able to bear another fight with him, but I needn't have worried. He didn't want to fight any more than I did.

"I'm so sorry. I had no right to act the way I did and I certainly had no right to say the things I said." He was calm, but I could also hear the emotion in his voice. "I hope you can forgive me."

I began to cry again. I wanted to jump into his arms and hug him, but thankfully I had the sense to realize that wouldn't have been the best thing for either one of us.

"Of course, Chris -"

He cut me off. "Actually, before you say anything else, please read this." He pulled a folded note from the back pocket of his jeans. "I had to write everything down, because I just didn't know if I'd have the guts..." His voice trailed off. "Read it." He handed it to me and backed away. "I'm going to walk to the rink and if you feel like joining me after you read it, then..." He was working hard not to give away any emotion. "And if not, I'll understand."

He turned and began walking away, and I immediately crossed to the stoop where he had been sitting just a couple of minutes prior and began reading.

Dear Abigail,
As I write this, I am sitting in your apartment (thank you for letting me stay in spite of everything) and glancing around and

*thinking of you. I am probably not in the best state of mind to write
a letter like this, but it needs to be done. When you get back tomorrow,
I have no idea what you will want to say to me, and that thought
worries me. But what really worries me is that I know what I will
want to say to you. I will want to say that you are making a big
mistake with Kennedy - not because he is a bad guy or the two of you
are incompatible or anything like that. I don't know him well enough
to surmise any of that yet, and frankly neither do you. I do know that
I don't like the guy, but that's my problem, not yours.*

*But you are making a mistake. You and I should be
together.*

I stopped reading for a moment. I remember being
filled with an overwhelming longing to have George there
with me because I just didn't feel like I could handle the
magnitude of that moment. I knew that if George were
there, he would make me laugh and put it all in perspective
for me. He would point out things I hadn't realized, and
blatantly disregard things which I thought were important,
but maybe weren't. But George wasn't there. I was alone
and in a very real situation that I couldn't laugh my way out
of. I was a little girl playing with big girl emotions. So I just
continued reading.

*But you are making a mistake. You and I should be
together. You think you aren't in love with me, and maybe you aren't,
but I think there is a very strong possibility that you are. That feeling
you had the first time we saw each other, the first time we touched, the
first time we skated, the first time we kissed - for that matter, the
second time we kissed... How do you know that feeling wasn't love?
I know that what I felt was much more than a physical attraction. If
you insist on believing that's all it was, then so be it. But I want you
to be sure.*

*I would have given it all up for you - I knew that right then
and there in that café in Vienna. Yes, I moved quickly. I guess I was
going through my slutty stage (sorry about that comment, by the way).
But I knew. I was sure that I would never love any woman the way I
love you. It was bigger than me, and it was bigger than skating, and
the Olympics...it was a once in a lifetime moment, and somehow I was
actually aware enough to know it. And I knew I couldn't let it be*

81

something that I looked back on and thought "What If...?" so yes, absolutely, I could find another skating partner.

But then you said we could have it all, and I was convinced. No, that's a lie. I wasn't convinced at all, but I wanted to be, because I absolutely wanted the Olympics, too. Not more than I wanted you, but pretty badly. So I could convince myself that we could have it all...eventually. Skating for five years, you for eternity. That seemed like a pretty good deal.

Accepting that bargain was where I made my mistake, and it didn't take me long to realize that. But rather than tell you that, or just kiss you again, I decided to be subtle. I gave you "Vienna," but by the time you got to the rink that morning (late, if you recall) I was exhausted and doubting, well, everything. And George was there, and you walked in laughing and so happy to be with him, and I didn't really know enough about him and your friendship with him to not feel threatened, and that didn't help my confidence level. But even through all of that, I really believed it was going to all work out, because I believed that you felt as strongly about me as I feel about you.

I didn't sleep on the flight from London this time. I just thought about you. I thought about us. And I decided that I was being stupid. Why couldn't we be partners on the ice and off? Because of a ridiculous rule I had created for myself when I was fourteen years old and didn't want to go out with Sandra Elson, my first partner? So I was going to tell you. I was going to tell you that I love you.

And then...Kennedy. I wasn't prepared to compete with anyone, Abigail, much less <u>him</u>, but I was going to do what I had to do. But you acted like we were just friends, and he talked about his future with you as if he were sure he would have one...and I didn't know how to handle it. So, obviously, I <u>didn't</u> handle it. I felt rejected and used, and I reacted horribly.

So all of that just to catch you up on my side of things, but what now? If you'll have me, I still want to skate with you. I do firmly believe that you and I have something no one else out there has, and I think we can go all the way. But some things are going to have to change. Just logistically speaking, it's too difficult doing things the way we are attempting to do them. It's bad enough that we have to handle the transcontinental aspect of it all, but trying to do that while I work a full-time job and you go to school? Impossible. The British Championships are around the corner and not only are we not competing, we didn't even give it a serious thought. How could we? We only have two routines in our repertoire, and one of them is "Vienna." And now apparently you have a boyfriend to take up even more of your time.

I called my commander this morning (remind me to pay you back for the international call) and quit the force. If you want to make an honest go at this, I'm sorry but I really think you have to quit school. We're so naturally good together that we've been tricking ourselves into thinking we're pulling it off. We're not.

If you are willing to give this all you've got, then I am too. But it's got to be all or nothing at this point. If you can put everything that has happened behind you, leave Brown, and commit to this with me 100%, let's do it. I promise to give you your space off of the ice. In fact, I'll have to, Abigail. I can't sit around while you talk about your plans to go visit him for the weekend, or while you talk about how happy you are. I'm sorry but I just can't do that. I wish I could be that sort of friend to you, but I can't. Not yet. But I can skate with you. I can make that work.

If, however, by some miraculous chance, reading this has made you realize what I already know - that you and I are meant to be together - then forget everything else I said! I will skate with you or not skate with you, live in England, live in Connecticut, live in Timbuktu...I don't care. I love you. The number one desire of my heart is to spend the next two thousand years with you.

I laughed through my tears – amused, touched, and a bit aggravated by his invoking of the "Two Thousand Years Clause" as we had begun to call it. Since that first day, crossing the Danube, "two thousand years" had come to represent our intensity and commitment to each other.

As I write this, I realize that if that's not what you want, I can't bear to have you tell me, so we have another interesting dilemma. Let's do this: I will be at the training center. If you love me, or you think you might love me, or you are at least interested in trying to figure out if you love me, meet me at the rink in your "Vienna" costume. If that door is closed but you are ready to put everything else aside and skate with me, then meet me at the rink wearing anything else - "Vienna" will be retired forever, literally and figuratively. But, if you're done with me and ready to move on with your life, well...don't go to the rink. I'll understand.

Regardless, let me say, for possibly the last time - I love you, Abigail Katherine Phelps. I always will.

Chris

I exhaled deeply and pulled a tissue from my pocket to wipe away the tears which had been flowing freely. And then I stood up and went inside my apartment to change my clothes.

11. SCENES FROM AN ITALIAN RESTAURANT

I was so genuinely devastated by Chris's letter. I hadn't realized just how much I cared about him and just how much I wanted, no, needed him to be a part of my life until I was faced with the prospect of losing him. I wanted to run to him and rush into his arms and tell him that. I wanted to tell him just how much I cared about him.

I went to the rink, and he quickly turned to face me as he heard me enter. He greeted me with a smile, which faltered for one brief moment when he saw me in my regular practice clothes, but he quickly forced the smile to return and skated over to me.

I wanted to say so much to him, but I knew that wasn't what he wanted. There would be time for that later. Thinking back, that may have been the first truly mature decision I ever made in my life.

We stared at each other for a few seconds, and then he spoke as if nothing had happened. "Late again. You're really going to have to work on that."

I smiled at him. "I will. Sorry."

He smiled back. "Oh well, I'm just glad you're here. Let's get to work."

And work we did. Since Chris didn't have a job to go back to, he decided to stay in the States an extra week, and we made up for the time we had lost on the ice, and then some. I called John and filled him in on everything that had happened, and he wasn't thrilled that I was dropping out of Brown. Neither was I, truthfully, but Chris was right. It had to be done if we were going to go anywhere with our skating.

While he wasn't delighted, John was at least supportive. He understood what we were trying to accomplish.

"It's a shame really," he said as we spoke on the phone that day. "I was looking forward to actually being on campus with you as my girlfriend." He had broken up with Christina as soon as he got back to Providence, and he seemed to have no qualms about us going public.

I, on the other hand, had a few qualms. "Are you kidding me? With the way photographers follow you around, and the way they follow me around, can you imagine how they would follow us around together?"

"Well, it's something we're going to have to get used to. Maybe not on campus, but everywhere else that we are together."

"And when will that be, John? You do realize that I'm not going to have a lot of time for dating for the next few years, don't you?"

"We'll make it work. We'll have some time on weekends."

"Sometimes." There was such a big part of me that wanted to just act like any other college girl and spend weekends hanging out with my boyfriend, but there was no turning back from the commitment Chris and I had made. Truthfully, in my heart of hearts, I didn't want to turn back.

John was trying to be reassuring, but I could tell he was worried about it all as well. "We'll make it work."

Chris went with me to Kentucky the following weekend. I was going to have to break to my parents the news that I was dropping out of Brown, and I needed the moral support. Chris didn't know, but while he wasn't around I also broke the news that I was dating John Kennedy. They handled the news about Brown much better than I had expected them to. Like everyone else, they weren't thrilled, but they understood. Apparently, even my parents thought that Chris and I had the potential to really go places with our skating. My dad made me promise to try to go back to school after I was done with skating, and that was pretty much that.

They were, surprisingly, much less understanding about my new boyfriend.

After a few seconds of stunned silence, which I was certain was attributable not to the fact that I was dating someone, but who I was dating, my mom spoke quietly. And she sounded confused.

"But, what about Chris?"

I thought that was a strange first question. "He knows about John, and I have guaranteed him that I won't let my relationship get in the way of skating."

"No, honey," my dad spoke up. "What your mom means is we thought you and Chris were...together."

I laughed, though I didn't find any of it funny at all. "Not you, too! Photographers, reporters, fans, and now my parents? Why does everyone think that we're together?"

My mom looked at my dad and then proceeded carefully. "Well, Abby, maybe it's because people believe what they want to believe. But maybe it's because we all think you *should* be."

I didn't understand it. I really didn't.

Tears began rolling down my cheeks. "Mom, why does everyone say that Chris and I should be together? That's all I ever hear from people, and I'm really getting tired of it."

My mother scooted her chair next to mine and put her arm around me. "Who else said it, baby?"

"Well...Chris, actually. He told me he's in love with me and that he is the one I should be with. But I love John, Mom. I really do. John's the guy I'm going to spend my life with."

I could tell my dad was hesitant to get too involved in the conversation, but he also couldn't resist. "Abby, I trust your judgment. I do. But you did just meet the guy. You and Chris know each other so well."

"Well, if that's all it's about, maybe I should just run off and marry George!" I was so fed up with the entire situation.

They both laughed, which just made me angrier. "Baby, we love George, you know that," my mom said through her chuckles. "But George isn't exactly the marrying kind, is he?" Even as a teenager, George Clooney insisted he was a bachelor for life. Before he moved to L.A., I often joked with him that he was going to have to leave Augusta soon, because every girl in the small town was either in love with him or they hated him, because they had once loved him.

"I'm just trying to make a point!" I shouted in frustration.

And with that, my parents knew it was time to drop the subject, and they left me alone to fume about the difficulty of my life - a life spent surrounded by remarkable men who loved me. You could say my perspective was a bit warped.

[FROM THE DESK OF DR. ALEC B. REDMOND You could say that, couldn't you? Now, the theme of multiple men in love with Abigail is a common one throughout the delusions. As I've stated, apart from the early exception, John Kennedy was never one of the men mentioned, but there were always multiple men. And very much like in this chapter, Abigail was always very clear that there was an obvious choice. There was never any real decision to be made. She may love two men, and they may love her, but there is never any real doubt as to whom she should be with, at least in her mind. Originally, I believed that represented some great love she had in her life, but she finally convinced me that there was no such love. I was left to believe that she only *desired* such love. I also feel strongly, after reading the last bit of her story, that the men surrounding her represent protection. But from what?]

Regardless, 1981 was a very productive year for Chris and me. It was amazing how much we were able to accomplish once we buckled down and devoted ourselves to skating, and it was refreshing that we didn't have time to focus on our personal issues when we were together. We got along very well, we worked together extremely well, and I think we both enjoyed our time together. At first we had to put effort into not being awkward around each other, and it took some work to perfect the delicate balance we required - we still wanted the sensual connection in our skating, but we couldn't allow it to affect us personally, as it had previously. We mostly achieved that, although we also accepted the fact that the attraction we each felt wasn't going away, and there would be times we would have to deliberately suppress that. But it did translate very well onto the ice.

We took on a coach full time in 1981, and we started gearing up to compete. However, unlike most competitive skaters, we also got the opportunity to perform in exhibitions frequently, due to the novelty of our pairing. Around that time, Chris and I began to really realize how good we were, and the rest of the world began to realize it too. I know that sounds very egotistical, and I don't mean for it to, but the fact is that Chris and I, when we skated together, were the best out there, and well on our way to being the best there ever was.

Our very first competition was to be the 1981 British Figure Skating Championships, held in Nottingham in November. We were completely ready for it and feeling very confident. Well, we were confident in our abilities. We weren't as confident when it came to guessing how we would be received by judges. We knew that audiences tended to love us, and with the competition being held in Nottingham, we would be competing on home ice, in front of Chris's hometown crowd. But we had begun to hear a lot of disparaging remarks from other skaters and coaches. A lot of it may have been mind games - you'd be surprised to learn just how much of that takes place anyway - but we also felt that a lot of it was legitimate lack of respect for what we were doing. I don't know that I understood it at the time, but I think I do now. They viewed us as a novelty act. To our peers, we were a joke.

Some of the top contenders from each discipline (men's and women's singles, pairs, and ice dancing) were invited to perform in an exhibition the evening before the Championships were to begin. There were no rules as to what had to be performed, no compulsory moves required, no time limit. Most of the skaters performed one of the routines they would be competing with - and looked at it as an additional chance to practice. A few didn't want to give it all away, so they performed one of their competitive pieces from the prior season.

I suppose Chris and I didn't play fair, though we certainly didn't break any rules, as there were none. We didn't even originally intend for it to go the way it went. We just made the most of the opportunity to not only impress the judges but to get the crowd firmly behind us - and intimidate our competitors. I believe it worked on all fronts, and since our competitors had set out to intimidate us first, we didn't feel bad about it in the least.

Our original plan for the exhibition was to skate to a vocal track version of "Summertime" from *Porgy and Bess*. We competed to an instrumental track of the song, so we felt it would be more exhibition-friendly without giving too much away. When we arrived at the Nottingham Ice Stadium, we began hearing buzz that a rival couple had learned we were performing "Summertime," and they were going to perform it first. We couldn't let that happen, obviously. It was our very first foray into the major competitive ranks, and we had to make a strong first impression. We had to show everyone that we were the real deal, no matter how non-traditional we were. The problem was that the only other music we had with us were our competitive numbers, and *The Stranger*, which we took everywhere.

We were a little (okay, more than a little) annoyed by the games which were being played, and the way we were being sabotaged and counted out. So, during our rink time before the exhibition, with dozens of other skaters and reporters and photographers all around, we rehearsed "Summertime," but when it was our turn to perform, "Scenes From An Italian Restaurant" blasted into the arena.

The song was, at that time, not extremely well known. "Vienna" had worked so well for us that we had messed around on the ice to every other song on the album, creating routines to some but mostly just warming up to them, tapping into the emotions which sprang from each melody. "Scenes" was seven-and-a-half minutes long, and we quite often used it as an exercise - building our endurance, practicing our most difficult footwork during the fast parts, and using the tempo and style changes to practice our emotional delivery. After a while, we realized we were practicing the same footwork and the same emotional delivery each time. What's more, the endurance issue became less and less of a challenge. We decided to create a program to the music, and it was incredibly difficult, but also incredibly moving. It was a story of young, innocent first love and the loss of that love. Marriage, divorce, old friends, catching up with those friends, realizing how much had changed, how much had stayed the same, and how much would never be the same again. It was right up our alley.

We didn't plan to ever perform it publicly. Chris and I loved to skate to "Scenes," and we did almost every single day that we were on the ice together, but it was, like I said, an exercise. And it was fun. I really do think, though neither of us realized it at the time, that Chris and I would get all of our emotions for each other out into the open while we were skating. We would pour every bit of the attraction, love, and unspoken words and sentiments into our skating, so that we could function as friends and partners and nothing more once the music stopped. It worked for us that way for years.

Skating to "Scenes" at the exhibition was risky. Scandalous even. The judges were present and they could have very easily thought we were acting above ourselves by performing such a long, non-traditional routine, and they could have punished us for it when the competition began. The crowd could have been expecting something completely different and been too confused to appreciate what they were seeing. And of course Chris and I could have messed up in royal fashion, on the most important stage with the highest level of risk to date.

As it was, we skated the routine perfectly, the crowd was silent - captivated - for seven-and-a-half minutes, and the judges rewarded us a few days later with our first British Figure Skating Championship. And "Scenes From An Italian Restaurant" began its ascent into Phelps and Dean folklore.

12. STREETLIFE SERENADER

Chris and I were riding high. After winning the British Championships in November of 1981, we went on to win the European Championships in January of '82 and the World Championships in March. John and I were riding pretty high as well. By the time we won the World Championships that year, John and I had been together for nearly two years, and the only thing that could have made us happier as a couple would have been more time together.

He faithfully drove to Simsbury every weekend that I was in the States. Occasionally he brought his mother or sister, Caroline, with him, which was great. Caroline and I became great friends. And credit to Chris: he may not have liked John, but he sure was an expert at charming the Kennedy ladies.

I'm certainly not one to talk about my sex life, but I do feel that it is an important part of the story in this case. So I must tell you: at this point in my life, I had no sex life. I was twenty-one years old, in a committed relationship with the most eligible bachelor in the world, and I was a virgin.

As much as I would like to tell you I was taking some moral high ground, or was trying to be a role model for the youth of America, that just wasn't the case.

John and I met, and then almost immediately Chris and I began focusing on training full time. From that point on, John and I only saw each other on the weekends, and that was only if it happened to be one of the weekends that Chris and I were in Connecticut, and of course that was only 40% of the time. Actually, once we started competing and really taking off, it was even less of the time because we had to travel for exhibitions and competitions. John would spend more time in Simsbury when he wasn't in school, but even when he was there, Chris and I trained hard.

John and I treasured our time together, and the physical was just never our priority. We talked and caught up, and just enjoyed being together, but that's not to say the attraction wasn't there. It absolutely was. The times when we, like any other young couple in love, started to get caught up in the physical and almost went somewhere with it, we always stopped because Chris was in the next room, or Mrs. Onassis was, or sometimes it just wasn't the romantic setting we wanted for our first time. After you spend so long waiting for your first time, you kind of feel like you need to make it special.

John flew to Copenhagen for the '82 World Championships and was there when we won. Previous to that trip, we hadn't really gone public to the world with our relationship. That also wasn't intentional. We certainly weren't hiding it, and everyone in our lives knew. I knew his friends and much of his family, and he knew mine. Everyone knew. We were a solid, committed couple, but we very rarely went out in public together - again because of how busy things were.

The closest the press had gotten to figuring things out was an exclusive scoop that John was no longer dating Christina Haag, and that came to light about seven months after the fact. Chris and I certainly didn't help them figure out the truth. We had mastered the art of the elusive answer when asked if we were dating each other. That had been a cornerstone since the beginning, so we'd had plenty of practice. One quote which got plenty of publicity was Chris's answer when asked if he was going to marry me.

"Not today," he said. "We have to skate today, so I don't think we'd have time." The press ate that up, and it had the added benefit of keeping them off the John and

Abby trail.

We did, however, finally get caught in Copenhagen. John had originally intended to take Caroline to Denmark with him, but at the last minute she had to cancel and he decided to go alone. If she had been able to go, I doubt that anyone would have strongly questioned why they were there. But John traveling across the world alone to go to the World Figure Skating Championships stood to raise a few eyebrows.

Like I said though, we weren't hiding, and when a reporter asked him, as he made his way into the arena, what he was doing there, John simply said, "I'm here to support my girlfriend."

He wouldn't comment further, but instant pandemonium broke out in the tabloids and other media outlets. JFK Jr. had a secret girlfriend! Suddenly, they were following his every move - even more so than usual. I didn't see him at all while the competition was ongoing since Chris and I had agreed very early on that we had to stay focused on each other and on the task at hand on competition days. But I knew John was there, of course. And if I hadn't known, I would have found out in the papers.

"Oh great," Chris said upon seeing John's quote in the paper. "That's just what we need. More distraction."

I went over to him and happily hugged him from behind. "I don't know what you're talking about. I for one couldn't be less distracted!"

He pulled away from me and rolled his eyes, but I could tell he was working to resist smiling at me. "Yeah, we'll see. You know it's just a matter of time until they figure out that it's you. I mean, who else could it be?"

"What do you mean? There are some pretty cute Russian girls here this year!" I teased.

That made Chris laugh. "Yeah! President Kennedy's son dating a Russian girl! Maybe he can do more to end the Cold War than his father ever could."

After the medal ceremony, I looked up into the stands and found John instantly, but I wasn't sure how to proceed. I really wanted to wave to him, or blow him a kiss, or run up and hug him or something, but it was so public. I knew that whatever I did would unleash the media firestorm. I needn't have wasted time trying to figure out what to do. John took care of that. As Chris and I skated off the ice together, John shouted, "I love you, Abby Phelps!"

There was a moment of hushed surprise all around the arena, and then the hoots and hollers began, and flashes from cameras began popping. John just smiled at me in the midst of it all, never wavering. He actually looked quite proud of himself - it was done on his terms. I was embarrassed for a brief moment, and then exhilarated that this man I loved so profoundly loved me just as much. I skated off the ice, thrilled to be finally going public, and not even caring about the grumbles I was certain to receive from Chris.

That evening, John and I finally had some time to be together. We had a very late, very public dinner, and then managed to escape the majority of the prying eyes to walk around Copenhagen mostly alone.

I knew that something was on his mind, even as adrenaline caused me to ramble on nonstop. I talked about what was next for Chris and me, what people had said to us afterward, how proud my parents were, the fact that Dorothy Hamill had hugged me, and on and on. He didn't talk much at all. Of course, I didn't give him much of a chance.

I could tell that regardless of how engaged he was in everything I was saying, he was also extremely preoccupied. But once I stopped talking long enough for him to get a word in, he had plenty to say.

We stopped by a lamppost along an abandoned street in the middle of the city. "Do you have any idea how much I love you?" he asked as he leaned in and kissed me.

"I think I have a pretty good idea, yes." I exhaled and grabbed his collar to pull him back. He had gone away too quickly.

His lips were almost mine, but at the last minute he pulled away again. He took a deep breath and smiled. "I'm trying to stay focused here, and you're not helping."

"Focused on what?" I asked as I grabbed him around the waist in another attempt to pull him closer. "Of all nights ever, this seems like the night you should be focused on *me*. I am a world champion, you know."

"Really? I hadn't heard," he whispered as he finally gave in and kissed me passionately. But then he pulled away - once again, far too soon. "Okay, I have to take a step back here so I can breathe." He laughed and reached behind his back to unlatch my fingers, and then he stepped away. And I pouted. He smiled but seemed very determined to no longer allow himself to be distracted from whatever it was that required his focus.

"Okay, fine," I sighed. "Breathe if you must."

"Here's the thing, Abby. I'm just not thrilled with the idea of one of the best nights of your life not having anything to do with me."

"It has *a lot* to do with you!" I spoke in a playful, flirty tone which matched his. "It's not every day that my boyfriend announces to the entire world that he loves me."

He laughed. "About that...I hope that didn't embarrass you. I was just so proud watching you out there, and I was tired of not being able to talk to you."

"Are you kidding me? That was great! Certainly took the pressure off of me. I was trying to decide whether or not to wave to you."

"Oh, a wave," he said as if the idea had never occurred to him. "Yes, I suppose a wave would have worked as well. Next time, I guess."

I giggled and grabbed hold of him, certain that he'd said what he needed to say and was ready to focus on kissing me. But he surprised me by immediately pulling away again.

"Sorry. Just give me a second, okay?" He suddenly looked nervous and I knew that the mood had shifted, though I didn't understand why. I nodded and waited for him to proceed. "Abby," he finally said, "the last two years have been the best of my life. And it's okay that we don't get as much time together as we would like, and it's okay that life is so busy, because this is just a small sliver of the rest of our lives together. I have known since the very first time I saw you that I was going to marry you someday, and I was going to be patient and wait until life settled down a bit, but I don't want to be patient. I don't want to wait. I feel like every day that I don't have the promise of you as my wife is a day that isn't quite as good as it could be."

He took a step away from me, reached into his coat pocket, and pulled out a small box before getting down on one knee. I covered my mouth as I gasped. I hadn't seen it coming at all.

"I love you. Will you please marry me?"

He opened the box to reveal a beautiful, classic emerald and diamond ring. It was breathtaking. *John* was breathtaking.

"This is the engagement ring that my father gave my mother. My mother gave it to me the day after you went to New York with me to meet her. The very first time she met you, she knew. Just like I knew."

He looked up at me expectantly. At least, I think he did. I could barely see through the tears. I couldn't speak and I couldn't move because I was so overwhelmed by the love I felt for him. He stood up and held my face in his hands, and he wiped away my tears.

"Please say you'll marry me, Abby."

I pulled him to me and kissed him, trying to convey with that kiss everything I wanted to say but couldn't, and then I did finally manage to say the only word that mattered.

"Yes."

13. WHEN IN ROME

John and I walked around Copenhagen until the sun came up. It was incredibly romantic. We talked about our plans for the future, what kind of wedding we wanted, how many kids we would have...all of the normal things for a young, newly engaged couple to discuss. Eventually the night had to end as the fatigue finally set in, and he escorted me back to my room in the skaters' dormitory.

We agreed to meet up later in the day after we both got some sleep, and then I settled into the most content and peaceful sleep I had ever had.

I awoke hours later to incessant pounding on the door. It took me a few seconds to remember where I was. Once I did, I remembered everything and quickly glanced at my left hand, partially expecting to discover it had all been a dream. A huge smile covered my face when I saw the ring on my finger.

The knocking continued and I rushed to open the door, certain it was John.

"Were you still asleep? Good grief, Abigail, it's almost noon." Chris's smile still reflected the joy of victory, and his joy only grew as he raised my blinds and watched me react to the harsh intrusion of sunlight.

"Yeah, sorry...I got in pretty late."

I suddenly realized I had to tell him about my engagement, and I knew I had to tell him immediately. He needed to be the first to know. He deserved that.

"Hey, don't apologize. Did you have a good time

last night?" Chris had been making a lot of effort in the previous months to be friends with me again, and overall we did pretty well. But he still struggled with the John conversations, and I had a doozy of a John conversation for him.

"Yes," I began hesitantly. "We had a great time. In fact, I need to talk to you about something, Chris." I was afraid it was going to be like when I first told him about John, except much, much worse.

"Does it have anything to do with the enormous ring on your finger?" He smiled at me, but it was a somewhat sad smile.

"Well, that was very observant of you," I said, somewhat flustered.

Chris pulled a local newspaper from the back pocket of his jeans. "Not really." He showed me the front page, with a Danish headline above a photo of John walking me back to my room. Off to the side was a zoomed-in photo of the ring on my hand, right next to a zoomed-in photo of the ring on Jacqueline Kennedy's hand in 1953. Well, that was fast.

Kærlighed og Ægteskab i København

"What does that say?" I asked, staring at the headline.

Chris handed the paper to me. "'Love and Marriage in Copenhagen,'" he sighed. "Once you go public, you really go public, don't you?"

I was in shock. "Chris, I'm so sorry. I really never would have imagined that you would find out this way."

He spoke quietly while smiling at me gently. "I know."

"I was going to tell you right away, I mean, right now. You were going to be the first person I told. And you still are, for that matter." I felt so guilty.

"I know."

We sat there, not saying a word, for a long time. Then Chris cleared his throat and began to speak. "I'm not exactly surprised, Abigail. It's been a couple of years, right? I figured it might happen eventually. So, do you have any idea when?"

I shrugged my shoulders. "Not really. We don't want to wait too long, but we also feel like we should wait until we can actually live in the same city. He'll be at Brown for another year, we'll be competing for another two...I don't know."

"You didn't ask my advice, but do you mind if I give it?"

Oh, my Cute Blonde Boy - still not realizing how much I valued him, and how important he was in my life. "Of course. You can say anything you want to say."

He laughed cautiously. "Oh, I think we both know that's not safe. But I do have one thing that I think I need to say. I think you should wait until after the Olympics. February of '84, less than two more years. You won't be able to be together full-time until then anyway, and once you get married, it won't be long until you want kids, and before you know it you'll have nine little Kennedys, and you'll always be on sailboats at the Cape." He smiled in response to my laughter and then continued, a bit more somberly. "The fact is, you promised to be mine until after Sarajevo."

He wasn't playing games, or trying to sabotage anything - he was just telling me how he really felt, and I appreciated it. And I knew it wasn't easy for him. After all, there had been a time when "after Sarajevo" was going to be our time to start building a life together.

"That sounds like a very fair, valid argument. I'll see what I can do."

If that had been the extent to which people in our lives gave us advice, John and I may have lived happily ever after.

«««§»»»

The following weekend, John took me to Hyannis Port, Massachusetts and the so-called Kennedy Compound to officially share the news of the engagement with his mother, sister, Uncle Ted, and whatever assortment of Kennedy cousins happened to be there. I was pretty excited about telling them all. I got along well with the relatives I had met, and the fact that I was wearing her engagement ring told me that the most important person in the room would be happy for us. Besides, I was pretty sure they all knew - but we wanted them to hear it from us.

During dinner, John stood up and got everyone's attention, but before he could say what he was prepared to say, Senator Ted Kennedy interrupted.

"John, why don't you have a seat? There are actually a few things I need to say."

John and I looked at each other, confused but not concerned.

"Actually," John stayed standing, "I would like to make an announcement, Uncle Teddy."

"I know. You want to announce that you plan to marry this young lady," Ted said as he smiled at me. "But let's face it. That won't be happening. Patrick, pass the stew to Ms. Phelps."

Patrick Kennedy, then fourteen years old, did what he was told without hesitation, and when I didn't take the bowl from him he set it down in front of me.

John sat down. He didn't understand what was happening any more than I did. I looked at Caroline and she kept her head down, eating her dinner. I looked at Mrs. Onassis, and she was watching John with concern, but she said nothing.

From his seat, John spoke again. "Uncle Teddy, I don't understand. It *will* be happening. I asked Abby to marry me and she said yes. I thought you would be happy for us. I for one am very happy." He grabbed my hand under the table.

I tried to disregard the nerves - fear, perhaps? - which was beginning to make its presence known in my heart and mind. There was nothing to worry about, I told myself. John loved me, and I loved him. We'd be just fine.

"Now listen here, John," the Senator spoke in his thick New England accent. "She's a very nice girl, and I think she has been very good for you for a time. But there is no future for you there." He spoke as if I were a career opportunity, and not a very good one.

John was growing indignant. "Why is there no future?" He let go of my hand and stood once more. "This is the woman I am going to spend the rest of my life with."

Ted stood up and slammed his hands down in front of him on the table. "No! You are the son of President John F. Kennedy, the nephew of Robert Kennedy, Attorney General of the United States, and you are the nephew of Senator Edward Kennedy. You were born into a great political dynasty, and your destiny is nothing less than the White House. Look at your mother, John. Your mother and your father are the example of what you and the woman you marry are aspiring to. You will be president one day, and your First Lady cannot be a Protestant figure skater whose career was built and whose life is spent in the arms of another man, representing another country. Your wife must leave no doubt as to her allegiance to this country, and your wife must be Catholic. You know that, and I am disappointed that you let it get this far. The two of you together certainly got your share of headlines in Copenhagen - and while I wish you had shown more discretion, we will be able to clean it up easily. At least the coverage was nothing compared to the years of speculation and scandal surrounding her relationship with Christopher Dean."

John opened his mouth to argue once more, but he sounded as if the wind had been knocked out of him. "Uncle Teddy, there's been speculation, but not scandal. What, she's not allowed to have men as friends?"

"Don't play dumb, John," Ted seethed. "You've seen the articles and the press conferences. And you've seen the way they are together on the ice, and the way he touches her, and the way he looks at her."

It wasn't fair. Nothing about it was fair, but what upset me the most, and what seemed the most unfair of all, was that Ted had latched onto the one minor chink in the armor of my relationship with John. Chris. John trusted me - I knew that - but that didn't change the fact that Chris was a bit of an unpopular topic in our relationship, and I refused to sit by and let Ted talk to John, about us, that way.

"Come now, Senator," I said, sounding much braver than I felt. "You of all people know that public perception, if believed to be true, has the capacity to ruin us. But thank goodness we have the ability to rise above it, and not allow it to shape what we know to be the truth. I'm certain that is something you understand well." I did everything short of invoking the names of Mary Jo Kopechne and Chappaquiddick, and he didn't look pleased. I'm assuming no one did, but my eyes didn't leave his.

His eyes flashed with anger and I had no doubt my attack had hit its target, so I was taken aback when he spoke again, and the words were cold, but calm. "You're clearly an intelligent girl, Miss Phelps. And I've said my final word on the matter."

That was all he said, and then he sat down and resumed eating his meal.

I hated him. I hated Ted Kennedy right then and there, and it was a hate which never went away. Twenty years later that man was still doing all he could to ruin my life. But even in that moment all those years ago, filled with hate for Ted, I was also filled with love for John, and I knew that he was about to stand up and put Ted in his place. John didn't even *want* to be president. He had never once mentioned that aspiration to me. Even if he did, I didn't see any reason I couldn't be First Lady someday.

I leaned over to John and whispered, "Tell him. Tell him you don't even want to be president."

John didn't look at me. He simply muttered the words which, for the first time, made it clear to me that no matter how much he loved me, it wasn't enough.

"It's not about what I want, Abby."

Everyone sat in silence, I sat in shock. I wanted to stand up and run out, but I couldn't make my legs move. John picked up his fork again, but he didn't eat. Finally, Mrs. Onassis said, "Why don't you take Abby home, John?"

I looked at her after she spoke, my eyes imploring her to stand up for her son and the woman he loved, and she smiled at me sadly, but then she looked away. By the time her eyes pulled away from mine, John was pulling my chair out so I could stand. He held my coat for me, which

I grabbed out of his hands, and then I stormed out and waited for him in the car.

[FROM THE DESK OF DR. ALEC B. REDMOND So according to Abigail's delusions, her antagonism with Ted Kennedy began in 1982, which is extremely interesting to me. Twenty years later, she continued the delusion. That sort of long form delusion is unusual. Usually the delusions are shaped and formed to fit the personality of the person as they go through time. Of course, the other possibility is that the delusion itself does not go back that far, but she created a backstory to facilitate the delusion which was prominent at the time of her admission to Cedar Springs. That seems more likely to me.]

John drove me the hour-and-a-half to Providence, Rhode Island, where we had already planned to stay at John's apartment for the night. Though neither of us had spoken the plan aloud, we had also planned to make love for the first time that night. We drove most of the way in silence, considering the many other plans we had made which were suddenly very much up in the air.

Finally, when we were almost to Brown, I couldn't take the silence any longer. On the drive I had gone over and over the conversation in my head, and I went from bewildered to hurt to angry. "How could you just sit there and take that?"

"You don't understand, Abby."

"No, I *don't* understand! Why don't you explain it to me?" I was all but shouting at him.

We pulled up to his apartment, he parked the car, and came around to open my door. I very deliberately opened it before he got there.

I continued my rant, "I felt like such a fool, John! I just knew you were going to stand up for me, and stand up for us. Stand up for yourself, at least. And you never did. On the first day you knew me, you were ready and willing to fight Chris because he said something disrespectful to me, and yet that man wrote me off as unworthy of you, and not good enough for America, actually, and you just sat there!"

"I know. I'm sorry." His voice was wavering, but the eye contact between us never did.

"Do you even love me, John?" I began to cry. Stupid tears, always betraying me.

"Yes. Of course I do, Abby. I love you with all my heart." He reached for me but I backed away.

"But not enough to defy Uncle Teddy?" I couldn't control the disgust which rolled off my tongue as I said the name.

"Being a Kennedy is more than being part of a family. It's a full-time job. No, I don't want to be president, but if the family - if Ted - has decided that he wants me to be, then my choice has been taken away. And he won't just step aside while I make a decision that he thinks will interfere."

"What will he do? What if we just told him to go to hell and eloped? What would he do? What could he possibly do?" I just didn't understand at all.

"Do you think that my father really wanted to be president? Do you think that was what he dreamt of as a kid? No! He wanted to be a writer. But after my Uncle Joe died, it was my father's turn, plain and simple. After my father died, it was Bobby's turn. And then Ted's. Well, I suppose I'm next. I'm sorry. I didn't realize... He had been very supportive of my relationship with you, but I don't think he realized how serious it was."

"So that's it?" I was gasping for air. "Because I'm not Catholic and because I do what he considers to be disgraceful things on the ice with another man, and because I skate for Great Britain because I *have* to, we're through?"

I knew he didn't want that to be the case, and he was hurting so badly, but he just wasn't willing to take on the Kennedy machine. "We don't have to be through."

"But you can't marry me?"

"No. I'm so sorry." Again he tried to reach for me, but I wouldn't let him touch me.

I took off the engagement ring which I had been so proud of just hours before, which suddenly represented so many reprehensible things to me. "I won't be your mistress, John." I put the ring in his hand, and walked away.

14. MIAMI 2017 (SEEN THE LIGHTS GO OUT ON BROADWAY)

Somehow, in the blurriness of the feeling that the world was collapsing around me, I managed to get a very expensive taxi ride to Simsbury. I didn't know what I would do once I got there. Chris was to fly home to England a couple of hours prior, and we had said our goodbyes before John and I left for Hyannis Port. My parents were in Kentucky. I assumed George was still in Los Angeles - he was living on a non-working actor's salary, which meant he was quite often sleeping on the couches or floors of friends, so we didn't get to talk much. And John was gone. For the first time in my life, I felt truly alone.

The competition season was over, and Chris and I had decided to take a month off from official training, though we both planned to work hard independently, of course. After the break, we would regroup in Simsbury and begin planning the follow-up to our remarkable breakthrough competitive season.

By the time the taxi dropped me off at my Simsbury apartment, I still didn't know what I was going to do. I didn't care.

I paid the driver and stepped out of the car. I stood there, maintaining my composure, as I had for the entire drive, until the car pulled away. And then I collapsed. I didn't faint - there wasn't even anything involuntary about it. I just finally allowed myself to feel the emotions which

I had been suppressing. I wasn't good enough for him. No, worse - he didn't believe that I was good enough for him. There wasn't an opinion in the entire Kennedy family - in the entire world - which I would have cared about if only John had loved me enough. If only John had thought I *was* enough...

I heard footsteps walking toward me, quickly and urgently. Then they became more of a run.

And then I was in his arms. I didn't have to look to see whose arms they were - so much of my life was spent in those arms. I trusted those arms. They had never let me fall.

"Oh, my sweet Abigail..." I remember him saying in soothing tones, and then I gave in to the grief, and eventually to sleep.

«««◊»»»

I awoke much like I had in Copenhagen - not to incessant knocking, but to the feeling that my most recent memories had been a dream. This time I was praying for that to be the case.

My eyelids fluttered open. It was dark. Still? Again? I didn't know. I looked around the room and recognized it as mine. Chris was sitting in the bed next to me, on top of the covers while I was under them, his neck bent back so that his head was resting on the wall, and he slept. I nudged him gently.

"Chris, lie down. That can't be comfortable." Barely conscious, he scooted down to a lying position next to me and continued to sleep. I went back to sleep too, resting my hand on his arm, just to feel a little less alone.

«««◊»»»

The sun was up and shining a little too brightly the next time I awoke.

"Good morning," Chris greeted me. I turned my head to where he was standing, by my dresser, putting away my clothes.

"Did you do my laundry?"

"Yes. Sorry. I needed something to do." Christopher Dean has never been happy unless he was accomplishing something.

"Don't apologize. Thanks." I smiled at him, the best smile I could muster.

"You're welcome." He didn't smile or look at me. He just kept folding.

Neither one of us knew how to begin the conversation which was about to take place, and I don't think either one of us really wanted to begin it, so I just enjoyed watching him for a moment. I was always fascinated by watching him, no matter what he was doing. The grace and poise and strength which he possessed on the ice somehow managed to be apparent in every menial task - even folding laundry.

"Why are you here, Chris?"

He looked over to me and his eyes met mine for the first time, and I saw the emotion he was trying to control, and I began to cry again. He hurried over to the bed and climbed in next to me and held me close.

"I'm so glad you're here," I sobbed. "But you were going home. Why are you here?"

He sighed. "I wish I could say that I just had a feeling you would need me. That would be awfully heroic of me, wouldn't it?"

"You are pretty heroic," I sniffed, an appreciative yet sad half-smile on my face.

"He called me." A disgust just like that I felt for Ted Kennedy resonated through every word Chris muttered about John. "He caught me here just before I headed out the door for the airport, actually."

"And he told you? I mean, about what happened?" I was hoping that he had, because I wasn't sure that I was up to the task.

"Not everything, but enough. It probably doesn't help the situation, but I had a few choice words for him..."

I could imagine how strongly Chris might defend me, and how he may have unleashed the hatred he had worked so hard to conceal for the past two years. "It helps a little bit, actually."

"Abigail, I'm so sorry. You know what I think about the guy, but...I know what *you* think about the guy, and I never would have wished this for you. Not in a million years."

I began to cry more and more against Chris's chest, while he rocked me and rubbed my hair and said nothing, which was exactly what I needed from him. And there, in the safest spot I knew, I fell asleep again.

«« ◊ »»

The next time I awoke, it was forced upon me.

"Wake up, sleepy head!" A voice startled me awake, loudly and somewhat obnoxiously. Where was the quiet, soothing British voice I had expected? I turned over, ready to punch the intruder, just to make it shut up.

"George!" I pulled him to me so tightly that it was surprising that I didn't strangle him.

He didn't try to get out of my death grip - he just hugged me back. "Wow, is it good to see you, kiddo," he said against my hair.

I pulled away from him and took a look. He looked good. He had filled out a lot and was looking much more like a man than he had the last time I had seen him. But it was no wonder. It had been so long.

"What in the world are you doing here? I've been trying to call you for weeks, but your number was disconnected, and my letters were returned, and I was starting to wonder if I'd ever see you again."

"Yeah, I'll tell you all about it later. We'll have plenty of time for that."

"Ahem," Chris cleared his throat at the door. "Sorry to interrupt the reunion, but I wanted to say goodbye. My taxi is here."

I stood up and walked over to him. "Where are you going? I hope you don't feel like you need to go because George is here."

"Abby," George interjected, "I'm here because Chris needs to go."

It clicked. "You got George here? Chris, I don't know what to say." The tears started to fall - again.

Chris set down his suitcase and pulled me to him for a hug. "Look, I would stay here forever if that was what you needed -"

"That is what I need," I interrupted him. "Please

don't go."

"No, Abigail, you need to be able to talk this all through with someone who isn't so..." He hesitated, trying to find the right words. "Personally invested. I am here for you. Always. But so is George. So have a few days with your best friend, get caught up, and then I will be back in a week, and you and I have a lot of work to do."

"No month-long break?" I was relieved, knowing that free time - time to think - wouldn't do me much good, but I did feel guilty that as a result, Chris was losing his break as well.

"No way. You're lucky I'm giving you a week."

I looked up at him, and I was filled with such affection and gratitude. "Thank you," I whispered.

He smiled down at me. "You're my partner. What's more, you just happen to be the most important person in my life. No thanks necessary."

With that, he gave me a hug, shook George's hand, picked up his suitcase and was on his way. And I swore to myself I would never tell him about the role he had unknowingly played in the drama at Hyannis Port. His selflessness and his friendship deserved so much better than that.

«««◊»»»

With George, I was able to pour out my heart. Chris was absolutely right: as much as I trusted Chris and felt that, when it came down to it, I could tell him anything, there were so many things that I wouldn't have wanted to tell him that I could feel free to tell George. Things like the way I had been made to feel so unworthy of the Kennedy name, and how it had felt to be sure that John loved me enough to put his uncle in his place, and the embarrassment I felt when I realized that wasn't true - not to mention the feeling of my heart breaking into a million pieces. Chris would want to fix it. George was okay just listening, and throwing in well-timed expletives in honor of Uncle Ted.

More than anything, I wouldn't have been able to tell Chris that I was still in love with John, and more than a little disappointed each time the phone rang and John wasn't on the other end. Chris wouldn't understand that. I didn't really understand it myself.

I did manage to get caught up on George's life when I wasn't hoarding all of our time with my tale of woe. He was still living in Los Angeles, still mostly out of work, but working as his Aunt Rosemary's chauffeur on occasion. I had missed one whole chapter in his life - he had gone back to Cincinnati and tried out for the Reds. Needless to say, he didn't make it, but the way he lit up telling me about it reminded me of the night we met, when he met all of his Cincinnati Reds heroes, and that made me happy.

From nowhere one evening, he broached the subject which he never really had before, though everyone else in my life had seen fit to.

"So, Chris is still in love with you, huh?" He continued to munch on his popcorn as we half-heartedly watched *The Love Boat*.

Because it was George, and because he was the only person who never nagged me about Chris, I felt okay just talking about it, and I didn't feel like I had to be on the defensive.

"I don't know. I don't really think so. We're really good friends now."

"Yeah, I could see that, but don't fool yourself. He's still got it pretty bad."

I wanted to act casual, so I kept eating popcorn too, eyes focused on Captain Stubing interacting with Don Ameche and Scott Baio. "Really? What makes you think that?"

"That was a pretty great thing he did, flying me here. And it was pretty selfless, you know? He wanted to be the one to be with you through this, but he knew that wasn't what you needed."

"True, but that's also something a good, caring friend might do." I don't know if I was trying to convince George or myself.

George never took his eyes off of the television. "I suppose so. I just don't think you should rule out the possibility that it is also something that a man in love would do. You know, a real man who cares enough about the woman he loves to fight for what is best for her, not himself." With that thinly veiled insult of John, he lifted my feet off of his lap, grabbed the empty popcorn bowl, and walked into the kitchen. "More butter this round? All right. Quit nagging!"

George flew out on Sunday morning, and Chris flew in that same afternoon. I greeted him at the airport with a sign that said "CUTE BLONDE BOY." He laughed when he saw it and gave me a huge hug in welcome.

"How are you?" He asked in a casual way, but I knew that what he meant was, "Are you still a weepy, broken woman who is going to continue to stain all of my shirts with her tears?"

"Better. Let's get to work," I said, determined not to drag Chris down with my pain.

He threw his arm around my shoulders and breathed an audible sigh of relief. "I can't tell you how glad I am to hear you say that!"

We got back to work, and worked more productively than we ever had. We were both so focused, but more than that we were enjoying being together. We breezed through the 1982/1983 season, again winning the British Championship, the European Championship, and the World Championship, and then suddenly before we knew it, a year had passed since my engagement. A year had passed since the *end* of my engagement.

John was in the news a lot in those days. He had graduated from Brown and was taking some time off to travel the world and work with Mother Teresa before going to law school, or maybe starting an acting career. All I knew was what I read in magazines. Oh, and he was dating Christina Haag again. Maybe *she* would make a suitable First Lady.

But Chris and I were in the news a lot, too. We were the front-runners heading into the Olympic season, and since John was out of the picture, the press was more interested than ever in the "Are They or Aren't They?" angle, which I couldn't help but enjoy just a little, if only out of spite for Ted.

For the record, we weren't. We spent every moment of our free time together, but we were the closest of friends, the closest of partners - nothing more.

After our second World Championship victory, we once again decided to forgo our month-long break, this time simply because we didn't want to be apart for a month. Additionally, it was time to get to work on the programs which would take us to the Olympics. What we had been waiting and working so hard for had finally arrived.

15. CARELESS TALK

I wasn't over John. Of course I wasn't. But it was one of the busiest and most exciting times of my life, and I got very good at burying things. Maybe a certain line in a song would make me think of him, or a particular food would bring back memories of a meal we had shared, but just as the emotions threatened to boil to the surface, I'd swallow them down. Do you know that feeling when you are trying not to cry, and trying to breathe, and trying to swallow all at once, and you have a difficult time doing any of it, much less all of it? That feeling in the back of your throat which seems to crush your tonsils and rise up to your ears? That was my normal feeling in 1983.

It didn't help that the world began noticing that John was no longer just a kid who represented the innocence the country had lost in November of 1963. He was no longer the little boy saluting his father's casket. He was no longer John-John.

He was JFK Jr.: beefcake. Mature women who had once cried for the fatherless boy and the memory of his carefree days crawling under President Kennedy's desk in the Oval Office suddenly, years before the word cougar meant anything other than a jungle cat, were having much more illicit thoughts involving John-John.

John's face - and John's body - began to sell more magazines than ever before, so he was on the cover of more magazines than a former fiancée could ever hope to avoid.

I was very grateful during that period that Chris was by my side. He was excellent at steering me away from newspaper stands and maneuvering himself between my eyes and televisions with John's face on them. I always knew what he was doing - at first he wasn't very subtle, and by the time he became more so, I was onto him. But I let him do it. Neither of us ever mentioned it, but I would thank him with a smile or by laying my head on his shoulder.

The unspoken communication between Chris and me was always powerful. George once said that Chris and I were the only people he knew who could finish each other's sentences before the sentences began. Obviously, that helped us on the ice as well. On the rare occasion when one of us missed a cue or skipped a step, the audience and judges never knew. We could read each other so well that it took no effort at all to get back in sync.

I was also grateful to have Chris by my side when we had to give interviews to the media. He was more timid than I was in front of the camera, so I quite often answered a lot of the questions, but he always piped up when he needed to. Most of the time, the questions were the same, and the answers were also pretty standard, with slight variations: How do you feel about your chances in Sarajevo? ("Well, we've worked hard, but so have all the other pairs. We just feel so fortunate to have the opportunity to compete with so many talented skaters.") What will you do after the Olympics? ("Right now we're just focused on preparing for the Games and haven't really thought that far ahead yet.") So tell us once and for all, are you two an item or aren't you? (*charming/ coy/ adorable laughter* "We have a great partnership! Let's leave it at that!")

A BBC Radio interview we did in April of 1983 threw a curveball at us.

The interview was going along pretty well. We'd gotten stuck and had to admit that we didn't have our music picked out for our Olympics long program yet, but other than that it was pretty standard. And then:

"So, Abigail, tell us your thoughts on this morning's announcement that your former fiancé John

Kennedy Jr. is engaged to be married."

Time stopped. I think my heart did too, for that matter. My brain was suddenly swimming in thoughts of hopping on a plane to the States and begging John to call off the wedding. Then the realization of how pathetic that was. Then wondering if George cared about me enough to murder Ted Kennedy if I asked him to. Then knowing that if he did, John would run back to me immediately. Then fear that he wouldn't.

The fear that he wouldn't, the epiphany that maybe John had actually moved on, and not just pretended to like I had, is where I almost got lost. Chris saved me again.

He grabbed my hand, which was sitting, shaking, on my knee under the desk in the broadcast studio. "Oh, come on now, Clive. Great Britain is gearing up to try and win its first Olympic gold medal in ice dancing and you want to talk about an American tabloid story? That's not very English of you!" Chris laughed, but there was a warning in his laughter.

Clive laughed too, forced to defend his national pride, but not ready to give up the scoop he was determined to get. "Well, in all fairness, ice dancing has only been an Olympic event since 1976, which makes this, oh let's see, only the third opportunity! And let's face it, I'm just asking the question on all my listeners' minds!"

Chris was outwardly calm, but I could tell by the way he was squeezing my hand that he was moments away from losing his composure. But he had bought me enough time.

"I don't mind answering the question," I lied in my most crowd-pleasing voice. "Actually, Clive, you've had the privilege of breaking the news to me." Chris put his hand on my back protectively, but never took his dagger-shooting eyes off of Clive.

"Really?" Clive feigned surprise. "I guess I would've assumed that he might have told you personally."

I laughed gently. "Is that so? Well, Clive, you must be one of the last good ones if you are considerate enough to call up all your exes and keep them current on the latest news."

I wanted to run. I had never felt so vulnerable in a public situation, and I wanted more than anything to get out of that studio before I suffocated. But I had to stay and play the game.

"So you and John didn't part as friends as you had us believe?" Ass.

"Actually," Chris said through clenched teeth, "we don't make a habit of discussing our personal affairs at all, so you must be leading yourself in your beliefs."

I was afraid Chris was going to jam the microphone down Clive's throat, so I thought it better just to answer the original question and hopefully we could be done, "John and I parted as a former couple - nothing more, nothing less - but I have great respect for him. I have moved on with my life, and he has clearly moved on with his. I wish him absolutely nothing but the best." I alternated between feelings of self-loathing, disgusted with myself for being as weak as I was, and loathing of the woman who was good enough for the man who was once mine.

Clive began to clap his hands in applause. "Well done!"

I looked at Chris, not understanding, but Chris continued to look only at Clive.

Clive continued his wrap-up of the interview, "Special thanks to my guests, Abigail Phelps and Christopher Dean, for being such good sports on this April Fools' Day."

It was April 1st. The bastard.

The On Air light switched off as Clive chuckled to himself, "Thanks again for being so game!"

I was speechless and dumbfounded. My knees began to tremble and I was glad that I was sitting down, since my legs never would have been able to hold me.

Chris was suddenly not sitting next to me. He leaned over the desk, knocked Clive's microphone to the floor and grabbed the front of his shirt with both hands and pulled him over the desk, taking Clive very much by surprise.

"You made it up?"

"Let go of me." Clive was looking into the sound booth for assistance, and he received none.

"Answer me!"

"Yes, I made it up! Just trying to get a rise. Harmless April Fools' joke!"

"If you weren't such a complete waste of time and space, I think I would kill you." Chris shoved Clive back into his chair. "Let's go, Abigail." He put one arm around my waist, the other held my arm and he shuttled me out of the BBC building. We didn't agree to another interview, apart from the required short conversations immediately following competitions, for nearly a year.

For about a month, we acted as if nothing had happened, until Chris brought it up for the first time one May morning as we jogged through Simsbury.

"You know that someday it's not going to be just some loser's April Fools' Day joke."

I knew that. Since April 1st, I had thought about little else than the way it had felt to hear that John was getting married, and how my first instinct had been to do whatever was necessary to get him back. I wasn't proud of that. Nevertheless, I hadn't been able to stop wondering if there *was* a way to get him back. Would I settle for being the president's mistress if the president was John?

"Shut up and see if you can keep up, Dean." I picked up the pace and Chris followed, and I continued to feel the pain from the bottom of my throat, through my tonsils, all the way up to my ears.

16. GOT TO BEGIN AGAIN

Choosing the music for our Olympic season felt, to Chris and me, like naming a child. Whatever we chose would be stuck with us for life, and much like a child's name, it isn't advisable to pick something because it's trendy, or fits in with the times.

Ravel's *Bolero* was not trendy, per se - it had premiered fifty-five years prior - but we were instantly in love with the piece. As we sat and listened to the copy we had borrowed from the BBC's collection (they seemed to think they owed us a favor or two), Chris and I stared at each other, eyes wide and jaws dropped. We had found our Olympic music. We had named our child.

The only problem was the length: seventeen minutes. The Olympic long program had to be four minutes, with only ten seconds of wiggle room on either side. We hired an orchestrator to trim it for us, while ensuring that it didn't lose any of the thematic elements we needed, but after it had been trimmed as much as possible, and we refused to budge any more, we were still eighteen seconds long.

As I was lacing up my skates at the Nottingham ice rink one morning, Chris ran in looking as if he had won the lottery, shaking a book at me with a joyous expression on his face. He'd spent hours reading through the Olympic rule book, trying to find a loophole, and at last he'd found one: the clock didn't start until a blade touched the ice.

"We'll start on our knees and stay that way for

eighteen seconds," he said to me, as if that made everything so clear.

"They aren't going to give us a medal for *not* skating, Chris." I thought it was the stupidest idea I had ever heard.

"Eighteen seconds, Abigail. It's not breaking the rules at all."

"But it's not the intent of the rules either. They'll be fed up with us before our blades hit the ice. There has to be another way. Sorry, I just think we should play it safe this time."

Chris turned around and walked out on me as he often did when he was trying not to strangle me, which should have made me angry but usually just made me laugh.

In the end, he was right of course, though I fought him until the bitter end. And while we broke none of the technical rules of Olympic ice dancing, we broke all of the unwritten ones. We stayed on our knees for the first eighteen seconds. While on our knees, we almost kissed, making this routine, like others before it, a little more sensual than the figure skating world was used to. We used only one piece of music, with one tempo throughout, rather than a medley of contrasting pieces. We had a story, like with most of our other routines, rather than a series of impressive moves. And we died at the end.

It was a *Romeo and Juliet*-type story: two young lovers unable to be together but refusing to be apart, making the journey together to the mouth of a volcano, which they threw themselves into together. We certainly had a flair for the dramatic in those days!

We won every competition that season, leading to the Olympics. In fact, leading into the Games Phelps and Dean had *never* placed lower than first. We were certainly expected to carry the winning streak out of Sarajevo with us, but our record just made us more nervous. We had an enormous target on our backs, and every other pair there wanted nothing more than to be the ones to dethrone us.

In an attempt to protect the built-in tension and suspense which builds throughout the routine, we didn't perform, compete with, or even rehearse *Bolero* in public in its full Olympic form. Now, we couldn't mess with it too much, of course. The reactions of the audience and the scores of the judges were needed as insight so that we could improve what needed improving before Sarajevo, but we did little things differently. Chris would spin me in a different direction, or I would lean against him where I hadn't previously and, most notably, leading up to the Olympics, the death at the end was almost casual and cold - though no one seemed to think so at the time. Only we knew how we were really going to do it - and it was going to be more intense than anything anyone ever expected to see on the ice.

We were leading somewhat comfortably heading into the long program, but that didn't help with the nerves at all. If anything, it made them worse. Chris and I sat silently in the dressing room, five minutes from our time to go on and skate *Bolero*. Or rather, I sat, Chris paced. And as I sat there, going step-by-step through my choreography in my head, as I always did before a competition, another thought entered my mind. It wasn't welcome, and I tried with all my might to get rid of it and focus on the most important moment of my career, which was just minutes away. But the thought wouldn't go away.

"Chris," I spoke quietly and hesitantly.

He looked at me, almost startled. We never spoke to each other in that time frame before we took the ice.

I didn't wait for a verbal acknowledgement that he was listening. "What's next?"

He looked down at his skates. "What do you mean?"

He knew exactly what I meant.

"Is this the last time we'll ever skate together?" My eyes filled with tears. Why did I have to think about it in that very moment?

"No," he said quietly, still looking at his skates. "We'll have the medalists' exhibition tomorrow night." Short of an actual volcanic eruption interrupting our performance, we were all but guaranteed a medal.

"And then *that's* the last time?"

He looked up at me finally, and came a step closer. "It doesn't have to be. We can compete longer, or we can go professional - do shows, and tour, and travel the world together." He was smiling that irresistible smile which I enjoyed so much.

"Ms. Phelps, Mr. Dean," a young man with a clipboard and a headset peeked his head in the door. "You go on the ice in two minutes. Good luck to you both."

Chris closed the gap between us and was suddenly in front of me with his hands on my arms. "Abigail, don't forget the other option. Think about how we felt five years ago when we met, and the future was so unknown, and the idea of this partnership was insane, and our respective nations had thrown us away, and no one believed in us. But you and I believed in us. We knew then that we would compete at these Olympics, and here we are. And we're not just competing. They expect us to win this thing."

"Ninety seconds," the young man said as he passed the door again.

"Chris, we need to go." I felt really uncomfortable in that moment. We had a ritual before we went on the ice. We didn't talk at all, and when we got our time warning, we went immediately to the ice, holding hands, but still not talking. And then there was a certain way we always placed our blade guards, just off the ice, and we didn't talk until we got our scores. I was really regretting starting the conversation. Immediately before our long program at the Olympics, most likely our final competition, at the end of an undefeated career, didn't seem like the right time to test out a new tradition.

Chris didn't start towards the ice as I thought he should. "Five years ago, Abigail, we knew two things. We knew that we were better than everyone else thought we were, and we knew that we wanted to be together. Well, we were right about the first thing. Maybe it's time to come back around to the second one, too."

"Ms. Phelps, Mr. Dean, I really must insist that you go to the ice now." The young man was beginning to look as nervous as I felt.

"Chris..."

"I know, I know. I know this isn't the time. I know we need to go skate, and I'm ready. But I just need you to know that no matter what happens - if we win gold, or if we trip over our skates on the way out - I have loved being your partner. But I'm still willing to give it all up to be with you. I can't think of anything I *wouldn't* give up to be with you. I'm still in love with you, Abigail. And after all this time, I can't really have any doubt that I always will be."

He put his hand behind my waist and my breath caught in my throat as he pulled me to him. He leaned in until his lips were just inches from mine, and suddenly I was back in Vienna. I felt like the teenage girl I had been the first time Chris kissed me. I wanted him just like I had wanted him then, and I couldn't for the life of me figure out how I had managed to resist him for five years.

I put my arms around him to pull him closer, but the spell was broken by the young man with the clipboard, who was getting very angry. "They will be calling your names in thirty seconds. Go! Go, go, go!!"

That did it. The reality finally set in, and Chris and I looked at each other with wide eyes and took off running for the ice together. We got there just as the announcer's voice called out, "Representing Great Britain, Abigail Phelps and Christopher Dean."

It was so odd. Chris and I were usually the consummate professionals, yet there we were, getting ready to skate onto the Olympic ice to perform the most dramatic ice dancing performance anyone had ever seen, and we were flushed and suppressing giggles.

We skated to our opening position, center rink, and as we got down on our knees, Chris whispered "I love you" in my ear. In the age of YouTube, you can actually see it if you look closely, but of course no one noticed at the time. But it was all I needed. I was ready to portray the lovers of *Bolero*.

And then, a few seconds later, the moment reached new levels of intensity when the "almost kiss" became a kiss. Chris and I both leaned in just half an inch more each, and his lips brushed against mine lightly. The rest of the routine grew in its desperation and passion with each touch and glance. The wonderful thing was we weren't distracted by it in the least. Quite the contrary. It just fueled the flame of the story we were telling. We didn't notice the crowd, or the judges, or the television cameras which were feeding our performance to millions of people worldwide. Chris and I were alone in the world, climbing a volcano to our deaths.

It was interesting to watch film of the performance later and realize that the silence I was aware of in the arena wasn't just an effect of focusing on Chris and blocking out the rest of the world. The crowd really didn't make a sound for almost the entire performance, but that changed the moment we died on the ice. The music reached its dramatic conclusion, and Chris and I were lying on the ice, when the audience erupted. We stood to take our bows, and were rewarded with a standing ovation. Dozens - maybe hundreds - of bouquets of flowers were thrown to the ice.

Needless to say, the audience enjoyed the show, but I really didn't know how we had skated technically. Had we actually remembered the choreography or just gotten lost in each other? That's a bit of an exaggeration, but it really was all a bit of a blur. I had no idea how well the judges would think we had performed.

There were so many people handing us flowers that we didn't even make it off the ice before the scores were revealed. And the crowd was so loud that I wasn't even able to hear the technical marks, but I really wasn't too worried about those anyway. The artistic marks carried the most weight in the long program, and Chris and I were always technically clean. The risk was in the artistic interpretation.

Chris and I found each other on one side of the ice and put our arms around each other just as the gasping moved throughout the crowd. We looked up at our scores and couldn't believe what we saw.

6.0   6.0   6.0   6.0   6.0   6.0   6.0   6.0   6.0

Chris hugged me and kissed me on the cheek. We were in complete shock. No one had ever received a full set of perfect marks at the Olympics before. The two skaters who had been written off by their home countries had just proven themselves to be the greatest ice dancers of all time.

What had transpired between us - the attraction, the kiss, Chris telling me he still loved me - certainly wasn't forgotten, but it also wasn't what we were thinking about in that moment. Sure, it played into the event as a whole, but at that very moment, we were Olympic champions. We had just earned a gold medal. All of the years of getting up earlier than everyone else so I could train, all of the parties I hadn't gone to, the last several years of moving to Connecticut and commuting to England, dropping out of Brown...it had all been for that very moment as we stood on the ice, staring at more perfect marks than anyone had ever seen together at the Olympics. I was overwhelmed by the emotion of it all.

And in the midst of all of that, following what would go on to become the most legendary and iconic performance in the history of figure skating, what Christopher Dean said to me was, "I told you that starting on our knees would work."

I laughed. "Yes, okay, you were right! You're always right, Chris!" And suddenly I felt very strongly that he had been right about us as well.

There were other skaters left to skate, but it didn't matter. No one could possibly catch us. We were gold medalists.

There wasn't a lot of time between the end of the competition and the medal ceremony, and in that time Chris and I didn't have an opportunity to talk to each other much at all. There were interviews and procedural discussions during which the Olympic organizers laid out for us what we needed to do during the medal ceremony, for the next evening's Medalists' Exhibition, and so on.

We were swarmed by friends and family, competitors and supporters. It was chaotic and exhilarating, and exhausting. Chris was somewhere doing something – we couldn't possibly keep track of each other with all that was going on – when I spoke with Brian Boitano for the first time. Brian was an American singles skater who finished a very promising 5th in Sarajevo, and was widely considered the future of the United States team.

After he congratulated me and introduced himself, he said, "Pretty good year for the Americans, wouldn't you say?" 1984 was indeed a good year for the USFSA. Scott Hamilton walked away with gold in singles, Rosalynn Sumners placed 2nd among the ladies, and Kitty and Peter Carruthers were awarded the silver in pairs. Only in ice dancing did the USFSA fail to medal, though they placed 4th and 5th just under us and the two top Soviet teams. So I couldn't help but wonder what I was missing when Brian said, "Medals in all four disciplines. I wonder when that last happened."

"No, actually," I corrected him, "Klimova and Ponomarenko moved ahead of Blumberg and Seibert with their original dance. Unfortunately the U.S. team finished just off the podium in ice dancing."

He shook his head. "I didn't say anything about the U.S. team. I said it was a pretty good year for the Americans."

I laughed. "Oh, well, if you're talking about me, I think you're the only one who remembers I'm not British."

"Nope," he said seriously. "I'm not the only one. You're one of us."

I found myself getting misty-eyed, so I said goodbye with, "Thank you for that."

A few minutes later as Chris and I sat with an interviewer for ABC Sports prior to the medal ceremony, it was pointed out to us that it was Valentine's Day. We really hadn't realized. In retrospect, there was something very special about winning with that performance on February 14th, and that stayed with us. Even now, so many years later, after everything we've been through together and separately since 1984, Chris and I always call or send each other a card on February 14th - Bolero Day as we call it.

And then it was time for the medal ceremony. We were both filled with complete joy, of course, but I was surprised to feel a momentary twinge of sadness when "God Save The Queen" began to play for us. My conversation with Brian was fresh in my mind, and I couldn't help but think of how nice it would have been to represent the United States. But then I wouldn't be with Chris, I told myself. And then what everyone had been trying to make me understand for five years finally hit home. If the USFSA had thought I was good enough to make it as a singles skater at the Olympic level, they probably would have been wrong. I was meant to have a partner. I was meant to skate with Christopher Dean, and in that powerful moment I finally accepted that, and I was so grateful.

And then something caught my eye which made the moment more powerful than I ever could have imagined. In the center of the crowd, halfway up the stands, a giant flag was being waved. It wasn't the Union Jack, though plenty of them were being proudly displayed as well. It was Old Glory, and it was being hoisted by Brian Boitano. And surrounding him, cheering and shouting my name, were the members of the United States figure skating team.

The tears began to fall - tears of happiness and pride and loving my life. Standing in front of Chris on the podium, alternating between staring up at the hanging flag of the country which had adopted me and glancing at the waving flag of my home country, I wasn't thinking about any of the pain of the last couple of years. I honestly wasn't thinking about John, for the first time in a very long time. I leaned my head back and rested it on Chris, and he reached down and held my right hand in his.

In that moment, I had everything I had ever wanted.

17. LEAVE A TENDER MOMENT ALONE

Chris and I concluded our gold medal obligations for the day and finally made it back to the Olympic Village. We hadn't been alone since the dressing room prior to the long program, so we hadn't finished our conversation. I can't speak for Chris, but it wasn't something that I had been thinking about, from the moment we saw our scores on. And I think it was the same way for him. We were very much in the moment and there was no preoccupation with romantic possibilities.

But there, in the Olympic Village, as Chris walked me to my room, it got very quiet between the two of us, as the memories of almost kissing in the dressing room, and his profession of love, came back with a vengeance. As we walked past, other Olympians would shout congratulations or applaud, and we would wave or smile or thank them, but I believe we thought only of each other.

I can tell you *exactly* what I was thinking: I wanted to be back in Chris's arms. Feelings and emotions and desires which I had experienced through the diminished lens of a teenager when Chris had kissed me in Vienna suddenly felt very adult. In Vienna I hadn't understood why I blushed so much, and why my legs were a little shaky. There in Sarajevo, though I was still sexually inexperienced, I looked at Chris through the eyes of a woman for the first time, and I knew exactly why I was blushing, and why my legs were shaky, and why I took every opportunity I could to get a little closer to him, or brush against him.

We weren't speaking, and we also didn't dare touch each other too much. All eyes were on us at all times. We were the royal couple of the 1984 Olympics, and it was almost uncomfortable being in public feeling the way I was feeling. In my heightened state of awareness, I was certain that the sexual tension between Chris and me was so thick that everyone would notice. Looking back, of course, I know that was absurd. If anyone would notice anything, it probably would have been that we weren't as talkative with each other as we normally were, but I doubt anyone would have guessed the reason why.

The moment we got to my room, I quickly looked down the hallway to make sure no one was around, and then smiled at Chris and asked if he would like to come in.

Chris smiled back at me. "I don't think that's a good idea."

What? That wasn't what he was supposed to say. "Why not?"

Chris looked down at his feet and exhibited a level of shyness I hadn't seen in him since the first time we met. "Frankly, Abigail, I'm not certain that I will be able to control myself if I'm alone with you right now."

That did it for me. I grabbed him by the front of his coat and pulled him to me, and his lips were on mine instantly. He pushed his body against mine, and I was exquisitely trapped between Chris and the door to my room. I wanted to get him through the door, but there was no chance that I was going to pull away from him even long enough to dig my keys out of my bag.

The hours of waiting to complete that almost-kiss in the dressing room, not to mention the years of waiting for everything else, had built upon themselves until we were both very nearly at our breaking point. Every touch set my skin on fire. Neither of us wanted to pull out of the kiss, even to breathe, to the extent that I thought I was going to hyperventilate - and I didn't care. Breathing wasn't worth the sacrifice.

I'm not entirely convinced that we wouldn't have had sex right there in the hallway if Scott Hamilton hadn't happened to walk by. As I mentioned, Scott was also a new gold medalist that year, and Chris and I had both come to view him as not only a great, fun, kind-hearted guy and an amazingly talented and entertaining skater, but a good friend as well. He is still a close friend to us both.

We didn't even notice that anyone was in the hallway at first, until Scott cleared his throat. Chris and I jumped away from each other like two kids caught in the act, which of course was pretty much exactly what we were.

Poor Scott looked so embarrassed, and yet amused. "Hey, Abby. Chris. Sorry to interrupt."

I thought about trying to create an excuse, but really what could it have been?

Scott continued, "I just wanted to let you know there is an ISU guy wandering around the Village looking for you, asking everyone if they've seen you."

Chris frowned. "What else could they possibly want us to do today?"

"Well, actually," Scott clarified, "they're just looking for Abby."

Chris and I looked at each other, wondering what this could be about, but mostly hating the idea of being separated.

Scott continued, "He's actually headed this way, so I thought I should give you a little advance notice." He smiled and his face flushed a bit.

I laughed. "How did you know that we would need some advance notice?"

"I walked by a few minutes ago," he said, smiling sheepishly. How long had we been at it? "You didn't notice, I'm sure, but I thought you probably didn't want the ISU to stumble upon the two of you..."

I gave Scott a hug. "We owe you one."

He laughed. "No biggie. And congrats, by the way. You may not realize it, but you guys just changed the entire sport out there today."

We accepted his congratulations, and offered ours in return, and then Chris kept talking with Scott. But I stopped paying attention, for down the hallway I saw, walking toward us, my old friend Sven, a tall lanky teenager, and a very intimidating-looking burly bodyguard-type guy.

As they approached, Scott sneaked off and was gone by the time Sven reached us. He greeted us as if we were his long-lost children with whom he had been longing to reunite. "Abigail! Christopher! Wonderful!" He awkwardly hummed the first few bars of *Bolero*. "That was just wonderful! I was so very proud of you and so delighted that our experiment went so well. It is a wonderful thing for the figure skating community. There could be no better demonstration of peace and cooperation among ISU nations than what we saw today. I knew that it would be so!"

"Actually," Chris said with no small amount of hostility, which he had been holding onto for years, I figured, "I'm fairly certain that you didn't think we would ever accomplish anything. Am I remembering correctly that you only agreed to let us be eligible for competition because Abigail wouldn't be involved otherwise?"

I put my hand on Chris's arm and squeezed gently, proud of him for standing up to Sven in a way that I didn't have the guts to.

All Sven said in response was, "Nonsense! Anyway, Abigail, I would like for you to meet someone."

I had almost forgotten the very young but very tall boy who Sven had brought with him. He had said nothing, and wasn't even watching the people around him.

"This is Sergei Grinkov. Sergei is a pairs skater from the Soviet Union. Sergei, this is Abigail Phelps."

The large third man translated what had just been said into Russian for Sergei. Sergei spoke back to him, and then the interpreter said to me, "Mr. Grinkov says, 'Ms. Phelps, it is an honor to meet you.'" He turned to Chris. "And he also says, 'Mr. Dean, it is also an honor to meet you. You are everything I aspire to be as a figure skating partner.'"

Chris turned and smiled as he reached out and shook Sergei's hand. "It's very nice to meet you Sergei." That was then translated.

Before I go any further, let me just tell you that in 1984 Sergei spoke no English. He began learning, and I soon started learning Russian, but it would be quite a while

131

before he and I communicated at all without the assistance of an interpreter, or at the very least a Russian-English dictionary. But I am just going to write Sergei's conversations in English. For a while, just assume that they were spoken through an interpreter unless stated otherwise.

Now back to 1984. I think at that point, Chris assumed, like I did, that Sergei was a big fan and happened to be a personal friend of Sven's family, or something to that effect. Neither one of us saw what was coming.

Sven turned completely away from Chris before he spoke. "Abigail, would you please come have a private conversation with Sergei and me?"

I had no idea what was happening, but I had a bad feeling about it all of a sudden. I reached down and grabbed Chris's hand. "Actually, there is nothing that you could say to me that you couldn't say in front of Chris."

Sven glanced down at our joined hands and then raised his glance to Chris's eyes. Chris didn't pull his eyes away from Sven or his hand away from me for even a moment. Sven did not look pleased, and we really didn't care. We figured we were one exhibition performance away from being done with the ISU anyway.

"Fine. Seeing the success that Phelps and Dean have had, the Soviet Union would be interested in pairing one of their skaters with an American as well. Obviously, this is a demonstration of peace on a much larger scale than that of the United States and Great Britain, and I think it is very important that we make this happen."

I didn't understand what any of it had to do with me, but Chris seemed to. "Are you kidding me?"

I looked at him, not Sven, for an explanation. "What?"

He pulled me slightly aside and spoke quietly. "The Soviet Union is asking for you."

Sven was hovering, but I looked only at Chris. "No. That can't be it."

"Yes, that is it, actually," Sven interjected in his usual kind but impatient way. "This is a very different situation than what we did with you and Christopher. This isn't a fun experiment. We aren't looking for exhibition skaters. The Soviet Union has dominated pairs skating for many years, and Sergei is their rising star - the best we have seen - but they haven't been able to find a skater worthy of him."

It was all so much more ridiculous than the pairing with Chris had ever been. "Well, *I'm* certainly not worthy of him. I'm an ice dancer. I used to jump, but I don't anymore. I don't know if I still can. What's more, Chris and I are Olympic gold medalists and we fully intend to retire together, one way or another. I'm sorry, but I already have a partner." Chris squeezed my hand and I felt his support and pride.

Sven still appeared impatient, but not worried. "Here is the situation, Abigail. The Soviet Union only wants you. If you don't agree to do this, they will pull all of their skaters out of the 1988 Olympics in Calgary, and perhaps beyond. If we lose the Soviet skaters, Olympic figure skating will die. Beyond that, I'm just not certain that your refusal to cooperate would assist in Cold War relations."

Chris laughed loudly. "This is insane! You are putting the outcome of the Cold War on her shoulders?"

Sven stayed as serious as ever. "It's not just me, Christopher. Abigail, President Reagan would like to speak with you on the phone this evening. He would very much like for you to do this for the United States."

I thought I was going to pass out. "It's figure skating! That's all it is. It's a sport where people move around on blades on the ice. That's all it is!"

For the first time since the introductions, Sergei spoke through his interpreter. "No, it's much more than that." Sergei asked if he could speak with Chris and me privately. The three of us, along with Sergei's interpreter, went into my room and Sergei told us that if I didn't agree to skate with him, he was going to lose his sports funding. Top athletes in the Soviet Union were given extra funding since they couldn't work paying jobs. Sergei's father was deceased, and his sports funding was all that provided for his mother and his sister. He begged me to consider pairing with him. He apologized for the situation, though he said it was out of his control as well.

If he lost his sports funding, he would have to get a job, which would basically mean his skating dreams would be dashed. I couldn't begin to understand what it was like living under the rule of the Soviet Union and I realized in that moment just how good I had it. I looked at Chris, who was as moved by Sergei's story as I was. We both liked Sergei right away. There was a sincerity to him which you don't see in many people. He was seventeen years old, I was twenty-two, but I knew that he was mature beyond his years. He hadn't had any choice but to be the man of his family from an early age.

Chris and I communicated without words, as we so often did, and we both knew that as ridiculous as it all was, I had to do it. Not for America, and certainly not for the Soviet Union or the ISU, but for Sergei Grinkov.

18. THROUGH THE LONG NIGHT

I received word about an hour later that my phone call with President Reagan had been postponed which, in Chris's opinion, just confirmed his belief that there had never been a call scheduled at all. That did all seem a bit dramatic and far-fetched to me, but there was no denying that there seemed to be something very politically and diplomatically profound about the entire thing.

Regardless, I don't really think that Ronald Reagan, "The Great Communicator," would have been as persuasive as Sergei Grinkov. There was just something about Sergei, and Chris saw it too, from the very beginning. Sergei was someone you could trust - not only to tell you the truth but also to do what was right. He worked hard — so much harder than Chris or I had ever thought about working. It was different for him. He was part of the Soviet Machine. They put him on the ice when he was three years old, and when he showed some natural talent, it was decided for him that he would grow up to be a figure skater. He didn't get to ask his mom if he could figure skate instead of play hockey, as Chris had, and he wasn't encouraged to have a backup plan in case skating didn't work out, as I had been. He had no choices.

Fortunately, he did love being on the ice. He had started as a singles skater, as I had, but it was quickly discovered that he was very strong - stronger than any of the other skaters his age - so they made him try pairs skating. While ice dancing requires that the male be strong enough to lift his partner, in pairs the male also has to perform jumps, almost on par with the singles skaters, and throw his partner. Sergei excelled at all of it. He wasn't the best jumper among the male singles skaters, but he was far better than most of the male pairs skaters. And he could throw a partner further, higher, and faster than anyone else his age.

The problem was finding a female skater who could keep up with him. By the time he was seventeen, Sergei had had six partners, and they were all the best of the best. But they weren't good enough. The Soviets were faced with what they perceived as an embarrassing dilemma: let Sergei work with an inferior partner and struggle it out but probably never reach greatness in pairs skating, move Sergei back to singles and lose out on the best pairs skater they had ever had in exchange for a mediocre singles skater, or cancel Sergei's program altogether and admit defeat.

But then Chris and I caught their eye. They scheduled a meeting with the ISU and told Sven and his counterparts that they were interested in a similar arrangement. Sven was terribly excited and began brainstorming with them as to who the perfect partner would be, but then the Soviets made it clear that they desired an arrangement more similar to what Chris and I had than they had originally indicated. I heard from a couple of sources later that Sven did actually try to keep it from happening. He said that I wasn't a very strong skater outside of ice dancing, he said that I was too old for Sergei, and not small enough to be thrown. All of it was true, but they didn't care. They issued their ultimatum regarding pulling the Soviet skaters out of Calgary, and Sven consented.

So many of the specifics of the arrangement differed from what the United States and Great Britain had landed upon. For instance, we would skate for the Soviet Union. There was no choice. However, as a consolation, the ISU would drop the 60/40 rule regarding training time in the two countries. In fact, the Soviet Union wanted us to train in the States because the ice conditions were better.

I was pleased with that, of course. Sergei would relocate to Simsbury, but we would work under a Soviet coach.

Chris and I decided that the February 15th Medalists' Exhibition would be our final skate together. There certainly was a sadness about that, but we also both felt then that we were definitely going to be together as a couple, so it wasn't as if it was the end for us. We both chose to look at it as a new beginning.

Chris and I talked it all out until 3:00 in the morning in the commons area of the Village until we could barely keep our eyes open. Sven had seen to it that the normal curfew was lifted for us, as it was officially our last night as partners, and we had a lot to discuss. As Chris walked me back to our room, the sexual tension from the same walk hours earlier was temporarily gone, and in its place a physical, mental, and emotional exhaustion like I had never known. We did hold hands as we walked, and it felt safe and comforting. I kept telling myself that it would all be okay, and Chris kept telling me that too, but it didn't feel okay.

I thought about all that Chris and I had shared. I thought about Vienna, as I so often did, but I thought of different memories from the usual ones. I thought about the first fight that Chris and I had, on the bridge crossing the Danube, when Chris refused to join my pity party, and instead told me that he was planning on competing in Sarajevo, regardless of what anyone else thought. I thought about being on the ice with him as he taught me the choreography for "Vienna" - by the time he was done, I felt that my entire life had been building toward becoming an ice dancer. I thought about the way he laughed at my reaction the first time his arm had to cross between my legs for a lift. I thought about so many things, and while I knew that Chris and I would still be together, I was sad to say goodbye to Phelps and Dean.

But in other ways, it felt like a perfect ending. We had won every competition that we had ever entered together. We were actually retiring undefeated – how many athletes of any sport get to do that? We had made history with *Bolero*, and no one was arguing against the opinion that

137

we were the best ice dancers - maybe the best figure skaters of any discipline - that there had ever been. If we had continued on together, anything we could have done together on the ice would have been a letdown, right?

We got to my room, and I did suddenly blush at the memory of our passionate activity against the door, but I was certainly too tired to do anything other than think about it at that moment. Chris leaned in to kiss me good night, and did so gently on my lips. It wasn't lost on me that it was the first time Chris and I had kissed without it being heated and intense and sexual, and that made that kiss exciting in a different way. It felt like we were embarking on a real relationship. Indeed, Chris and I had taken very large steps in our relationship that Valentine's Day.

«««§»»»

At the Exhibition on the 15th, the mood was somber for Chris and me, but the audience didn't know that they were witnessing what we thought would be our last time on the ice together. Originally, we had planned to skate to John Lennon's "Imagine" but at the last minute we decided to retire with something we loved - something which represented us, at least as far as we were concerned. We decided to skate, one last time, to "Scenes From An Italian Restaurant."

We took to the ice and were greeted by an outrageously enthusiastic audience. That was wonderful, and meant so much to us, but it wasn't exactly a surprise. Audiences had always loved us. But what happened once our music began surprised us beyond belief.

They sang along.

There were thousands of people in the audience, and they all seemed to know the words to the previously obscure Billy Joel song that Chris and I loved so much. It seemed to unite the crowd, as people from all nations who spoke all languages sang along, mostly in English. It energized Chris and me, and made us very emotional at times.

We skated all seven-and-a-half minutes, and I swear most of those people knew the whole thing! We didn't understand it, but we loved it. And though no one knew it, we were saying goodbye. And through their singing, Chris and I felt as if the world was telling us, as we had told each other over and over the night before, that it was all going to be okay.

We left the ice after waving to the devoted crowd and soaking in their love, trying to savor the feeling of being with them, and the feeling of being with each other. By the time we reached the dressing room of the arena, Chris was fighting the emotion and I had already lost my battle. My tears were flowing freely.

He pulled me to him and held me close and let me cry, as he had so many times in the five years of our partnership.

"Hey, look," he pulled away at the sight of a pile of telegrams sitting on the table. We grabbed them and sat down to open them together. We received telegrams from notables from the entertainment industry such as Gene Kelly and Julie Andrews congratulating us on our Olympic victory. We received one from Buckingham Palace and one from the White House, though I really had a difficult time believing that either Queen Elizabeth or President Reagan actually knew who we were.

As I was reading aloud one from Rosemary Clooney, in which she congratulated us and also passed on love from George, Chris stopped me and handed me the telegram he was holding. It was from Robert Redford, and it was addressed to me alone. I was instantly beside myself that Robert Redford knew who I was and had taken the time to write, but as I read I quickly realized it wasn't just another congratulatory note.

Dear Abigail,

First, let me congratulate you on your gold medal. To be honest, I don't usually watch skating, but I enjoyed your program. In fact, I've enjoyed all of your programs that I've seen. I just happened to be watching your performance of Bolero *with a friend, Sydney Pollack. Sydney is a director and an actor and we are getting geared up to work on a film together in Africa, based on the life and writings of Isak Dinesen. Syd and I both think you may be perfect for a role in it. If you have any interest in acting (which you do so well on the ice anyway) why don't you give me a call when you get back to the States? We would love to talk to you about it.*

Again - congrats.

Bob Redford

And then Robert Redford gave me his home phone number. Surely this was not my life.

"What do you make of that?" Chris asked after I read the note aloud.

I shrugged my shoulders. "I have no idea."

"Well, you didn't ask me but I think you should go for it. I for one would love to see you on the big screen."

"Oh," I blew it off, "I'm sure it would just be some little something."

"Maybe, but it could be fun for you. And besides, your parents are always saying you should have a back-up career. You know," he smiled an adorable, mischievous smile at me. "In case this whole skating thing doesn't work out."

After the Closing Ceremonies, Chris and I had to say goodbye at the airport, as we had so many times before, but there was definitely a difference. There was, of course, the difference of being more than friends, though we hadn't really talked about what we were. We both had so much business and publicity to deal with over our last few days in Sarajevo that we just hadn't had the time.

But there at the airport, that difference was nothing compared to the fact that we didn't know when we would see each other again. Previously, our schedule had been completely laid out for the season, or the year even. As we walked to the gates for our flights - his ultimately to London, mine ultimately to New York City - for the very first time the next flight to see each other wasn't scheduled.

We were sure to get to the airport early enough that we would have plenty of time together. As we walked through the terminal, Chris had his arm around me, we held hands, he would occasionally lean down and kiss me, we would whisper to each other and giggle...and we didn't care that every person in the airport knew us, and we didn't care that photographs were being taken. We knew that there would be photos of us in the papers the next day, but we didn't feel like we had anything to hide. And even if we had, I don't think we would have been able to bear the sacrifice of not touching each other.

My flight had the earlier scheduled departure, so we sat at my gate talking for the better part of an hour. By the time my flight began boarding, I didn't know how I was possibly going to be able to leave him.

"Why are there so many things standing between us being together? Why is there always something new in our way?" I was crying, as I did so often.

Chris smiled and pulled me into a hug. "Abigail, as far as I'm concerned there has only ever been one obstacle: you not wanting to be with me. That was the only thing that could stop us from being together. If that's gone, I'm not worried about the rest."

"I want to be with you now, but now I have to skate with someone else, and I have to travel with someone else. What are you going to do? Are you going to get another partner?" The idea made me insanely jealous, yet I knew that he probably wasn't ready to give up skating altogether at the age of twenty-seven.

"No, I don't want to skate with anyone else. I think I might try coaching, or maybe choreographing."

Of course! "Chris, you are already the best choreographer in the world!" I took just a second to think before I proceeded with telling him the thought I was having. I wanted to make sure I knew what I was saying, and wasn't just speaking out of emotion. No, it was exactly what I wanted. I pulled out of his embrace and looked up at him. "You can choreograph in the States. Move to Simsbury and live with me." He looked a bit taken aback and I worried I was moving too fast - though it had been five years! "Or don't live with me, but date me. Whatever. *Be* with me."

I was so afraid he would say no, and I just didn't know if I could bear it.

He thought for a moment, staring into my eyes the entire time, and then he said, simply, "Maybe."

Well, he hadn't said no, but I had really been hoping for yes. Tears welled up in my eyes again.

"Hey, don't cry about maybe!" He wiped away a tear rolling slowly down my cheek. "I love the idea. I do. I just think we should proceed with caution. I know we've been waiting to be together for years, but on an actual romance front, this is all pretty new, and that's a huge decision. I'm definitely leaning toward yes, but I think we should both think about it a little more and talk about it a little more, and not make a last minute, emotional decision two minutes before you board a plane. Okay?"

I smiled at him. Maybe was starting to sound more like yes. "Okay."

"Okay." He wiped away the last of my tears. "Now, you need to go get on that plane. But I will call you tomorrow, and then we will talk about the future."

I picked up my bag and put the strap over my shoulder, and prepared to walk away from him as bravely as I could. "Okay. Tomorrow." I tilted my head up and kissed him goodbye. "Chris, thank you. Thank you for *Bolero*. Thank you for not giving up on me when I couldn't see what was right in front of me, and thank you for not giving up on me when the rest of the world had."

"Oh, come on now," he said with a smile as he tucked a strand of my hair behind my ear. "The world had not given up on you. Only the United States."

"Much better," I laughed and then took a deep breath as I stared up into the eyes of my Cute Blonde Boy. "Thank you for loving me."

He cupped my face in his hands and kissed me one last time, and it was a kiss to remember. "God help me, I do love you, Abigail Phelps. Now, get on that plane, get some rest, call Robert Redford when you get home, and I'll talk to you tomorrow."

Yes. This really was my life.

19. YOU PICKED A REAL BAD TIME

I tried to sleep on the flight from Sarajevo to Munich, and again from Munich to New York, but I couldn't. There were so many things running through my mind, not the least of which was how much I missed Chris. By the time the plane landed at JFK, I was tempted to catch the next plane to London, but I was too tired to follow through with it. Instead, I took a cab to Simsbury, determined to get some sleep and save ambitious romantic gestures for another day.

I finally fell asleep in the back of the taxi, before the Manhattan skyline was even out of sight.

"Miss, you're home," the driver alerted me, bringing me back to reality from a dream I had been having in which Chris and I had decided to give up skating and become trapeze artists instead. Glad to be awake, but anxious to fall asleep again and hopefully move on to a better dream, ideally still about Chris, I paid the driver, grabbed my things, and walked into my apartment.

I opened the door and knew he was there before I saw him. I don't know how I knew, I just did. I didn't want him to be there. Actually, the thought that ran through my head was, "Seriously? Just when I've finally moved on?"

"What are you doing here?" I asked the question, but I didn't move any further into the room. I think I was afraid to see him. Chris wasn't there to throw himself between me and the sight of him, and I feared the return of the pain in my throat, through my tonsils, up to my ears…

"Hi, Abby. I just want to talk. Please." John walked into the foyer of my apartment, but kept a safe distance.

And there he was. For the first time in two years I was standing face to face with the man who had betrayed me so horribly, and scarred me so deeply. The sight of him brought it all back, as I had known it would, and as Chris had known it would, but the reality hurt so much worse than any of those magazine covers ever could have.

"How did you get in here?"

John grinned sheepishly. "Lucky for me, your landlord has a fifteen-year-old daughter."

I groaned. "Oh, fantastic. My security is in the hands of a hormonal teenager with a JFK Jr. poster on her wall."

John looked hurt by that. "Your security? I'm not going to hurt you, Abby. I'm sorry that I did it this way, but I have to talk to you, and I guessed you wouldn't agree to meet with me otherwise."

"*Now* you want to talk, John? There were all sorts of things I wanted you to say in Hyannis Port. There have even been a few things I would have liked to have heard you say since then. But now you want to talk?" I moved past him into my bedroom and began feverishly unpacking my luggage. I was so determined not to cry, not to let him see how weak I was. How weak he had made me.

"I know," he said quietly. "I'm so sorry, for so many things. Can we please just sit and talk for a minute?"

I had no idea what he wanted to talk about, but I knew it was going to hurt, and I didn't want to hurt anymore. "I don't think that's a good idea."

He continued to keep his safe distance, and I appreciated that, but I didn't appreciate that he seemed determined to talk, regardless of what I said.

"Congratulations on the Olympics, by the way. I was so proud of you and happy for you." That was sincere - I didn't doubt that. He had always been incredibly supportive of my skating. But times had changed and my natural response to his sincere expression of support was to try to hurt him.

"John, you should know that I'm with Chris now."

That did it.

He stepped back a couple of steps, but never took his eyes off of me. "With him, as in...*with* him?"

"You didn't expect me to sit around waiting for you, did you? Oh wait, you didn't want me anyway. I guess I should have just crumbled up and died. That's probably what most women would do for you, right, John?" I had so much anger and pain bottled up inside, and I was ready to hurl it at him with all the strength I could muster.

He was shaken. "No, of course not. I'm sorry, I'm just a little surprised is all. I'm not surprised you moved on. I wanted you to. That's why I didn't contact you sooner. I just didn't realize..."

"You're surprised it's him? Why *wouldn't* it be him? I would have been with him a long time ago if you hadn't gotten in the way and wasted two years of my life!" Even as I said it, that one felt wrong.

He seemed to soak that in for a moment. "You're right." He sighed. "This isn't how I wanted this to go."

I looked at him with tears in my eyes, defeated. "I would have done anything to be with you. I would have sacrificed from my life anyone, and anything." The tears fell freely. "You destroyed me, John."

Tears welled up in John's eyes too, which just sent me further over the edge. I had never seen him cry. "I know. I'm so sorry."

We stared at each other in silence for several seconds, thinking about everything that had happened, and everything we had lost.

John finally broke the silence, so softly. "Do you love him?"

I thought about that, first trying to decide what I should tell him, and then realizing that I didn't know if I loved Chris or not. I loved him in certain ways, obviously, and I was attracted to him almost to the point of obsession at times. But did I love him? I decided to answer as honestly as I could, without showing him all of my cards.

"I'm getting there." That sounded so stupid. I had to give more credence to my relationship with Chris than that. "He has been there for me through…everything," I said, hoping John understood the subtext as it related to him. "And we have gotten extremely close." I smiled a little, thinking about what an understatement that was. "He's my partner. In every way."

"I guess, what I really need to know," he said quietly, looking down at his feet, "is if you're happy."

I had no idea how to reply to that, so I settled on honesty again. "I hadn't been. Not since Hyannis Port." I always referred to my break-up with John as Hyannis Port. It always hurt a little less when I didn't have to say his name. "But something clicked in Sarajevo. Standing on the podium, with Chris, I realized that I had spent so much time thinking about what I had lost that I wasn't paying attention to what I had. And what I had, what I *have*, is a man who has loved me since the beginning and loves me still. And he and I fight more than you and I ever did, and we irritate each other, and he pushes me harder than I like to be pushed sometimes, but he's brilliant and he's funny and he protects me and he respects me." I think we both heard the unspoken "unlike you." I wish I could have just stopped there. "So I was happy. I was happy until I saw you again."

John's eyes locked with mine. "Because you still love me?" There wasn't anything egotistical about the way he said it, and he didn't say it with his normal confidence, but he had heard it in my voice. Thinking that I might still love him was an unexpected realization for him, and he asked with hope.

I didn't want to love him, and right then I would have given anything to be able to honestly tell him that I didn't. But what he had said that day in his mother's apartment was true for me as well. As long as I lived, John would be my heart - whether I liked it or not.

"Yes," I said quietly. "I wish I didn't." I took a deep breath as I rubbed my eyes. "But that doesn't change anything. Not a single thing."

"I still love you, too."

Somehow I already knew that, but it didn't make it any less painful to hear. And suddenly I knew this was a conversation I shouldn't be having on as little sleep as I'd had.

"What do you want, John? I haven't slept in what feels like two weeks, I miss Chris, I've got to get ready to skate with this Russian guy, I'm supposed to be calling Robert Redford, and I have to deal with you on top of it all. This really isn't a good time for me, so can we please get on with it?"

"Please explain the Russian guy and Robert Redford." He looked very confused.

I didn't feel like getting into it. Not with him. "No. Just tell me what you want to talk about and then let me go to bed."

"How about this?" He took one step closer and I countered by backing away a step. He held his hands up as if to show that he meant no harm. "You go to bed. I will just sit in the living room and quietly watch TV while you take a nap, and then we can talk a little after you get some rest. Okay?"

I felt like that wasn't a very good idea, but I was too tired to push for anything else. So I consented, and then I slept for an eternity - and I wish I could say I dreamt of Chris.

I felt like a new woman when I finally awoke. I immediately knew that I had been out for hours, but I didn't know how many. When I heard the knocking on my front door, I went to answer it, feeling like I was in complete control of my sensibilities, finally, but unfortunately not yet remembering that John was there. I wish I had remembered.

I opened the door, and could barely believe my eyes. There, looking disheveled and exhausted - yet elated and sexier than ever - was Christopher Dean, and before I could even register what was happening, I was in his arms and he was kissing me like we hadn't seen each other in years rather than a day or so. I finally pulled away because I wanted to look at him and make sure I wasn't dreaming.

"What are you doing here?" I was ecstatic.

He walked in and set his stuff down, making himself at home like he always did, which I loved. Then he grabbed me again and pulled me close to him.

"I just couldn't do it. I couldn't go back to England. Why would I? The person I love most in the world had just gotten on a plane to the States." He smiled at me, and I melted. And while he talked I reached up and felt his unshaven face. I'd never seen him look so scruffy and unkempt, and I liked it. I liked it a lot. "So I booked the next flight, but it was cancelled, after I waited five hours, so I got on the next flight after that, and here I am!"

"So...how long are you staying?" I hoped I was finally going to get the "yes" that I had wanted to hear at the airport.

"As long as you'll have me, I suppose. That is," he looked at me questioningly, "if the offer still stands."

I think I actually squealed. I threw my arms around his neck and he lifted me off the ground and twirled me. "Yes! Of course the offer still stands!"

And then I heard the door knob twist from the inside of the bathroom, and it all came rushing back. I wanted to pull Chris outside, or warn him, or just make John go away, but there was no time for any of that. From my bathroom, out walked the body of Adonis clothed only in a towel around his waist. Great.

Chris reacted first. "What the hell?" He said it in John's direction, and then looked to me for the answer.

I knew then that it wasn't intentional on John's part. He didn't come out like that to try to ruin my moment with Chris. I could tell by his expression that he'd had no idea Chris, or anyone, had come into my apartment, and I don't think he even knew I was awake. He actually seemed to realize the magnitude of his bad timing immediately, and he felt horrible.

"Hey, Chris, don't get the wrong idea. Abby's been sleeping, and I just came to talk. I fell asleep on the couch and took a shower when I -" That was as far as John got before Chris punched him in the jaw.

My hands flew to my mouth and then I went over to check on John, whose lip was bleeding pretty badly.

"Chris, nothing happened! I promise you, nothing happened." I was imploring him to believe me.

"I know." Chris was holding his fist and pacing the room.

I stepped away from John and went to Chris. "If you know, then why did you do that?"

Chris ran his good hand through his hair, like he always did when he was frustrated with me. "That was just for the past."

And as strange as it sounds, that was the moment I first realized I was in love with him. Yes, John was standing there, and there was no doubt in my mind that I was still in love with him, too. And yes, it was a rather barbaric moment in the history that Chris, John, and I share. But it was also the most protective and noble thing I had ever seen, and in so many ways it represented the road to being together which Chris and I had taken.

John stood up from where Chris had knocked him down, but he didn't fight back. He just tried to make things better - better for me, that is - and that selflessness didn't help my conflicted emotions.

"Chris, I deserved that. I deserve much more than that, and while I'd prefer if you don't hit me again, if you need to yell at me or whatever, I get that. But don't take my being here out on Abby. She didn't know I was coming, and she probably didn't know I'd really still be here when she got up, but she told me you two are together, and you've made her happy again. And I thank you for that."

Chris laughed bitterly. "You *thank* me? Well, I'm so glad I could help," Chris said sarcastically. "You pompous ass. You don't have any idea what the last two years have been like for her. And now you've decided it's time to just waltz back into her life?"

"Hey, let's just go sit down and talk." I grabbed his hands and looked into his eyes, pleading with him to focus on me and not John. "The past doesn't matter."

"Doesn't it? Really, Abigail?" He said it quietly, with so much pain in his eyes. Though I understood that he wasn't thrilled about encountering John mostly naked in my apartment, if he believed me that nothing happened, I didn't really understand why he was so upset.

I shook my head. "No, not to me."

And then, he drove the nail in my coffin.

He looked into my eyes and held my face in his hands, and asked the one question to which I had no defense. "Do you still love him, Abigail?"

Why did people keep asking me that? I wanted to scream, "I love you!" at the top of my lungs. Why didn't he ask who I wanted to be with, or which of them I would kick out of my apartment and never see again if it were up to me? Anything but the one question he asked. I couldn't lie to him, but I didn't want to tell him the truth. And I knew that after five years, professing my love to Chris at that very moment wouldn't seem very genuine, though my feelings certainly were.

John tried to step in. He knew that I was still in love with him - I had stupidly told him so. And he knew that, as of the night before, I didn't think I was in love with Chris. I think he also knew I wouldn't lie to my partner. I never had.

"I'm serious, you were all she talked about last night. She's moved on -"

John was cut off again, but at least it wasn't by a fist.

"Shut. Up." Chris spoke slowly through clenched teeth, and then turned back to me. "I need to know, Abigail. I know you want to be with me. I know you've moved on. But do you still love him?"

The tears began to fall, and I couldn't speak, so I just nodded my head sadly.

Chris sighed and pulled me against his chest, and then, just between him and me, though John was still in the room, he whispered into my ear and broke my heart. "I will always love you, Abigail, but I can't do this again. I can't sit around waiting for you to realize that the deeper connection is still there, and all three of us in this room know it's still there. I can't bear the pain of losing you to him again."

I pulled away and through my tears I pleaded with him. "You won't lose me to him, Chris!"

He rested his forehead against mine. "I will. Please don't make me go through that again. Let me go now, okay?"

I probably should have told him no, and finally told him that I loved him, but I think that somewhere inside of me I knew he was right. I knew that John and I weren't getting back together - it wasn't that simple - but I also knew that, like Chris had said, that deeper connection still existed. And it always would. Chris deserved better than I was able to give.

My only reply was to sob, and feel the world crash down around me once more. Chris pulled me against his chest again, kissed the top of my head, and said, "I wish I was the type of man who would take what I could get. I love you so much that I *should* just take what I can get. But at the end of the day," he lifted my head in his hands again and looked me in the eyes, "I love you too much for my own good, I suppose." He tried to force a smile, and then he kissed me gently on the lips. "Goodbye, Abigail." He pulled away from me, grabbed his luggage, and he was gone.

[FROM THE DESK OF DR. ALEC B. REDMOND Abigail seems to know something of loss, doesn't she? It's more than just a recurring theme - it seems to shape the created character of Abigail Phelps. As a psychiatrist, I am still very intrigued by the protection aspect of it all. The character of Abigail, just like the woman I know, is strong and at times even fierce, and yet she wants to be protected. It was in the very moment when Chris stood up for her that she realized the depth of her feelings for him. Perhaps the real Abigail has never had that in her life. She finds that characteristic attractive and desirable in a man. Could it all boil down to not having a strong male influence during her childhood? Perhaps. I will discuss that with her at length during our next session. Additionally, I do have to say that as a reader I couldn't help but cheer, just a little, when Chris knocked John to the ground. Well done, Cute Blonde Boy.]

20. YOU'RE ONLY HUMAN (SECOND WIND)

The pain of losing Chris was so different from the pain of losing John. With John, I had felt nothing. My innocence and joy vacated my body, and in their place a cynical, jaded, bitter young woman took up residence for a time. The pain had been so intense that the only way to cope was to ignore.

When Chris left, I felt each emotion clearly - sadness, loneliness, anger. Actually, the anger was the common thread between the two break-ups, and in both cases, John Kennedy was on the receiving end.

I stood there, in my living room just where Chris had left me, for several minutes, crying and thinking. I tried to decide if I should run after him or if it would only make things worse. I wondered if he would cool off for a few days and then call me. I wondered if he was gone from my life for good. I thought only of Chris until John spoke.

"Abby, I'm so sorry. What can I do? How can I help?"

And that's when the anger began. I turned to him with fire in my eyes. "How is it possible? How is it possible that you could destroy my life two times in such a short span of time?"

"Destroy your life? Look, I'm sorry that I came out when I did and was in the wrong place at the wrong time, but the fact that I was here wasn't really the problem, was it?"

I didn't want him to argue with me, I just wanted

him to let me beat up on him a little bit. I wasn't expecting him to point out the obvious.

"No, the problem is that you screwed me over so completely that somehow I'm so messed up that I can hate you and love you at the same time. And that's how you destroyed my life. Again. Now will you please leave?"

John sighed, "Let me say what I came to say, and then I'll go."

"Whatever," I groaned. "Just get on with it. Dazzle me with whatever it is you have to say."

He looked nervous all of a sudden. "Can we sit?"

His nervousness made me nervous, so I sat, and John sat in a chair across the room from me.

"Okay, here it is," he began. "I'm not expecting what I say to make you forgive me, or make things better, or anything really. But I need you to know. I need you to know that from the moment you took off your engagement ring at Brown that night, absolutely everything that I have done in my life has been with the goal of someday convincing you to come back to me."

Well, that was unexpected. "Getting back with Christina was an attempt to get me back?" How stupid did he think I was, and how stupid was I for admitting that I'd been paying enough attention to know that he was back with Christina?

"I'm not back with Christina, and I never was. Christina and I are friends. We were friends before we ever dated and we've become friends again. She appears with me publicly so that the world thinks we are together." He seemed to really be focusing on how he said every word, as if trying to pass along some unspoken code word. "So that *everyone* thinks we're together."

I had no idea what he was talking about, and then suddenly, I did.

I jumped up from my seat, not believing that he was telling me what I knew he was telling me. "So that Ted thinks you're together?"

He just nodded. "Abby, I handled everything so badly that night, and I can't tell you how much I regret it. But what I was trying to tell you, and didn't know how to tell you, was that Ted won't let anything, or anyone, stand in the way of me being president, if that's really what he wants. The best possible thing for us to do was exactly what we did then - just part ways and move on. But I couldn't move on. I tried. So I started thinking about ways to get you back, but every time I seriously considered it, I knew that Ted wouldn't allow it."

It all sounded very menacing and scary. I knew I hated Ted Kennedy, and it wasn't difficult to surmise that he wasn't very fond of me, but I really never realized it was that serious. "What would he do?"

John shrugged. "I really don't know. But nothing is more important to him than the White House. Well, the White House and the family. But what he doesn't realize is that nothing is more important to me than you, and the moment he did what he did, and I lost you, well...he lost me."

We sat there in silence as I took it all in. Would Ted Kennedy have me killed if I didn't leave John alone? Surely not, but John was certainly worried about something. Had he stayed away to protect me? And if so, did that change anything? As I much I didn't want to admit it, I knew the answer before I even fully formulated the question in my mind. Yes. It changed everything.

"Okay," I finally spoke again, "so what's your plan? You pretend to date Christina to get the scent off the trail, but how does that really help?"

"I have a plan, but not a lot of specifics yet," he admitted. "The basic idea is to become as un-presidential as I can." He smiled, I think genuinely pleased by the thought.

Tears welled up in my eyes again. As much as it moved me to know how strongly he still felt about me, and how much he wanted to be with me again - how much he had *always* wanted to be with me - I was still thinking of Chris and the emptiness which existed in my life if he was no longer in it.

"John, up until a few minutes ago, I was convinced my future was with Chris. I'm not ready to be with you. I'm just not there."

He stood and crossed the room to me and held my hands in his. I flinched at his touch, but I didn't pull away. "Oh, Abby, I know that. I wouldn't ask you for that. Not yet. Actually, what I'm asking right now is if you're willing to try being my friend. And will you allow me to be yours?"

"Your friend?" I didn't understand the game plan at all.

"Yes. Let's get to know each other again. Let's just spend a little time together and try to move past the hurt, and see if you can ever forgive me. Let's just start there. Please."

We had both grown up so much in the two years prior - that hit me in that moment. And it was almost unfathomable how much life had changed in just four years. In February of 1984, he was twenty-three and I was twenty-two, but it felt like a lifetime since we met as teenagers on the campus of Brown. And I realized that maybe John and I were capable of an adult friendship, and maybe - just maybe - down the road a bit I would be capable of exhibiting the forgiveness he was hoping for.

"So we start over?" I asked, just to clarify one more time.

John pulled his hands off of mine and then stuck out his right hand towards me. "I'm John Kennedy."

I shook his hand with a smile and repeated my line from our ancient history. "Of course I know who you are, John."

We moved slowly in our friendship, but we started talking on the phone every couple of days, and then every day. We got caught up on the events in our lives that we had each missed out on, and amazingly he let me cry to him about missing Chris. And it was John who reminded me, in early March, that I had said something about needing to call Robert Redford. I had completely forgotten.

With a nervous stomach, I picked up the phone one evening and dialed the number on the telegram. A professional-sounding female answered, and when I told her who was calling, she said she would transfer me at once. Really?

He picked up almost immediately after. I knew his voice so well. There weren't many bigger stars in the world.

"Abigail! I'd about given up on you!" He had laughter in his voice and I liked him right away.

"I'm so sorry, Mr. Redford -"

He cut me off. "Bob."

Well, that just didn't feel right. "Okay. Bob. I'm sorry. Things were kind of crazy after the Olympics."

"I bet! Hey, no, that's fine. No apology necessary. So, let me tell you what we're doing here." And he went on to tell me all about *Out of Africa*. "So, the part we're thinking of for you is a young American heiress. She's a distraction to my character, Denys, basically. It's a small part, but pivotal, and might be a great foot in the door for you. Would you like to do a screen test for us?"

I thought about telling him that I had never acted before and I didn't know if I could, and I had never been on film, except for television coverage of skating...but then I realized he already knew all of that and he was interested in me anyway.

"Sure! I'd love to."

"Great. We'll fly you out to L.A. next week if that works for you. You'll need us to arrange a place to stay, I'm guessing?"

I thought about that quickly. I might get to see George! "No, actually, I think I'll see if I can stay with Rosemary Clooney." I realized how random that sounded. "She's my best friend's aunt," I clarified.

Bob laughed. "You've got connections! You and Hollywood will get along just fine."

I flew to California the following Monday, and George was there to pick me up at the airport. We quickly got caught up on everything in the car on the way to Rosemary's house. I think he was as sad as I was that Chris and I weren't together, and he wasn't thrilled that John was back in the picture, even as a friend, but of course he was as supportive as ever when it came right down to it.

His career was finally starting to take off, it seemed. He had filmed a pilot which had been picked up for a television series called *E/R*, which of course didn't end up bringing him quite the fame that *ER* did a decade later, but at the time we were sure it was his big break and we were over the moon about it.

I felt kind of guilty telling him all about the movie that I was there to audition for. It wasn't a sure thing, of course, but Robert Redford had called me personally asking me to consider playing a love interest of his in a major Hollywood production. Meanwhile George had filmed one bad TV pilot after another for years. But he didn't look at it that way. He was thrilled for me.

Rosemary, as it turned out, was in New York performing for a few weeks, but she told George and her household staff to wait on me hand and foot and make sure I had a good time.

On Wednesday I met with Sydney Pollack and Robert Redford. Redford was even more beautiful in person than he was in the movies, but he was just as nice as could be to me and I felt immediately comfortable with him and Syd. I read the scene with Bob, and it went really well. Even I could tell it went well, and I knew nothing about any of it!

They got me in costume and makeup and we did a screen test, and again, it went well.

Syd looked at Bob, a bit frustrated. "It's just too bad there isn't a bigger American role. She's good. And actually there's almost too much chemistry between the two of you for her to play the character. I think it will be distracting."

I was standing right there, and hearing them talk about me I felt uncomfortable for the first time.

Bob turned to me. "We definitely want you for the film, but like Syd was saying, when you want the audience to be rooting against a romantic pairing, it's not a good idea for the pairing to be as appealing as you and I apparently are on screen. We just wish we had something bigger. Unfortunately, most of the female roles are British."

Mostly just goofing off, in my best British dialect I said, "Yes, that is rather unfortunate, isn't it?"

I laughed. They didn't.

"That was perfect. Can you do that all the time?"

Syd asked.

I kept the accent going. "Of course. Don't forget, I spent most of my life for the last five years with a British skating partner, and I had to live in Great Britain 60% of the time."

Bob looked at Syd and then back at me. "You can't do Danish, can you?"

I didn't understand why that mattered, but it just so happened that I could. In a pretty good, though I say it myself, Danish dialect, I said, "I'm not sure if you knew, but I happened to have had a very public engagement in Copenhagen a couple of years ago." I smiled at them. It felt like a parlor game, and it made me think of Chris. I liked to annoy him by adopting the dialect of whichever nation we happened to be performing or competing in.

Syd walked over and hugged me, and patted Bob on the back. "Well, well," Syd said in disbelief. "What do you know?" I didn't understand what was happening, but apparently that was the moment Syd and Bob knew they'd found their Karen Blixen, who of course published books under the name Isak Dinesen.

George picked me up an hour later and I told him that I had been cast in my first film, which didn't seem to surprise him. He was excited for me and said he was taking me out for a celebratory dinner - Rosemary's treat, though she was still out of town. He did seem slightly more surprised to learn I had scored the lead, but he couldn't have been nearly as surprised as I was.

I got back to Simsbury on Saturday, and Sergei arrived for a short-term visit on Sunday. We weren't scheduled to begin training together full-time until the fall, which I had to have pushed back to late winter, since I would be in Africa filming. That didn't bother him at all, though the Soviet administrators seemed less easy-going. I didn't care.

On that, Sergei's first trip to the United States, we were supposed to have some promotional photos taken, which we did, and do some basic workouts together, which we also did. The Soviets didn't care if we got to know each other or not, but I did, so one day I managed to steal Sergei away - just him, me, and his interpreter - and we drove to Manhattan. Though we didn't talk very much, since it took a fair amount of effort, I felt like I got to know him very well in those precious few hours of down time. We went to the Statue of Liberty and the top of the Empire State Building, we ate hot dogs from a street vendor, and we laughed at his confusion as he tried to understand the subway signs. That day meant a lot to me.

By the end of his trip, I felt very protective of Sergei Grinkov. I considered him a friend, but also a project. It became my mission to see joy on Sergei's face every single day that I spent with him. He had a smile which could light up the world, and when I saw that smile - which came in spite of the struggles he faced at home and the burdens which were placed on his young shoulders - the world was right again.

FROM THE DESK OF DR. ALEC B. REDMOND
Cedar Springs Hospital
Colorado Springs, Colorado

The acting is quite often found in Abigail's delusions, and the root of that seems to be Abigail's own acting experience, though obviously she wasn't actually taking roles away from Meryl Streep. The following is an excerpt of a conversation which Abigail and I had in a 2005 session.

Alec B. Redmond: What were your original aspirations for yourself?

Abigail Phelps: You mean career-wise?

ABR: Yes.

AP: Oh, I don't know.

ABR: You don't know?

AP: I know, but…I wanted to be a writer. That's actually what I thought I would do.

ABR: Well, you're a bit of a writer now, aren't you?

AP: I don't think that counts!

ABR: I think it does. So, what would you have written? The great American novel?

AP: No, plays. Screenplays. I love movies, theater, television…whatever. I like conversations.

ABR: Did you ever do any acting?

AP: Well, that's an interesting question. Yes. I'm going to say yes, absolutely. I actually did a fair amount of acting when I was younger. Too young, really.

ABR: Too young? Were you a child actor?

AP: (laughter) No! Not that young, but young.

ABR: Were you any good?

AP: I think I was, actually.

ABR: Then why did you quit? I mean, I assume you quit? Are you sneaking off and doing local productions on the weekends?

AP: No. The acting is well and firmly in my past. It got to the point that it was time to put away certain parts of my life and focus on others.

21. I DON'T WANT TO BE ALONE

A couple of days after being cast in *Out Of Africa*, the reality began to set in, and I was terrified. What was I thinking? I had no idea how to be an actor! I'd never taken a single acting class, at least not since basic drama curriculum in high school, and I truthfully didn't even know if I could keep a Danish dialect going through an entire film. I was convinced that either Sydney Pollack and Robert Redford were out of their minds, or I had somehow seriously mislead them - and I did actually try to set it all straight on more than one occasion. By the time we started filming in Kenya, I'm sure they thought I was the one who had lost my mind. Sydney would just laugh it off with a "You're going to be great, kid! I'm betting my film on it." Somehow, that didn't help at all.

Bob, on the other hand, let me indulge in my paranoia, and then would kindly offer a counter-argument to ever reason I knew I was wrong for the movie. He was very sweet with me from the very beginning of our acquaintance, and we became good friends before filming ever began. In the end, that was how I got through the whole experience.

Bob had to shoot the majority of his scenes early in the process to accommodate his schedule for *Legal Eagles*, which he was scheduled to star in next, alongside Debra Winger and Daryl Hannah. That, of course, meant that our scenes together were in the can before I ever shot a scene without him. He got me through. He would offer kind but honest feedback, and offer me tips and pointers, and as we worked together, and I took the Robert Redford Master Class in Acting, my confidence grew. Within a few weeks, I felt like an actress.

That didn't mean I was prepared for the love scenes. I knew they were coming, of course, and I accepted that, but when the day came, and I had to spend hours on end naked in bed with Robert Redford, I felt more nervous than I had ever felt about anything. Ever. I kept my robe on as long as Syd would allow, and though he was very kind and patient, I do think there were moments when he really wished he hadn't hired a first-time actress.

Finally, as I was on the verge of vomiting due to my nerves, Bob took me into his trailer so that we could have a moment alone. He told me that he still got nervous about love scenes too, even though he had done so many. That didn't really help me the way he had meant for it to. To me, what that said was they really were something to worry about. It wasn't just me!

But what he finally said that did the trick, or at least got me functional, was "Every time you went onto the ice with Christopher Dean, you acted out a love scene. Bolero was a four-minute love scene. The only difference is this one will be about a minute long when all is said and done. Oh," he said with a smile, "and you won't be wearing any clothes."

I laughed, and then I thought about that for a moment. That was how the world viewed Chris and me? A love scene every time we stepped on the ice? It was true. The only part Bob was wrong about was there was no acting involved in my love scenes with Chris. So, with thoughts of Chris and how much I missed him running rampant in my mind, Bob and I filmed our passionate love scene in the Kenyan night, and I just had to shut off the part of my brain that told me I was acting.

For every film or television show I have ever acted in since *Out of Africa*, there has been some review, usually multiple reviews, which talk about what a natural actor I am - that I make it seem effortless, that you forget you're watching someone playing a role and you feel like you are looking at a snapshot of someone's life. I have gotten a lot of recognition and praise for that over the years - and a lot of awards, actually. But for the first time, I'm going to give away my secret. I don't know how to be an actor. Not at all. I'm not acting in a way that makes it look like I'm not acting. I'm just not acting!

Here's the thing: I never had to act when I was on the ice. As a singles skater, I was always focused on the technical aspect of it all, and my inability to create a character or demonstrate the emotion of a piece is probably why I was never better than I was. With Chris, we were never acting. From "Vienna" on, we were full of repressed sexual desire for each other, in addition to our friendship and a lot of drama going on in our lives at any given moment. And of course Chris was in love with me every single time we stepped on the ice together, and though I never quite met him there until we were no longer skating together, the feelings I did have for him were extraordinarily deep. With Sergei, our developing friendship shaped the way we began together on the ice, and as the relationship grew and changed, our skating did too.

Now let me tell you one more little secret. This is all the same reason that I quite often make multiple movies with the same actor. I love going onto a set and my relationship with my male counterpart is already firmly in place, and I just have to adapt a bit to make it work for the script. Don't let the awards fool you - I'm not a skilled actress and I never have been!

But in Africa, it was all new and I had to figure it out as I went along. Thank God for Robert Redford! And when he left Kenya, and left me behind to finish filming without him, I missed him greatly and felt his absence every day. And the more I missed him, the more I missed Chris, because I didn't have a constant companion and friend on set to keep me thinking of other things. I think that feeling of loneliness and of being lost in the wilderness completely shaped my portrayal of Karen Blixen.

Towards the end of production we had to shoot for a couple of weeks in England. I knew it was coming up, so I decided to take a chance and write to Chris, to see if I could see him. I had come to accept that our romantic relationship was over. As much as it hurt, and as much as I still wanted him, and wanted to be with him, I also understood his perspective and I couldn't blame him for it. John and I were getting along very well then, months after he had come back into my life, but at that stage I really believed that we'd never again be more than friends. I didn't see that we were building toward being together again. I just felt that we were building toward forgiveness and understanding.

But I knew that I couldn't ask Chris to trust me on that, and even if I did, and even if he decided to give our relationship another chance, I knew that Chris would never be okay with John being in my life. There was nothing territorial about it, and it certainly wasn't your normal everyday insecurity. No, Chris had been through the fire with me - the fire which John had lit. I knew that he wouldn't understand why I would even want to be friends with someone who had hurt me so deeply, first of all, and beyond that, he knew, better than anyone, the depth of my feelings.

It had taken so much for Chris to work past my choosing John over him in the first place. He first became my friend again, and then took the chance on revealing his heart to me once more, knowing there was a possibility I would crush it a second time. Of course, I hadn't, and in fact our timing was completely in sync, for the first time, and we were ready to move past the pain and fall into each other again. And then he took an even bigger risk by showing up at my door that day, prepared to leave his life in England and start a new one with me in Connecticut.

And what was on the other side of that door but the person he hated most in the world.

Chris and I hadn't talked since, but I knew him well enough to know how any conversation we could have would play out, so I hadn't contacted him. I gave him some time and space, and really I hoped that he would contact me, because I knew that when he was ready he would. I knew that we would get past it, because I knew that he didn't want to live his life without me in it any more than I wanted to live mine without him.

But I got tired of waiting, so I wrote him a letter from Kenya.

Dear Chris,

Hi, old friend. Depending upon your state of mind right now, I know that there is a very good chance that you won't be thrilled to receive this letter. I understand that, but I do ask that you read it. I have just a couple of things that I need to say.

First of all, I miss you. But don't worry - this letter is not an attempt to get you back. I didn't understand why you were so upset that day, but I do now. And I know that you know I was telling you the truth when I told you nothing happened with John. Nothing has happened with John, still. I know you believe that, but I also know that you don't understand why I would even talk to him, or allow him within 100 yards. I don't know that I can explain it. All I know is that if I can ever find a way to truly resolve the pain and resentment from Hyannis Port, I'll be a better person for it. So I'm trying to resolve it.

Here's the thing, Chris: nothing in my life feels right without you. And I have tried to be very mature about this whole thing and give you your space, but you know that maturity is not always an easy thing for me! There just has to be a scenario in which we come out of this together. I have thought about it coming out any other way, and I just can't comprehend that as our reality.

You've probably taken your last chance on me romantically. I get that. I don't like it, but I get it. I'm sorry that I have hurt you so many times. I never meant to. I think you know that.

Even though being happy and together and in love may never be in the cards for us, I refuse to believe that friendship isn't. You are my family and my home, in so many ways. You're my partner. And if I have to look at you and pretend that I don't have stronger feelings for you, and pretend that I don't get weak in the knees every time I look at you, then I am willing to do that. But I am not willing to lose you from my life.

I will be in England in two weeks, on the 24th. We will mostly be in remote areas, but we do have two days in London. (I took your advice and called Robert Redford. I guess you'll get to see me on the big screen after all, if you're interested...) I would love to see

165

you. I will work my schedule however I have to so that we can have dinner or a cup of coffee. Or anything.

I'm including the address for the production company in London. If you reply to that address, they'll forward it on to me. It would mean a great deal to me if we could just talk for a few minutes.

I miss you.

Love, Your Abigail

I sent it off with much apprehension. I was so worried that I wouldn't hear back from him at all, but the day we arrived in England, an assistant from the production office handed me an envelope.

Hi Abby,

I stopped right there. I had feverishly opened the letter, so excited to hear from him and somehow certain that he and I would be okay, and that we were still friends and we would be back to normal, or at least a new version of normal, in no time. But in his greeting, he called me Abby. And all of my expectations changed. It seems like such an unimportant little thing, but I remembered the day we first met, when he said he liked the idea of always being the one to call me Abigail. And he had been. For five years, he had always called me Abigail. Somehow it had always represented how close we were, and how flirty we were, and how special we were to each other. Suddenly, I was just Abby?

Hi Abby,

I'm so glad that you are doing the film. I'm sure you'll be wonderful.

I'm afraid I won't be able to meet with you while you are here. I could make excuses, and tell you how terribly busy I am, but after all we have been through together, you deserve better than that. So I'll give you the truth. You may be able to pretend there aren't stronger feelings between us, and you may be able to pretend that we don't want to rip each other's clothes off (my version of "weak in the knees" - call a spade a spade) every time we see each other, but I'm not there yet.

And yes, for the record, I believe you that nothing happened between you and him. I really do know and believe that you were committed to me, and I do appreciate that, but, like I said that night, I also just believe it's a matter of time.

I know that on some level you are wondering what the difference is. If I believe you that nothing was happening, why did it suddenly all just have to end? But I also think you already know the answer to that. One moment he was out of your life and I had no reason to believe he would ever be back in it. The next, he was there. I can't believe that you didn't want to kill the guy on sight, frankly. I did. But that's neither here nor there. He was there. And I knew I was on the way out.

It might not have happened right away, or even soon. And I know, I know, I know that you had no intention of that happening. But it would have. So, as hard as it was, it had to end when it did - before I moved in with you, and before we made love, and got married, and had kids... All of these things on the horizon... And I just wouldn't be able to stand being that guy - the guy standing in the way of your happiness.

I don't hold anything against you. Quite the opposite. With you, I had the five most extraordinary years of my life. Thank you for that. And I don't know, maybe someday we can sit down for dinner, or a cup of coffee, but I'm not there yet. I'm trying to learn to function without you. I need to do that <u>without you</u>. I hope you understand.

I wish you nothing but the best. Between the movie, and the Calgary Olympics in four years (I know you'll be there), and the complete media obsession with all things Phelps, I have no doubt that I will be able to keep track of you. Know that even though I am not there to support you in person, I am always on your side. And I am so proud of what we created together, and I am so proud of you and all you have accomplished and will continue to accomplish. Thank you for the honor of being your partner. I would do it all again without hesitation. But since that isn't an option, it's time to move on. Be happy, be successful, and above all guard your heart. A heart like that doesn't come along every day, and it deserves better than what it's gone through the past few years.

Always,
Chris

He really was out of my life. I had tried to prepare

myself, but it didn't work. I sat in my trailer and read his letter three, four, five times, and each time it hurt more, but each time I also cried a little less. I think I realized then that Chris had given me a gift. I wanted him in my life, and that never changed. But for the first time in my adult life, he wasn't an option. And that changed everything. I certainly didn't know then if it would be a good thing or a bad thing, but I felt the tide of my life change. I knew that I was embarking on a new chapter.

And I knew that Christopher Dean was in the world not hating me. He still respected me, and he still loved me, as I did him. And that was the greatest gift of all. Like he said, if we had moved forward, how much harder it would have been...

So I completed filming on *Out of Africa*, and I began training with Sergei Grinkov, and the following year I had more praise heaped on me than I knew what to do with. *Out of Africa* won the Oscar for Best Picture, and I was nominated for Best Actress. Sergei and I won our first World Championship in pairs skating. I was successful in everything I did, but I guarded my heart too, as Chris had advised. John and I proceeded into a cautious friendship, but with Chris's words always in the back of my mind, I didn't really let him in.

The only thing I couldn't do was be happy, and I couldn't help but hope that Chris, knowing me like he did, would know that, as he followed my successes. And I couldn't help but hope that he would know it was because I missed him, and although I had never told him, I hoped that he would know how very much I loved him. And I guess in some small way during that time in my life, the thought that he might just know how important he was to me did bring me the greatest happiness I could hope for.

22. BLONDE OVER BLUE

So, like I said, in 1985 I was on top of the world. My very first acting role ever had resulted in awards and nominations galore. I got offered many other roles after the gigantic success of *Out of Africa*, but I turned them all down. It was very flattering, but I considered acting a one-time thing. It had been the right circumstances at the right time, with Robert Redford and Sydney Pollack, and I got to go to Kenya and meet interesting people and see animals in the wild which I had previously only seen in the zoo. It was amazing and I knew I would treasure it always, but I didn't get bitten by the acting bug at that point.

I think I had really done it, at least in part, to stay busy and keep my mind off of my disastrous personal life. I was so lonely. I was in my mid-twenties, still a virgin, and messing up every relationship I had. But then again, I'd only dated the two guys. And had I really *dated* either of them? Chris and I became a couple just days before we broke up. Five years of build-up, and then it all went to hell in a matter of hours. John and I had been together for two years, but those two years were spent trying to squeeze in a dinner together while I was training for the Olympics and he was finishing college.

I was such a romantic failure. It was George who pointed that out to me, in the way that only a true best friend can. I'll never forget it. We were at the Academy Awards - our first of many together - held that year at the Dorothy Chandler Pavilion in Los Angeles. It was a fun and relaxed evening for us - he was there as a spectator, and so was I. I knew that there was absolutely no chance I would win, and that's not just me being humble. *Out of Africa* was a huge hit, of course, and the film received eleven nominations, matched only by *The Color Purple*. There was a very good chance that the film would win a lot of Oscars, and it did - it won seven, unmatched by anything - but I had been nominated for lots of awards all through the season, and I lost everything. Well, that's not true. They liked me in Italy. But that was great for me. The pressure was off, and George and I had a great time.

As we sat there during the commercial break right before they announced Best Actress, George leaned over to me and said, "Do you have a speech ready?"

I laughed. "You mean my It-Was-An-Honor-Being-Nominated Speech? Yes, tried and true and ready to go!"

"No, I'm serious, what if you win this thing? What are you going to say?"

"I haven't even thought about it," I lied.

"You're lying." George cocked his eyebrow at me and smiled that Clooney smile. "Here's what I think. I think you're sure you won't win - and okay, you probably won't - but you prepared a speech which says everything you're afraid to say, because then at least if you don't say it, it's not your fault. You were prepared to, but the award went to...who? Jessica Lange? Are we betting on Jessica Lange this time? I forget."

I looked at him and I was pretty annoyed. I wasn't annoyed that he was saying what he was saying - George and I have the right to say anything to each other if it is said in love. I was just annoyed because he was right.

"Do you really want to hear it?" I pulled a little note card out of my handbag.

"I really do."

So I began reading my acceptance speech to him - the one I had never intended for anyone to hear. I read it very quietly so no one would hear and think that I was practicing. How vain that would be!

"Thank you all. I'd like to thank the Academy for

170

this great honor." I looked up at George with a look that I hoped expressed how stupid I felt. He just smiled at me, enjoying himself a little too much. I continued, "I'm up here alone, and that feels wrong. I'm a girl who needs a partner -"

George smiled smugly. "I knew it."

The orchestra began to play the music indicating the ceremony was continuing, and F. Murray Abraham took to the stage to present the award for Best Actress. George and I kept whispering.

"Knew what? I think it's a nice speech. I talk about how much I loved being Bob's partner in this film. And I talk about -"

"Chris. You talk about Chris, don't you?" I silently tucked the paper back into my clutch as the color rose to my cheeks. "You're so dramatic, Abby! You always have been. Ten bucks says you quote some 'Vienna' lyrics in there." I wish I'd thought of that. "Why don't you just tell him you love him? You know that if you called him up and told him you are head over heels in love with him and that you are fine with never seeing John again, the two of you could be together and you could cut out all of the drama. But you can't do that."

"And the nominees are..."

We stopped talking, knowing that the cameras would be on me soon.

"Abigail Phelps. *Out of Africa.*"

I kept looking straight ahead and smiled while the other nominees were announced. After Geraldine Page was announced as the winner, and I applauded and looked thrilled for Geraldine, whom I had never met in my life, and never even seen in a movie, including the one for which she had just beaten me to an Oscar, George started talking again.

"You owe me fifty bucks."

I let out a loud laugh, which thankfully couldn't be heard over Geraldine's ovation. "You did not pick Geraldine Page. You picked Jessica Lange. You just said so. And I picked Whoopi Goldberg. We both lose. Now, as you were saying?"

"Now, to present the award for Best Actor: Sally Field."

"You're not willing to give up all the drama. You love that they both love you. You love that they hate each other because of how much they love you, and that's why you don't date. You're afraid that if you just dated some nice, normal guy who maybe you didn't love at first sight but who you could get to know and maybe fall in love with, you know, the way most people do it, then you would be bored. Because that's just not how you do things. And that's okay. I accept that about you. And when you're old and gray and alone and not understanding why John and Chris don't fight over you anymore, I'll still visit you. And we'll sit together and watch *Out of Africa* and *Bolero* and reflect on your golden days. I won't even bring my twenty-two-year-old girlfriend around, because I am your best friend and don't want to make you feel bad about yourself."

"And the winner is...William Hurt for Kiss of the Spider Woman*!"*

I applauded William Hurt's victory, kept facing forward, and leaned over and talked to George out of the corner of my mouth. "I will kill you one day. It may be while you sleep, it may not."

George laughed and I couldn't help but smile. He put his arm around me and pulled me close.

"You really do think I am a complete romantic failure, don't you?"

"Yes," he said, putting his head against mine. "But you're my romantic failure. Now," he sat up and began looking around the pavilion, "how much will you give me if I can get Geraldine Page's phone number?"

We sat back and watched Sydney Pollack win Best Director and *Out of Africa* win Best Picture, and there, on top of the world, I suddenly had a very real desire for something boring to happen in my life.

Well, Sergei wasn't boring, but Sergei was normal. With him there was no drama. Even John said that Sergei was the best thing that ever could have happened to me. When Sergei and I trained, we focused on, well...training! There wasn't an underlying sexual tension - not in the least.

I can honestly say that in 1985, I was not the slightest bit attracted to him. It's not that he wasn't attractive - he was a good-looking kid. But that's the thing. He was a kid. By the summer of that year, I was twenty-four and he was eighteen. A few years down the road, six years didn't seem like too big of an age difference between us. But when he was still a teenager, and I was simultaneously in love with a twenty-five-year-old and a twenty-seven-year-old, well...Sergei seemed like a baby.

He was, however, extremely mature, and as we got better at communicating, I grew to see just what a smart, funny, and insightful guy he was. He was trying to learn English, I was trying to learn Russian, and what we each discovered was we had a better ear for foreign languages than we had a tongue for them. We both got to the point that we could understand a lot of words which were said, but we couldn't speak very many of them ourselves. At least not in complete sentences. Quite often, Sergei would speak in simple Russian sentences, combined with a bit of pantomime, and I would be able to figure out what he was saying. And I would do the same in English. If people happened to be walking past, they probably thought we were insane.

Regardless, it helped our friendship develop. One of us would laugh at the other's attempt, and we would both laugh at all of the laughter. We talked about our lives a lot. Sergei would start with one sentence: "Ваш ум занят" which means, "Your mind is occupied." That was his way of asking what was bothering me, because he could always tell when something was. And I would tell him about Chris, and about John. Of course he quickly learned to recognize their names in English, so he knew who I was talking about. But it always made him laugh when I used actions or gestures to describe people, so whenever possible, just to make Sergei laugh, John's name would be said while I saluted, like the image of little toddler John that even the Soviets were familiar with. And I would say Chris's name while throwing myself on the ground like the ending of *Bolero*. Of course, that required a little more effort, but if you ever saw Sergei laugh, you would understand.

I would ask for his advice, and he would say, in broken English and a very heavy Russian dialect, "What George say?" He knew that I talked to George about everything, and that George had no doubt already given his opinion on whatever subject was at hand - and Sergei thought George was the funniest person in the world. By the time Sergei and I were partners, I was doing all right on money, thanks to *Out of Africa*, but mostly thanks to a commercial endorsement or two. I flew George out to Connecticut fairly often - that was my indulgence. And George would spend as much time talking with Sergei as he would with me, because the two of them got along so well. Sergei thought George could do no wrong, and whether the question was "Should I try sending another letter to Chris?" or "John wants to see me this weekend. What do you think?" or "Should I have pancakes or waffles?" Sergei's answer was usually, "What George say?" And every single time we would crack up laughing.

One weekend that summer, I paid to fly Sergei to Moscow to visit his mother and sister. He tried to refuse the offer, but in the end I didn't give him much choice. He hadn't been home in so long and it made me happy to be able to do that for him. But, I confess, I had an ulterior motive.

Bob Redford had called. He was in New York re-shooting a few scenes for *Legal Eagles* due to some film quality issues, and after he wrapped, he was meeting with his good friends Paul Newman and Joanne Woodward, who lived in Westport, Connecticut. He said he would love to see me, and also he had been telling Paul and Joanne about what a good time he and I had in Kenya, and they would love to meet me. He suggested I take the train to Manhattan and visit the set, and he would take me to dinner that evening, and then after he did a little bit of work the next day, I could ride to Connecticut with him, meet Paul and Joanne, and then he would take me home to Simsbury.

Now, I've so calmly recalled that memory, but there was nothing calm about it at the time. Robert

Redford wanted to take me to dinner. Okay, as cool as that was (and still is), Bob is my friend. I could mostly keep my feet on the ground about dinner with Bob. But Paul Newman and Joanne Woodward wanted to meet me? That was insane. I took him up on the offer immediately. But even as wonderful as all of that was, that wasn't all I had planned while Sergei was away. I had piled ulterior motives upon ulterior motives.

I had really begun enjoying my time with John again. We were still just friends, and cautious friends at that, but the defenses had slowly begun to slip away. I was, more and more all the time, beginning to remember what had been so fantastic about our relationship. What's more, I discovered things about him that I had never known, and I actually liked him even more than I ever had before.

Nevertheless, I was very careful about letting him know any of that, so when he would call, sometimes I would agree to see him, sometimes I wouldn't. I always made him go to the effort and I never would. But I figured I could probably get away with a casual visit. I mean, I was going to be in Manhattan anyway...

I took the Amtrak to the city and the subway to John's apartment. He looked good that day. Of course, he always looked good, but I remember thinking, on that particular day, that he looked better than I could remember him ever looking. I pretty instantly knew that was a bad sign.

We walked to the *Legal Eagles* set together, which was just about eight blocks from where John lived, and on the way we laughed and we talked, and I fought the temptation to tell him how I was feeling. But as I watched him navigate his way through downtown New York - so JFK Jr., and yet so normal - I knew that something inside of me had changed. I wasn't ready to be with him again, but I was ready to forgive him. I had forgiven him already, actually, and I was ready to tell him. And I was ready to discuss what came next.

"John." I stopped him when we were a block away from the set.

He turned to me. "Yeah?"

And I didn't say anything. I didn't know what to say, and whatever I wanted to say, I didn't want to say it there, in the middle of the hustle and bustle of a New York afternoon. But I was certainly looking at him differently than I had in the fifteen months we had been talking again, forging a friendship. I don't think he had any idea that I was as far along as I was, and he didn't pick up on anything.

"Nothing," I said, determined to bring it up the next time we were alone. "I'm just happy to see you."

He smiled. "Really?"

I smiled back. "Yeah, really."

He laughed. "Well, what do you know?" I think that alone was enough to make him pretty happy.

We resumed walking and arrived to the set a couple of buoyant people. Bob saw me right away and waved and hurried over to greet me with a hug. It was so good to see him again. In addition to his friendship, I just had such a soft spot for him because of everything he had taught me and all of the experiences we shared in Kenya.

I introduced him to John, but it turned out they had met years prior at some benefit or something - I forgot I was mingling with the power players. And then came the moment when everything changed.

Bob waved to someone who was apparently coming up behind me, and motioned them over.

"Hey, I'd like you to meet some people. This is Abby Phelps, who I met on safari." He smiled and I laughed. "And this is John Kennedy. Abby, John, this is Daryl Hannah."

23. IF I ONLY HAD THE WORDS (TO TELL YOU)

Daryl Hannah. Women should not be allowed to look as good as Daryl Hannah looked in the 1980's. She had the complexion and bone structure of a Grecian goddess, her hair effortlessly looked like that of a porcelain doll, and her tall, slender, athletic build caught the eye of every man, and every woman for that matter, within range. More than any of that, what really made her stick out in a crowd was the confidence she exuded. She looked comfortable in her own skin in a way that I had never been. Women should not be allowed to look like that. It's not good for the egos of the rest of us.

Daryl greeted us after Bob made the introductions. "Abby, it's so nice to meet you. I really loved your work in *Out of Africa.*"

I smiled. "Thank you. I loved your work in, well, so many things! *Splash* comes instantly to mind, of course."

"Aww, thank you." She seemed humble and down-to-earth and kind, and I remember in that very moment thinking that maybe Daryl Hannah and I could be friends. It was the only time I ever had that thought.

She turned to John. "And of course I know who you are, John."

What? That was my line. That was what I had said to John when we first met, and then again when we started over. I looked quickly at John, certain that he would look at me and we would pass a secret glance, communicating the significance of that line which only he and I knew. But he was looking at her, complimenting her on some insignificant art house film that I had never seen, and that I didn't think John really had either.

It wasn't like I held a trademark on "Of course I know who you are" or anything. I realize that now and I realized it then, but it seemed so flirty when she said it. And how could he not look at me? Was none of that as special to him as it was to me?

These are the thoughts which were running through my head and I was quickly getting lost in them. Meanwhile, she was laughing at something hilarious John had said, and I had missed it, so I wasn't laughing. I was still staring at John, not understanding why he hadn't looked at me yet.

"Everything okay, Abby?" Bob noticed I wasn't enjoying the moment the way everyone else was. At least someone noticed something.

"Yes. Fine. Just wondering where the ladies room is." I had to get away and think for a minute. I didn't know what I needed to think about, but I knew I needed to think.

Bob began to direct me, and then Daryl jumped in and said, "Actually, I need to go too. I'll show you."

Great.

"Oh, perfect. Thanks." As Daryl started walking away, I turned to John and smiled what I hoped was a seductive smile. "Be okay without me for a minute?"

"Sure." He was talking to me, but watching her walk away. I wanted to snap my fingers and break the spell, but instead, in a bit of a huff, I turned and followed after her.

We were barely through the restroom door before Daryl dove right in. "So, can I ask you a question?"

"Sure, I guess."

"Is John available?"

She had just met him, literally five minutes prior! Was she insane? And then I had a flashback to five minutes after John and I met. And then I was remembering five minutes after Chris and I met. Were all women like that? I really thought it was just me with those two guys, because of the instant connections we'd had. Then again, maybe Daryl Hannah was going through her slutty stage.

"Umm, what do you mean?" I stalled.

Daryl fixed her hair in the mirror, not that it needed fixing. "Is he dating anyone?"

I had no idea what to say. "Well..."

She covered her mouth in horror. "Oh, I'm so sorry! Are the two of you dating?"

I had to keep stalling. I really didn't know how to handle the situation. "You mean, now? Are John and I dating now?"

"I remember now! I remember seeing something in some magazine or other. You two *were* together weren't you?" She looked so proud of herself for remembering. Good for you, Daryl!

"We were, yes - for a long time. We were engaged, actually."

"That's right!" She crossed her arms and looked at me inquisitively. "But you're not together now?"

I couldn't tell her that we were still in love with each other, and that he was busily working on some non-specific plan to become less presidential, and that there was a slight chance that Ted Kennedy would hire someone to kill me, and that we had been working on getting back together, and that I was getting closer and closer to being ready for that with each passing moment. I couldn't tell her any of that, so I just said, "No. We're not together now."

"Then do you mind if I ask him out? I know it's quick, but I really think we connected back there." She started fixing her hair again.

I wanted to tell her no, and make something up if I had to. He had a girlfriend. He was working so hard to get his law degree that he didn't really have time to date. He was considering becoming a priest. Whatever. But in the end I couldn't do it. You see, the problem was, they *had* connected. It was obvious. And John had spent more than a year trying to be the best friend to me that he could possibly be. In spite of the fact that he was still in love with me, or perhaps because of that fact, he had let me cry on his shoulder about Chris. He had listened as I talked about filming love scenes with Robert Redford. He resisted the temptation to put his arm around me at the movies. When he kissed me goodnight, it was always on the cheek. And why? Because I wasn't ready for anything more. I held him off, always at an arm's length.

I couldn't have it both ways.

"No," I said, much more bravely than I felt. "I don't mind."

We walked back to the spot where we had left John and Bob, and they were still chatting. Daryl stood there with renewed purpose once we got back. She had a mission.

Both of the men greeted us when we returned. John smiled at Daryl, but he winked at me. I relaxed, but just slightly.

"Well," Bob spoke to me, "I should be able to get out of here in just a few minutes if you would still like to grab some dinner tonight."

"Yes, of course." I smiled at him. I had almost forgotten the purpose of the trip, but I was very much looking forward to getting caught up with my friend.

Bob turned to John and Daryl. "Why don't the two of you join us?"

Oh no. Please no. I didn't think I would be able to stand watching her drool over John all night long.

Daryl didn't respond right away, she just looked at John to see what his decision would be.

"Thanks, but I think I'll pass. Maybe another time. I would really hate to get in the way of the two of you getting all caught up and remembering your days in the wild together." He smiled and I melted. We were still so in tune with each other.

"Have it your way," Bob said with a smile. "Daryl, how about you?"

She kept looking at John. "I don't think so. Not tonight. I'm pretty tired."

"Do you have a long way to travel home?" John asked her.

"No, actually, I just live a few blocks from here. West." She might as well have been batting her eyelashes, twirling her hair, and showing a little leg, I thought.

"Oh, me too. Why don't I walk you home?"

What? Umm...what? That didn't go at all the way it was supposed to.

"That would be great, thanks." She looked so smug, or at least that was my interpretation. "Let me just grab my stuff. I'll be right back." And with that she bounced off.

Bob put his hand on my arm. "I'll go wrap up and then we can go too."

And then I had John to myself for a moment. I wanted him to say, "Hey, nothing to worry about there." Or "Rather than get a hotel room, why don't you just stay at my place tonight?" Instead, what he said was, "Daryl's nice, isn't she?"

"Sure." I could see the writing on the wall.

"You sure you're okay?" He seemed to really look at me for the first time since Daryl's appearance.

I sighed. "I'm fine. She's going to ask you out."

John laughed. "What? What makes you think that?"

"In the restroom she asked me if it was okay." I wanted to cry and run away.

"Oh." He processed the information for a moment. "And what did you say?"

The threatening tears started to burn as I looked into John's eyes. "I don't have any right to say no, do I?"

"Okay, ready if you are!" She was back.

John continued looking at me for a few seconds. I think he wanted me to say, "Don't go." I think he wanted me to tell him that I was ready to be with him again, and I was tempted to. But I was tempted to because I was jealous. I didn't want him to leave with Daryl Hannah. I had spent more than a year not allowing him to be with me, but that didn't mean that I wanted him to be with anyone else.

And the fact is that I was close. I was so close to being ready to give him another chance, but when I did, what would that life look like? Would we be constantly hiding from Ted, and the world? Would there ever come a day when we could truly be together? When we could get married? Have kids? What kind of life could we ever have together, when we were forbidden from being together at all?

We had become friends. We were *allowed* to be friends. I had forgiven him. I trusted him again. But I couldn't give in to my love for him again. Not because I was protecting my heart, but because I didn't see how the life we could have together could really be any kind of life at all.

"Abby?" John looked deep into my eyes, giving me one last chance to claim him as my own. My ego appreciated the consideration. All I had to do was say the word, and the Grecian goddess would walk home alone.

I cleared my throat, never taking my eyes away from John's. "You two be careful. It looks like it might rain."

He looked away, disappointed and hurt. "Yeah, you be careful too. Have fun." He turned to Daryl, and put his arm out very chivalrously. "Shall we?"

She took his arm with a laugh. "We shall! Nice to meet you, Abby," she called over her shoulder as they walked away.

I watched them go, and in spite of myself, I couldn't help but notice how good they looked together. Of course they did. Both of them were more attractive than anyone had the right to be.

But so was Robert Redford, and by the time he walked back over to me and asked if I was ready to go, I was determined to follow John's advice and have some fun.

24. HONESTY

Let me tell you, having dinner with Bob Redford is something that everyone should experience at least once in their lives. It is equal parts therapy, entertainment, and education. There are still times when I feel like the world is unraveling, and nothing gets me functional again more quickly than calling up Bob and asking him to dinner. I used to joke with him that I was going to write a play called *Dinner With Redford*, and it would just be him on a stage, sitting at a two-person table facing the audience. There would be roses and candles on the table, and a bottle of wine close by, and Bob would spend two-and-a-half hours eating and talking to the audience, and at the end everyone would walk away feeling like they had a little more direction in their lives.

We left the set with his arm around my shoulders and a good-natured, "So, what are you in the mood for, kid?"

He always called me kid. Actually, he still calls me kid, and I'm roughly the age now that he was then! I think he probably would have called me kid even if he were only a few days older, rather than the nearly quarter century that he has over me. Bob seems to understand my naiveté. It's why he took me under his wing in Kenya, and it's why he feels free to lecture me and give me advice to this day. But I welcome his lectures and his advice, and he is always capable of turning things around for me.

I think he looked at me as a protégé, yes, but I also

know that he truly considered me a friend, even then. And while he may quite often pass along words of wisdom to me, he also never treats me as anything other than an equal and a peer.

He took me to a snazzy Upper East Side jazz club that he knew well, and we were seated in a cozy little booth in a dark corner. I let him order a drink for me, since I didn't really know what I liked apart from Chardonnay and wine coolers. And before you judge, remember that it was the 1980's, thus the wine coolers, but also, I was an athlete. I had never done a lot of drinking. Chardonnay was what I would order when I had to order a drink, because I didn't really know the name of anything else.

Bob ordered me a Singapore Sling. I hadn't bothered to mention that little detail about not doing a lot of drinking, and I loved the Singapore Sling. I think I was on my second before we ordered dinner, and then the conversation began.

"John and Daryl seemed to hit it off, didn't they?" Bob took a sip of his scotch but never took his eyes off of me.

I probably would have spit out my drink if it hadn't been too good to waste, but I did choke on it a little bit, which was every bit as humiliating. "Did they? I guess I didn't notice."

He leaned forward. "You forget. Everything you know about acting, you learned from me." He was smiling kindly. "I'm not buying it."

"It's nothing. It's just complicated." I did really want to talk about it, actually. I usually only got to talk about John to George, who was long distance, and Sergei, who only had a basic comprehension of the English language. But as well as Bob and I had gotten along in Kenya, and as much as I considered him a friend, talking about John still seemed a little too personal.

"Abby, you find a relationship, be it romantic or platonic, which isn't complicated, and then that will be a valid argument. Until then..."

I hadn't prepared myself for vulnerability that evening, but suddenly I was off and running. I told him everything. I told him about how John and I met, and I told him about Chris. I told him about Hyannis Port. I told him about the two years of hell, and I told him about John finally coming back into my life, just when I was finally accepting the idea of my life without him in it. I told him about the friendship John and I had been building, and I told him about Daryl asking me if it was okay to go out with John.

"So, you're all caught up," I said in conclusion, just as the waiter brought us our dinner, and my third Singapore Sling.

Bob had patiently listened to all of it. He seemed to think it all through for a moment, and then he asked, "So you love them both? John and Chris, I mean."

"Yes."

"And you were, at one time or another, very happy with each of them?"

"Absolutely."

"And neither one of them has stopped loving you."

"To my knowledge," I interrupted.

"Okay, to your knowledge. So, who do you love more?"

I choked on my drink for a second time. No one had ever asked me that before. "I don't love either of them more than the other. I just love them differently."

He took a bite of his asparagus. "See I don't believe that. If they were both standing in front of you, and all was forgiven, and you could have either one of them and live happily ever after - no family in the way, no distance in the way, no other guy in the way - you must know who you would choose."

I was looking to him for guidance and he was saying things that George had never said, and therefore that Sergei had never said, and I was suddenly convinced that Robert Redford had all the answers.

"Who would I choose?" I wasn't thinking aloud. I was asking him.

He laughed. "How the hell am I supposed to know? But I don't think that you can move forward until *you* know. Chris walked out of your life. This is a guy who didn't abandon you even when things were at the absolute worst. This is a guy who was prepared to play second fiddle just so he could have you in his life. This is a guy who put your needs first time and time again. So it just seems strange to me that he ran for the hills the first time in a while that it looked like he might not come out on top."

I had never thought about Chris leaving as a selfish act on his part. Not at all. But until that moment, I also hadn't realized that maybe he didn't leave just because he didn't want to lose me again. Maybe he left so that I wouldn't have to choose.

I was feeling the alcohol. Things were just a little fuzzy. I had never been drunk before, and as I ordered another Singapore Sling, the thought occurred to me that maybe while having such a serious conversation wasn't the best time to give being drunk a try.

"Well, that just makes everything more complicated!" I cried out. "In one way that makes me think I should be with John, because even Chris thought that was the way it was going to go, and I should just let Chris be free. But, in another way it makes me think I should be with Chris. If he is willing to sacrifice that much just so I can be happy..."

"But hold on a minute," Bob said as he finished off his fiftyhundredth drink, for all I knew - but he sure carried it better than I did. "Now let's think about John for a minute. He stayed away from you - the woman he loves - for two years, just so he could protect you. And in your apartment that night, he was ready to walk away so that you could be with Chris. He took the punch like a man, and still tried to convince Chris to stay - for your sake. And he's been going to a lot of effort to earn your trust again."

"Yes, but he went home with Daryl Hannah tonight," I said bitterly.

"No," he corrected me. "He walked Daryl Hannah home tonight. That's all you know as fact. Don't get ahead of yourself. But even if he did go home with her, you can't expect him to just sit around waiting, can you? I mean, you've dated some in the meantime, right?"

I stared at him blankly.

"No one?" He looked at me in disbelief.

"No one - just those two. I've never been interested in anyone else."

He sat back in his chair. "Well, I don't know what to tell you about that one, kid."

We finished dinner and made our arrangements for the next day's trip to Westport, and then I fell into a taxi to head to my hotel. At the last minute, I asked the driver to take the next right, and I had him drop me off at John's instead.

I staggered in the door, past the doorman.

"Would you like for me to buzz him, Miss Phelps?" he asked as he went to push the button on the elevator for me.

"Nah. Thanks, Conrad. I think I'll surprise him this time."

As the elevator made its way to the top floor, I think I really realized where I was for the first time, and I wasn't entirely sure what I was doing there. But I was excited to see John, and hoped that I wouldn't see Daryl as well.

I took a deep breath before knocking on the door, then I heard the familiar shuffle - steps getting closer to the door, and then stopping and looking through the peephole, and then chains and locks being cleared out of the way.

John opened the door wearing pajama pants and no shirt. His hair was rumpled and his eyes were barely open.

"Abby? Is everything okay?"

"Everything's fine. Can I come in? Did I wake you? Sorry, I didn't mean to wake you." Nerves and alcohol were combining to make me talk very quickly.

"It's fine," he yawned. "What time is it anyway?" He opened the door so I could enter, as I looked at my watch. Wow. Really?

"Oh, John, it's 1:30. I'm sorry. I'll just go and let you get some sleep." I still didn't know if Daryl was there, and the more I thought about it, if she was, I didn't really want to know.

I turned to head back out the door, but John held

my arm and stopped me. "Don't be silly. It's not every day that you show up at my door in the middle of the night, so you must have had a reason. What's going on? Did you have fun tonight?"

"See, that's the thing." I started to cross to the couch, but I tripped over my own feet as I did. John caught me.

A smile crept across his face as he held me and looked down at me. "Abigail Katherine Phelps, are you drunk?"

I just laid there like dead weight in his arms and started giggling. "Maybe a little."

He helped me upright, the smile still plastered on his face. "Well, well, well. I didn't think I would ever see the day. So, yes, it is probably safe to say you had fun."

"Well, like I was saying, that's the thing. I should have been having fun. It was good seeing Bob. But something was stopping me from having too much fun." My inhibitions were completely gone.

John couldn't read me very well in my inebriated state, and he had no idea what I was talking about. "Which was...?"

I scooted up as close as I could get to him, and stood on my toes and whispered in his ear, "I couldn't stop thinking about you." Then I kissed his ear, down his neck, and to his collarbone.

He tensed up immediately. "Abby? What are you doing?" He breathed the words more than said them.

Rather than answer, I made my way to his lips and kissed him for the first time in so long. There was one brief, shocked moment in which he didn't respond, and then he swooped me into his arms and carried me to the couch. He set me down, and I scooted down to a laying position, and he was instantly on top of me. Ridiculously, in that moment I remember jubilantly thinking, "Well, I guess Daryl's not here!"

We were all over each other, making up for lost time. It was so much more intense and passionate than it had ever been when we were together. He wanted me every bit as much as I wanted him, and we kissed with desperation. It was as if we were afraid to stop, because the moment might pass, or someone might be standing in our way again, or we would have to wait a few more years...

But then suddenly he did stop. He stood up and crossed the room until he was at the opposite wall, and he stood there trying to catch his breath.

I pushed myself up a bit so I was resting on my elbows. "Hey," I panted with a smile. "Where'd you go?"

"I'm sorry, Abby. I can't do this."

I stood up. "I knew it! You did sleep with her, didn't you?" I was accusatory and angry and hurt, all at once.

John was just confused. "Sleep with who?"

"Daryl." I gave him a look which I hoped said, "What kind of fool do you take me for?"

"What? No! I walked her home. What..." He walked half the length of the room. "Is that what this is about? Are you trying to mark your territory or something?"

I'd screwed up. My brain was so fuzzy that none of it made sense, but I instantly knew I'd screwed up. But at least my inhibitions were still missing in action, and while that can often be a bad thing, in this case it led to me telling the truth. A truth which was long overdue.

"No!" I walked to him and met him in the middle of the room. "I'm sorry. I'm such an idiot. It's not about marking my territory, but it is about the way I felt thinking that you might be with her. It was all I could think about all night. I mean, why *wouldn't* you sleep with her, John? You saw her."

"Yes, I saw her. What's your point?"

"She's beautiful! She's perfect! She's...she's..." I couldn't think of a word to trump perfect.

"Yes, she is very attractive. And yes, I am very attracted to her. And yes, she is also smart and funny and kind and talking on the way to her place we discovered that we have a lot in common. But I'm going to ask again: What's your point?"

I began to cry. "You're attracted to her?"

"Yes, Abby, I'm attracted to her. Hell, I think on

some level *you're* attracted to her. What's wrong with that? Why are you so insecure all of a sudden?" He just stood there with his arms crossed, trying to figure me out.

"All of a sudden? You think that I'm just insecure all of a sudden? There has never been one single moment of one single day when I have understood why you would want anything to do with me. There is nothing 'all of a sudden' about this, John. So add to that the perfection of Daryl Hannah, and I am practically collapsing under the weight of my inferiority."

"So it's not about marking your territory, it's about trying to make yourself feel better? You think that maybe, for one moment, my attention is on some woman other than you, and you just can't stand it?"

I didn't know how to make him understand. I knew that he thought I was being petty and immature, but I really don't think I was. I just wasn't handling it all in the best possible way - again mostly thanks to the Singapore Slings. But what I was feeling was legitimate, and I had to make him understand that.

"A few years ago," I began hesitantly, not wanting to remember the pain, "Chris and I were on some stupid little radio show on the BBC, hosted by some stupid little man. It was all going along like every other interview, and then this stupid little man asked me if I wanted to comment on the announcement of your engagement. It had just been announced, he said. Well, I told him I hadn't heard, and he talked about how surprised he was that you hadn't called me to tell me before the world found out. And in that moment, with Chris by my side and the whole of the United Kingdom listening, I just shut down. Chris knew that I was dying inside. He tried to turn the conversation back to skating, but that stupid little man would have none of it. Meanwhile I was trying to figure out if it was too late to get you back. If I begged you to take me back, would you? And I was so ashamed of myself for thinking like that. You had been the one who said we couldn't get married, you had been the one who humiliated me, and taken the most joyous, complete time of my life and turned it into a time of knowing I wasn't good enough for you. I had never understood why you would want anything to do with me, but I had never questioned it. And then, you destroyed me. And I was left to pick up the shambles of my broken life. Yet there I was, trying to think of anything that I could do to get you back. To convince you that this woman you were about to marry, whoever she was, could never love you like I did."

John had tears streaming down his cheeks. "I don't understand..."

I shivered at the memory. "It was April Fools' Day. It was a stupid little man's stupid little joke, but the effect that had on me was huge. When you left me, or when you let me leave you, rather, I discovered that I wasn't good enough for you. But that day, April 1, 1983, I discovered that I wasn't even good enough for myself. So yes, I'm a bit insecure. Sorry."

I felt the chill coming back into my heart, and I didn't want it there. I fought it as hard as I could, and I broke down into heaving sobs and collapsed into a heap in the middle of John's priceless Persian rug. I was in so much pain, but it was so different from all of the other pain that I had experienced. I really was fighting. I refused to give in to the fear and the insecurity and the void again, but it was so hard...

John was suddenly on the floor with me, holding me close, crying with me. "Look at me. Look at me, Abby!" He held my face in both of his hands and forced me to raise my head. "Now, you listen to me. I did not sleep with Daryl Hannah. I did not *think* about sleeping with Daryl Hannah. Yes, she's beautiful, and all of those other things that I said, but she is nothing compared to you. You are the most gorgeous creature I have ever seen, and when you smile at me I feel like it's you and me against the world. I wake up thinking of you and I go to sleep thinking of you, and I never stop all day long. You are my entire world. You are my heart. I was so stupid to let you walk away that day, and I have never stopped regretting it, but I just didn't know - I don't know - what he'll do, Abby. And it was so selfish of me, and I'm sorry, but I had to let you go because I knew you would move on. I knew you could get over me, but I knew that I could never get over anything happening to you, especially if I could have prevented it. I'm so sorry for what I have done to you. You deserve so much better. And the only reason I stopped back there on the couch a few minutes ago is because I want you to have better for your first time than my couch in the middle of the night when you may be too drunk to really remember it in the morning. That's why I stopped, Abby. Not because I don't want you, because I do, and not because I was thinking of anyone else. Sometimes I really do wish I could think of someone else, but I just haven't had any luck with that."

I continued to sob. I believed every word he said, and I think that night I finally began to truly heal. I thought I had before, but I had just buried it deeper and deeper until I thought it was gone. That night it all rose to the surface. Every last bit of it.

I cried for hours - I just couldn't stop - but the pain did start to ease, slowly. John held me all night, there on his priceless Persian rug which I had stained with my tears, and when we finally fell asleep as the sun was coming up over the Manhattan skyline, I knew that the next time I awoke, everything would be different. I didn't know if that would be a good thing or a bad thing, but I did know that John and I would never be the same again.

25. TOMORROW IS TODAY

There wasn't really a moment when I awoke. It was more just a general awareness. And as I became more and more aware, I was able to put together the pieces and remember where I was and what had happened. The first thing I became aware of was the hard floor I was sleeping on, and then the ache in my throat, unlike any I had ever felt. And then I heard the Manhattan traffic, and that made my head hurt, and suddenly it was all back with a vengeance. I had never had a hangover before, and right then and there on John's floor, I promised myself I never would again. It was a promise I broke, but it took me years to do it.

I started to sit up, but I had barely budged before John called to me from across the room. "Whoa, whoa...hang on. Don't move."

Too late. I thought my head might implode.

"Here, drink this." He handed me some cold and green thing, which looked disgusting, and I looked at him apprehensively. I can't be sure, but I really think he was trying not to laugh at me. At least he knew better than to actually do it.

"What is it?" I thought I was going to vomit just looking at it.

"Don't ask. Just trust me. Drink it fast so you don't taste it too much." He really was enjoying himself. "And you might want to hold your nose so you don't smell it either."

I did as he suggested and, holding my nose, downed the frothy poison he had prepared for me. I don't have words in my vocabulary to describe how gross it was. After I finished off the glass, John placed a pillow under my head and told me to lie on my side and stare at the wall.

"Is all of this to help with the hangover, or just for your personal amusement?"

He smiled as he gently brushed my hair out of my face. "Both." He leaned down and kissed me on the forehead. "Now, stare at the wall, don't talk, and don't move."

I did as I was told, and about ten minutes later I began to feel alive again. And as I began to feel alive, more memories came flooding back - the ones which weren't as directly related to the hangover.

He had held me all night long. As I cried and couldn't quite gain control of my emotions for hours, he held me and comforted me, and let me say everything I needed to say. And it had to have hurt him as badly as it hurt me. I'd gotten it all out. I didn't remember everything, and I still don't. He never would tell me what I had said that I didn't already remember, but I knew that there were some missing pieces. I've always assumed that those missing pieces were either things which would hurt too much if they were brought up again, or things that I wouldn't even believe I had said. I'm pretty sure that all of the unspoken, devastating thoughts I had ever had about John weren't unspoken after that night. But they were never spoken of again.

"I think I feel better. Can I sit up?"

"Yes, but slowly." He helped me upright and then assessed my reaction to see how I was really feeling. And I was okay. After that he helped me to the couch, and before too long I felt completely normal.

"What was in that drink? You should bottle that stuff up and sell it as a miracle hangover cure." I had graduated to orange juice, which tasted much better.

He smiled. "Top secret."

I smiled back at him, remembering what he had said. "When you smile at me I feel like it's you and me against the world." I knew what he meant. We sat there in silence, smiling at each other for way too long. And then I remembered one more thing.

"Oh no! What time is it?" I looked down at my watch, and began to panic.

"Hey, hey. It's Saturday. Sergei's in Moscow. You don't have anywhere to be. Would you like some more orange juice?" He stood up and walked into the kitchen.

"No, no, no." It was twenty minutes past noon. "I was supposed to meet with Bob this morning. We were going to Westport." I had stood up Butch, Sundance, and Joanne Woodward. That doesn't happen every day.

"It's fine." John brought in another glass of juice, not having waited for my answer. "I called Redford. He completely understood and promised to take you to meet Paul and Joanne another day. Actually, he felt pretty responsible for the state you were in. I got the impression that you were really knocking them back last night."

I wouldn't allow him to get any more pleasure from laughing at me right then. Besides, I knew I was missing something in there. "How did you get his phone number?"

"Do you need another pillow?" he asked, clearly trying to change the subject.

My jaw dropped. "You got it from Daryl, didn't you?"

His smile faded. "You're mad. I knew you'd be mad, but hear me out. I think you'll be a lot less mad when I tell you what I said to her..."

I was intrigued. "Go on."

"Well, it's no big deal, actually. I just called her up, because she gave me her number last night. And before you ask, I did not give her mine. But I just asked if I could have his number, and she said yes, but said she was curious as to why, and I said, 'Well, the fact is, Abby is supposed to meet up with him in a little bit, but she's still asleep. And we got so little sleep last night that I don't have the heart to wake her.'" John looked equal parts proud of himself and fearful of my reaction.

My eyes must have been the size of saucers. "John! You made it sound like we...like we...you know!" Damn it.

My inhibitions were back.

The fearful part disappeared and he decided it was safe to be proud of himself. "What? Slept together? Well, we did," he teased.

He scooted a little closer, and I started blushing. "Yes, technically, but she's not going to think that it was under the circumstances that it was under."

"Do you care what she thinks? Because I really don't." A strand of my hair came loose from my ponytail and he put it behind my ear. "I don't care what anyone thinks."

"Apart from Ted, you mean." He dropped his hand and sighed. "No, no, wait." I immediately picked his hand back up and held it in mine. "I'm sorry. I didn't mean for that to sound the way it sounded. I just mean it as fact. I know that you have to care what Ted thinks. I get that now. I do finally understand that, John. I'm sorry it took me so long -"

He cut me off. "No, Abby, don't you dare apologize to me. For anything. I'm the one who is sorry."

I knew I didn't want to head down that path again. It was done. It was over. "Thank you for last night. I know that must have been difficult for you, to sit through my rehashing of all of that, but it's over now. John," I said softly, scooting closer to him and holding his hand tightly. "I forgive you. I 100% forgive you, and I say that without any hesitation or trepidation. I forgive you. I trust you. It's over and done. It's in the past, and it's going to stay there. Forever." I pulled him to me and hugged him, and he held me without saying a word. "Now you just need to forgive yourself," I added.

He pulled away and looked me in the eyes. "That's going to be tough."

"I know. But you have to find a way to do it. Do you know why?"

He just shook his head sadly.

"Because the sooner you do, the sooner we can move on and start working on my plan."

He arched his eyebrow at me. "What plan is that?"

"My plan to make you less presidential. I'm taking

over. You have supposedly been making yourself less presidential for a while now, but how? By playing flag football in Central Park without a shirt on? You do realize that women are allowed to vote in this country now, don't you Mr. Kennedy?" I reached over to his end table and grabbed a notebook and a pen. I opened to a blank page and at the top wrote, "Ways to Convince Americans That John Can't Be President."

He laughed when he saw what I wrote. "So what has to change there? Put on a shirt? I'm not crazy about that idea."

I pretended to consider it. "No, neither am I."

"Okay, well, I'm going to keep playing football. That's a given."

"Well, obviously."

"Hmm." He pondered for a moment. "I could flunk the bar exam."

I laughed. "We want to ruin your chances of ever being president, not of ever having gainful employment! I'm going to need you to support me when the International Skating Union runs out of countries to sell me to, you know. And by then, you'll have been disowned and we'll only own one home in Hyannis. And of course some property on the Vineyard. And we may have to trade this place in for something in Chelsea. So you must be able to get a job. That's a must."

"Fair enough," he said through his laughter.

"Well, I'll just leave the list here and we'll keep working on it."

"Okay." John was trying to keep a serious look on his face to match mine, but he wasn't succeeding, and I found myself trying to catch my breath. He was so cute. I know that calling John Kennedy Jr. cute is like calling the Pacific Ocean wet, but in that moment I was really taken by how cute he was. We hadn't been that relaxed together in four years. Actually, I don't know that we had ever been that relaxed together. You see, as horrible as everything had been, it had broken us so completely that we had no choice but to rebuild on a new foundation. The old foundation had been damaged beyond repair, and in its place was built a foundation of friendship. As teenagers, we had fallen in love so immediately that we had skipped the friendship stage, but in 1986, John and I were friends. We were amazingly good friends.

"John?"

He was still trying not to smile, certain that I was still joking around, but my thoughts had moved on. "Yes, Miss Phelps?"

"I love you."

The smile faded, and in its place was an expression which I will remember for as long as I live. Though he never said it, and I never asked, I think that may have been the moment in which John forgave himself.

"I love you, too."

I repositioned myself so that I could cuddle up next to him on the couch, and he placed his arm around me. We sat there for an eternity, not saying a word, just enjoying the fact that for at least that one brief shining moment, life was as it should be.

[FROM THE DESK OF DR. ALEC B. REDMOND Maybe this is just a novel. Just a work of fiction based on Abigail's delusions, but built upon with deliberate, creative, intensive effort. Maybe Abigail knows exactly what she is doing, and she is waiting for me to read her book and then go back to her at our next session, ready to send her back to Cedar Springs, and she will laugh and say, "Lighten up, Doc!" and then I will give her credit for being a creative mastermind. And then I will give myself credit for being the most successful psychiatrist in the history of delusional disorders. Now I am having a very difficult time believing that she doesn't know exactly what she is doing. Did you catch that last line? "One brief shining moment," as in "One brief shining moment that was known as Camelot." The Kennedy presidency. She just threw that in there as part of a delusion? And have her delusions really organized themselves to the extent that *Bolero* led to *Out of Africa*, which ultimately led to John and Daryl meeting? John and Daryl - an actual, long-time couple. That's not how delusions work. Abigail knows what she is doing. I'm just going to read her novel and go along for the ride, but she knows exactly what she is doing.]

26. WE DIDN'T START THE FIRE

John and I found an interesting, and overall pretty successful, balance in our relationship. We were completely, 100%, unwaveringly in love with each other, but we kept it mostly platonic and focused on the friendship aspect. That's not to say that there weren't meaningful, stolen glances, and that's not to say that once in a while, in the privacy of my home or his, a goodnight hug and kiss on the cheek didn't occasionally end up being slightly more, and that was always fine. Better than fine. Neither one of us was dating anyone else, or had any desire to.

Christina Haag was still his public "girlfriend" and she and I actually became very good friends as well. She and John were like brother and sister, but having dated previously it was no big deal for them to be just affectionate enough that the public and the media wholeheartedly believed they were together.

John and I were also finally accepted by the public as "just friends." That was important, of course, because if the world didn't believe it, we had no chance of Ted believing it. It helped that I got along so well with Christina. I occasionally tagged along as a third wheel, or we would "double date" and I would bring George or Sergei, and it just added more credibility to the "just friends" charade. And it also allowed John and me to spend more time together.

It was a very conscious decision to stay pretty

platonic in private as well. There were several reasons for it, but the biggest was it made it easier for us to stay platonic in public. We knew that if we were free to kiss or make love in our private time together, it would be all the more difficult to keep our hands off of each other in public. And honestly, it was enough of a challenge as it was.

It was a lot of work and a lot of sacrifice, but we both knew it would be worth it. We were biding our time - sacrificing a few years of being together so that we could have it all a little bit down the road.

We had a five-year plan, starting in 1986. By 1991, we would be married and starting a family. The plan for those years in between included the 1988 Calgary Olympics, followed by my retirement from figure skating. I would go back to Brown, or maybe even Harvard, just to suck up to Ted further (which, yes, disgusted me, but I would do what I had to do to be with John), and I would get my degree. Meanwhile, John would finish school, pass the bar exam, and start practicing law full-time. That doesn't sound very un-presidential, does it? Well, we had decided to go with a slightly different approach.

We realized that his attempts to appear less presidential could also just be written off as his rebellious phase, and with his looks and charisma, and family connections, he could be easily forgiven. It might not ultimately do any good. So he would still pursue his law career and be a model citizen who made his mother and the rest of his family proud. He was just going to go with a more direct approach. John was a very public citizen, and if he granted an interview, or so much as gave a one-sentence quote, it was guaranteed to be reprinted endlessly and read or heard by most of America. So, when asked if he would ever run for office, whereas he had previously said things like, "I have a great respect for those who give their lives to public service, and whether or not I have the fortitude to do that remains to be seen," he started saying instead, "I have a great respect for those who give their lives to public service, but I'm going to have to leave that to other members of my family. It's just not the life for me."

He agreed to appear at all sorts of charitable events, and did great things and gave large amounts of money to organizations he championed, but he refused to appear at political fundraisers, and he stopped endorsing candidates, even members of his own family. He distanced himself from politics completely, and Ted was not pleased, but I think that Ted accepted it to some extent, because John made it clear he just wasn't interested. At least he wasn't doing it so he could be with some Protestant figure skater.

But of course, he was doing it so he could be with some Protestant figure skater, and each time John was quoted distancing himself further and further from politics, I knew that it was really his way of telling me how much he loved me.

So we could wait a little longer to be together. We were sure of our love for each other and knew that nothing could stand in our way.

«««◊»»»

In February of 1988, Sergei and I headed to Calgary for the Winter Olympics. My experience in pairs skating, with Sergei, was so different from my experience in ice dancing, with Chris. Sergei and I didn't push the envelope artistically as Chris and I had. Instead, we pushed it technically. For instance, we were the first pair to complete a quadruple twist lift, which involved Sergei throwing me ridiculously high into the air where I would rotate four times, and then Sergei would catch me. It was also a different experience in that Sergei and I always competed and performed to classical music. We were very by-the-book in that regard - the Soviets wouldn't have it any other way. Of course there was also no sensuality like there had been between Chris and me.

Regardless, Sergei and I were the favorites leading into the Olympics. Again, unlike Chris and me, Sergei and I weren't undefeated heading to Calgary, but we hadn't lost often, and we always placed. Coming out of the 1987 season, we were at the top of our game.

With the Games being held in Canada, more of my supporters were able to get there since Calgary was infinitely more accessible than Sarajevo. Throughout the competition, Sergei and I had a pretty large cheering section. I had wanted to fly Sergei's mother and sister in, but he said his mother had never left her home, and she didn't want to go to. That made me sad, but Sergei seemed to be fine with it. It was just a way of life. I did ultimately get his sister Natalia there, and that seemed to mean a great deal to Sergei, which of course meant a great deal to me. And then there was my American fan base.

My parents were there, of course, and George was there with his girlfriend at the time, Kelly Preston. Bob came for the long program, and brought his daughter, Amy. And John was there. He brought Christina along to be safe, but that didn't bother me a bit - knowing he was in the stands was all that mattered.

Sergei and I were leading after the short program. Once again, I found myself in a situation where the gold medal was mine to lose. In 1988, I was more relaxed than I had been in 1984. To be honest, the only thing to worry about was falling or Sergei dropping me. Well, Sergei never dropped me, and I just didn't tend to fall very often. Sergei was the one who was nervous. It was his first Olympics, of course, and he had a lot more riding on a victory than I did. If he returned to Moscow with a gold medal, he and his family would be set for the rest of his life. If he didn't, well, he wasn't sure what would happen. But I was confident. Not cocky, just confident. I knew that Sergei and I were good enough to make it happen, and I believed in him more than I had ever believed in anyone. I didn't see that we could possibly fail.

An hour before we were to take the ice for the long program, I was pacing the hallway, going over our routine in my head, when someone coming around the corner bumped into me and I fell square on my tailbone. I was okay. I knew I would be sore in the morning, but I immediately took stock and knew that I wasn't injured to the point that it would affect my ability to compete.

As a hand appeared in front of my face to help me up, a very familiar Nottingham accent resonated in my ears. "Well, you do love meeting men this way, don't you?"

My eyes immediately went to his face, though sight

certainly wasn't necessary to know whom I had run into. I took his hand and stood up. "It's my version of a pickup line, I suppose. You'd think I could come up with something less painful, hmm?" I rubbed my tailbone, still assessing my condition.

"I am sorry about that. Are you okay? You go on soon, don't you?"

"I'm okay."

With that out of the way, we just stared at each other for a moment, uncertain how to proceed, not used to being uncomfortable with each other. We were no longer used to being with each other at all.

Chris broke the awkward silence. "Well, hello, by the way." He looked as if he were deciding whether or not to hug me, so I made the decision and grabbed him.

"Hi. It's good to see you." It was an awkward hug, but it *was* awfully good to see him. I pulled away. "What are you doing here?" For one fleeting moment I thought maybe he had come to be part of my cheering section.

"I've just started working with the Duchesnays." The Duchesnays were a French-Canadian brother and sister ice dance team, Paul and Isabelle. They made their appearance on the international ice dancing scene after Chris and I had already left.

"Oh, that's great, Chris." I smiled at him, and then it was awkward again. Neither one of us knew how to act or what to say.

"So," he began, "you and Sergei looked good out there in the short program. You're about to make history again tonight."

"We'll see." I had kind of stopped thinking about the history aspect of it all - potentially winning a medal in both partner disciplines, which had never been done. But it had also never been attempted, so as far as I was concerned, the history was already made. "I miss you." It just came out.

"I'm in a relationship..." He was shaking his head and shuffling his feet as he said it.

"No, Chris, I'm not trying to make this a big deal, or bring up our history, and I really don't want to make you uncomfortable. I'm happy that you're in a relationship. I am too. I just want you to know that being here, going through this whole Olympics thing again, I can't help but think of you and, as much as I love skating with Sergei, you and I both know that you and I were once-in-a-lifetime. I can't help but look back on it with fondness. That's all."

"Oh. Okay." He visibly relaxed. "I know what you mean."

Unfortunately I couldn't leave it at that. "But I miss you as my friend, too. I know you don't want to talk about any of this, and that's okay, but I've been dying to talk to you for so long and I have to say it while I can. I'm sorry for everything that happened, but I thank you so much for caring about me enough to -"

He cut me off by putting his finger to my lips. "I miss you too."

We stood there for a moment, and I wasn't torn in the least as to whom I wanted to be with. I was in love with John. John was my life, and he was my future, and not for one moment did I feel otherwise. But that doesn't change the fact that Chris's finger on my lips sent an electrical charge through me just like I had felt each time he had ever touched me.

He felt it too.

He pulled away with a red-faced, "I'm sorry."

No. I wasn't going to let this get in the way of potentially having him in my life again. "Chris, I'm twenty-six years old. And you're almost thirty now, my friend. I'm finally ready to own up to what you and I have between us, which is a lethal amount of sexual chemistry. It just is what it is. We've had it for almost a decade now. It's not going away, so let's just accept that and not let it stand in the way of being in each other's lives. You're with someone. I'm with someone. It doesn't change the fact that there is a part of us that still wants to, how did you say it? 'Rip each other's clothes off?' But we are also mature adults capable of controlling that desire, and we have both moved on, and it's time for you to come back into my life and be my friend."

For a second he tried not to smile, but in the end

he couldn't help it. "I'm not sorry I stayed away for four years, you know. I had to."

I smiled back. "I know."

He sighed. "Okay. Friends, hmm?" He seemed to be turning the idea over in his mind, and then he seemed to accept it. "So, not a lot of people know, and it really needs to stay that way for now, but the person I am in a relationship with is Isabelle Duchesnay. We just don't want to cause any media hoopla, since I'm their choreographer and everything."

I nodded. "Understood. It won't go any further. And, well...not a lot of people know, and it really needs to stay that way for now, but the person I'm in a relationship with is John Kennedy." I paused and looked up at him nervously. To his credit, his long-standing hatred of John was not evident on his face. "We just don't want Uncle Ted hiring a hit man to kill me or anything." I chuckled, trying to make an incredibly real, serious situation a little less intense.

Chris nodded, and thankfully choked down everything I'm sure he wanted to say. "Understood. But if we're going to be friends, I still don't want to be around Kennedy. Sorry. Some things I just can't let go."

I nodded once more. "I'm sure he'll prefer it that way too." Then I exhaled deeply and pulled him to me, and there was nothing awkward about that second hug. "I'm so glad to have you back."

Sergei and I easily won the gold medal. As we stood on the podium, more than anything I noticed the contrasts between that moment and the last time I had been on the Olympic podium. There was a different national anthem, of course, but I barely even noticed. Brian Boitano, who I'd met four years earlier in Sarajevo, was again in the crowd – this time as the men's gold medalist – and he was again waving the American flag and cheering for me. That made me smile, of course, but it didn't have the misty-eyed result that it had four years prior. The last four years had been for Sergei. I wasn't lost in my thoughts of how nice it would have been to be representing America - I didn't care about that anymore, or at least I didn't think I did. Most

Americans, with the exception of a certain Massachusetts senator, had embraced what I was doing. And I had never been very shy about letting people know that I hadn't been given much choice as to whether or not I would skate for the Soviet Union.

It was nice to have another gold medal, and of course it was gratifying to have all of the hard work pay off, but it really was all for Sergei. I kept glancing up at him as the anthem played, and I was touched by how much it all meant to him. And that was what really made me proud. I had helped him achieve that moment.

After, we were surrounded by all of our cheerleaders, hugging and celebrating. John gave me a platonic congratulatory hug and said, "I am so proud of you." And he quietly whispered, "I love you" in my ear. Even in the midst of our closest friends, the only ones who knew about the true status of our relationship were George and Christina, and John's sister Caroline. My parents didn't even know, and neither did Mrs. Onassis. And now Chris knew. I would have to find time to let John know that a little later.

I agreed to go professional with Sergei for a few months. I told him I didn't want to skate for much longer, but I was intrigued by the idea of professional skating. There was a lot of money to be had, of course, but what intrigued me the most was that I wouldn't be representing a country at all. We would just be Phelps and Grinkov, no Soviet Union attached. And then, I had a really crazy idea.

I knew that I was almost done skating, and I was certain my retirement was going to be permanent. I was going to go back to school and become a respectable Kennedy wife. But once the burden of the Soviet Union was lifted, I began to feel very nostalgic about figure skating. I was going to miss it. Not the politics, and certainly not the ISU, but I was going to miss being on the ice. Sergei didn't know the real reason that I was going to retire, but Chris did. We had begun talking regularly again. In fact, there was rarely a day that we didn't talk on the phone, and in the weeks following the Olympics, we got all caught up on four years of details of the other's life. It was during one of our daily phone calls that I hatched my scheme.

"Skate with me again, Chris. One last hurrah."

He laughed at me. "You're going to be skating with Sergei. Or have you just decided to dash the kid's hopes and dreams?"

I wasn't laughing. "No, I want to do both. It's just for a few months. The professional season will be over in August, and then I'll retire and you can keep choreographing and Sergei can get a new partner. But wouldn't it be great to skate together for just one more season? What a way to go out: with my two gold medal partners, who just happen to be two of my closest friends? I couldn't ask for a better send-off than that."

It took some convincing, but he eventually consented. Stepping back onto the ice with Chris felt like going home again. He, Sergei, and I all trained in Simsbury and entered the same competitions in pairs and in ice dancing. I was exhausted, but it was by far the most gratifying time I had ever spent on the ice.

Sergei and I, and Chris and I, won every competition we entered. Sergei and I stuck to mostly classical numbers, but I did get him to relax a bit in his choices. And I think he really started having fun on the ice. Chris choreographed all routines for both pairings, and he really took Sergei outside of his comfort zone for a while, but you couldn't argue with the results. Chris taught Sergei to embrace a more sensual side with me in his skating, and of course Christopher Dean was the master of skating sensually with me, so Sergei learned from the best.

The crowds loved everything we did, and they seemed thrilled to have Chris and me back, if even for a short time. In fact, I think the only two people who weren't thrilled were John Kennedy and Isabelle Duchesnay. Don't get me wrong, John understood and was supportive. He knew that I was preparing to give up everything I had ever known in order to be with him, and while I was happy to do that and was going to be doing exactly what I wanted, which was be with John, he wanted me to enjoy my last months on the ice. And he knew that skating with Chris was when I was really in my element. That didn't change the fact that there was still an insecurity within John relating to my attraction to Chris, but he trusted me, and I knew that we were well in control of our emotions.

Now Isabelle was a different story. I would sometimes call her Yoko, which Chris couldn't help but laugh at. She was always there, just like Yoko Ono had always been with John Lennon in the last days of The Beatles. She was at workouts, she was at practice, she was at training, and she was at competitions. She did not trust me one bit, and she didn't seem to trust Chris one bit if he was with me. But I just ignored her, and so did Chris. He was fascinated with Isabelle, but he knew she was difficult. But then, so was he, to most people. Not to me, of course, but to most people. So he and Isabelle made a perfect, high-maintenance pair, and they finally went public with their relationship in the spring of 1988. By then, everyone saw her with us all the time anyway, so it was pretty obvious.

In July of that year, Ted Kennedy asked John to introduce him at the Democratic National Convention. John first turned him down, but then Mrs. Onassis stepped in and told John, "This has nothing to do with politics. This is your family." He assured me it would be a brief introduction which he didn't even think would be televised. Of course I supported him and told him to do what he needed to do.

His last words to me before we hung up the phone the night before he spoke at the Convention were, "Don't worry, Abby. I may be so bad at public speaking that the family decides I need to go into a new family business. What should it be? I could be a plumber maybe? Will you still marry me if I unclog drains for a living? *Profiles in Plumbing* anyone? Or would that be *Plumbing in Courage?*"

I laughed. "Remember rule number one, John. You must be able to find gainful employment. As long as you can do that, of course I'll still marry you! But almost every job, even plumbing, requires some speaking, so don't screw up too badly out there tomorrow night!"

We laughed, and he promised to call me after the

Convention.

The next evening, I turned on the television, based on what he had said not really anticipating his part being televised, but I thought I would see, just in case.

Half an hour later, he was introduced, and the crowd went wild. He got a two-minute standing ovation before he ever opened his mouth, and once he did start speaking he went on to praise Uncle Teddy. I was in shock. "America is better because of the leadership of Edward Kennedy," he said. But are our lives better, John? How could he stand at the podium of the biggest political rally in the world and praise the man who had torn us apart?

He was an amazingly good public speaker. What's more, he looked damn near presidential. My heart had been stepped on.

Moments after he left the stage on my television screen, my phone rang. It was him, and he was completely fired up.

"Oh, Abby, it went so well. I can't believe how well it went. It was actually really fun." I wish I could have been happy for him.

"Yeah. You were great."

"Oh, you saw it? Great! Did you see the reaction I got? I really didn't expect it to be that much fun." He was so caught up in the moment, and he had completely lost track of the big picture.

"I'm glad you had fun. Of course, that probably did set us back a bit in our five-year plan." I was bitter, and I was so angry. I just didn't understand what he was thinking.

"What? Oh!" He laughed. "No, don't worry about that. This didn't mean anything to anyone."

I lost my cool. "Are you kidding me? You haven't been hearing what they are saying. I'm looking right now at Tom Brokaw talking with political experts about how polished you were, and how much the crowd loved you, and how much enthusiasm you generated, and how you are the future of the Democratic Party!"

John was silent on the other end of the phone.

I, meanwhile, was still fuming. "Say something!"

"Maybe there is a way we can have it all, Abby. It

might take a little longer than we thought, but maybe I can be in politics too."

"I need to know right now if you are choosing politics over me, John. Right this minute, I need to know."

"What? No, of course not! I love you. You're all that matters to me. You know that!"

I breathed a sigh of relief. Okay. It would be okay.

He continued, "I just don't think it's really fair for you to tell me I can't go into politics if that's what I'm meant to do. The life of a public servant requires sacrifices, Abby. You and I are no different."

"How dare you talk to me about sacrifices?" I seethed. I didn't know if Ted was brainwashing him or if he was just riding high on the wave of the world loving him, but I wasn't talking to the John I knew and loved. "I have done nothing but sacrifice to be with you. And now I'm not being fair? Go to hell, John." I hung up the phone.

The phone rang again immediately, but I wasn't about to pick up. His voice was suddenly on my answering machine. "Abby, pick up. Abby?" He waited. "I'm sorry I said that. I didn't mean it that way. But I am feeling really drawn to running for office, and I would like to talk to you about it. Please pick up the phone, Abby." He waited again. "Fine. Real mature, Phelps." And he hung up the phone.

Moments later he was on my screen again, being interviewed by Connie Chung. She talked to him about how rare it was for him to speak publicly like that, and asked him why he had agreed to do it. "Because Teddy asked. That's enough."

I talked to my TV screen: "So if Teddy just nicely asks you to dump me, will that be enough, John?"

And then she asked him if he was interested in entering politics. I silently pleaded with him. Please, John. Please. Five-year plan. Now's your chance. It was the biggest platform he was ever going to get.

But then I heard the words come from his mouth. "...I'll see what happens..."

We were done. I felt betrayed and hurt and confused, and so very angry. I turned off the television and started kicking things and throwing pillows. I had never been so livid in my entire life.

When the doorbell rang, I huffed over to the door and threw it open without looking to see who it was first. It was Chris.

He looked in and saw the mess I was leaving in my wake. "I just wanted to check on you."

Angry tears filled my eyes. "You saw?"

"I saw." He looked like he wanted to comfort me, but anger was not my usual reaction and I don't think he knew how. "Abigail, I am so sorry. But I'm sure he just got caught up in the moment, and..." Defending John was certainly not *his* usual reaction, and it was not something which came easily to him. And I really didn't want to hear it.

"Just shut up, Chris."

I pulled him roughly to me and kissed him. His lips instinctively met mine in their urgent plea for just a moment before he pulled away and held me at arms' length.

"Don't," he whispered, looking down at the floor. "You will regret this."

I knew he was right, and I didn't care. I wanted to forget about John and I wanted to get out all of the frustration and the pain that came with waiting and being patient for something which was never going to be. "I'll regret it? Won't you regret it?"

"Are you kidding me?" A decade's worth of wanting each other bubbled to the surface as his eyes met mine. "I could never regret being with you."

I couldn't take it any longer. I kissed him again, and he didn't resist. With his foot, he shut the door behind him then lifted me and carried me into my bedroom. And in an evening which was passionate and intense, and yet gentle and loving, I lost my virginity to the wrong man.

27. SHADES OF GREY

From the moment my eyes fluttered open early the next morning, I was bombarded with thoughts and memories and emotions. I felt so many things, all at once, and each time a thought popped into my head, there was a counter-argument which followed soon thereafter.

I'd cheated on John. But how can you cheat on someone who is only your boyfriend in private?

I hadn't given him a chance to explain. But what explanation could there possibly be which would make it any less painful, or make me feel any less betrayed?

It was going to make things so much more difficult with Chris. But we had both wanted each other for so long - maybe by getting it out of the way, we had cleared the way for an even closer friendship?

I really shouldn't have lost my virginity during a one-night stand with one of my closest friends. But in so many ways, didn't it make perfect sense that it was with him?

I'd thrown away everything that John and I had built. But hadn't he already thrown it away the moment he stepped onto that stage at the Convention?

I'd messed up. Okay. I couldn't argue with that one.

I rolled over in bed, not sure if Chris was still there. I really hoped it wasn't like the nights of indiscretion in movies. I didn't want to find a note on his pillow that said he couldn't stay, but he valued our time together and he wished me nothing but the best. I wouldn't be able to bear that. But I also didn't know if I would be able to bear the alternative: a naked Chris still lying next to me, thinking that we were going to be a couple.

I have to admit, I could bear the thought of the first part of that. There was just something about the combination of the two of us when Christopher Dean and I came together - be it on the ice or, apparently, in bed. We were potent together, and I was ashamed of myself, lying there thinking about just how much I had enjoyed the evening. And as I felt my cheeks warm, just like they had the first time I saw him, and the first time I skated with him, and the first time I kissed him, I forced myself to stop thinking in such graphic detail of the first time we made love. The only time, I mentally corrected myself.

Well, there was no note on the pillow, but there was no Chris, either. And then I smelled the coffee, and I smiled. Of course. Something in between. I got out of bed and dressed quickly, then with a bit of apprehension, very uncertain as to how it was all going to play out, I went out to the kitchen.

He looked good. He was in the clothes he had been wearing the night before, of course, but he had showered and his hair - that blonde hair which I loved - was disheveled and extremely sexy. He was leaning against the counter, reading the newspaper, drinking a cup of coffee. He looked cool and casual and pretty irresistible, actually.

He looked up and smiled as I entered the kitchen. "Good morning. I made some coffee. Are you hungry?"

"No, not really. Coffee sounds good though. Thanks." He poured me a cup and set it down on the table. I sat down, and he sat across from me.

It was strange. It probably should have been uncomfortable, but it wasn't. We just sat there, looking at each other and drinking our coffee, trying to figure out what to say, but not being in any hurry to say it.

"So, what are your plans for the day? Are you and Sergei working?" Chris opened with business as usual.

I smiled at his attempt to act as if nothing had changed. "No. Actually, I think you and I were supposed to…"

"Oh. That's right." He looked at his watch. "I'm supposed to meet you at the rink in forty-five minutes. I may be a little late." He smiled and looked down at the floor. "I didn't sleep very much last night. I'm kind of tired."

I started blushing again. "Nope. Sorry. You never let me get away with that. Late is late, regardless of how good you think your excuse is."

His laughter was easy and relaxed. "Oh, come on! I've waited ten years for an excuse this good!"

I picked up a dish towel and threw it at him, and laughed right along with him. And then, without meaning to, and without even thinking about what I was saying until it was too late, I turned very serious and asked him, "Was it worth the wait?"

He stopped laughing and looked up at me again. "Absolutely."

"Wasn't finally having sex supposed to help release some of the sexual tension? Why does it feel like there is more of it than there ever was before?" I paused, and started blushing again. "Okay, I didn't really mean to say that aloud."

Chris smiled, but I could tell he was trying not to laugh. "No, it's a very valid question, Miss Phelps. And I do actually know the answer." He leaned in as if he were about to reveal to me the answer to one of life's great questions. "The only time that having sex releases the sexual tension is when the sex isn't as good as you expect it to be."

I choked a bit on my coffee, and as my choking turned to laughter, he just kept talking.

"You see, we spent years and years wanting and waiting, so it was bound to be a disappointment. Right? Right?" He was determined to get a response out of me.

"Right," I said very earnestly.

"Right! So, the fact that it, well, wasn't, has left us both in a state of shock, satisfaction, and heightened sexual awareness. Now do you understand?" He winked at me.

"Yes, Mr. Dean. I think I understand. Thank you

for explaining it so clearly." I never would have thought we would be joking around like that the morning after.

Chris took a sip of his coffee. "You're very welcome."

"Can I ask another question?" I had to make sure we were on the same page, as much as I hated to ruin the carefree mood.

He nodded and waited for me to proceed.

"What did last night mean to you?" I knew what it meant to me. I needed to be assured that it didn't mean more to Chris.

He sighed. "Abigail, I have no delusions about what last night was, so don't worry." He reached across the table and took my hands in his. "Last night was amazing. And a long time coming. But I know that it was a moment. It was an inevitable moment that I'm so glad I got to share with you, and I have absolutely no regrets. Maybe I should, but I don't."

"Are we okay?" That was what mattered the most to me at that moment.

He sat back in his chair. "Yes, we're fine. In fact we're better than fine, don't you think?"

I thought about it for a moment. "Actually, yes."

"Good. I'm glad you see it my way. Now we know the secret. Sex once a decade apparently does the trick." He looked at the calendar on my wall. "Same time, same place, July 21, 1998?"

I started laughing again. "We'll see, won't we?"

"Now, I have a question for you. Are you going to tell him?"

I hadn't really thought about it. In my heart of hearts, I felt like John had chosen politics and Ted over me, and the moment that happened I figured he was out of my life. That's not what I wanted, but I didn't see how we could recover this time.

"I don't know," I answered honestly. "Are you going to tell Yoko? I mean, Isabelle?" I flashed him an innocent smile.

"Hell no! If she found out I got ice cream with you without her knowledge, I'd be a dead man. If she finds out

215

I slept with you, I don't know...something worse than death."

"Why are you with her, Chris?" I really didn't understand their relationship.

He smiled. "She's really not so bad when you aren't around. She just has some insecurities about you and me. I've told her there isn't anything to worry about, but for some reason she just doesn't believe me."

"Well," I exclaimed in mock bewilderment, "I can't believe she doesn't trust us more than that!"

"I know! What is her problem?"

We sat there in silence for another moment, feeling like horrible people and yet not really being able to muster up any true guilt or regret. And that just made us feel even more like horrible people.

"Well," he said as he stood up and took his empty coffee cup to the sink, "obviously whether you decide to tell him or not, I am completely behind you. But maybe give me a little warning. I don't think it would take much to convince him to kick my ass as it is. And the last time I punched him, he just took it. I don't know that I would be so lucky twice. I'm British, you know. I don't think I would stand a chance in an actual fight with a New Yorker." He walked over to my chair and leaned down and gave me a kiss on the cheek. "Still up for choreographing today?"

"Sure. Meet you there or want to go together?"

"I'll meet you there. I really should be seen in different clothes today."

"Good thinking," I laughed. "Okay. An hour?"

"An hour," he nodded. "Unless, I don't know...do you think if we doubled up we'd be good for twenty years?" he asked, looking from me to the bedroom.

I laughed and pushed him towards the front door. "I'll see you in an hour!"

He gave me one more kiss on the cheek, and a quick hug, and he was gone. And I was left in my apartment, first thinking about how everything with Chris had turned out better than I ever could have hoped, and then thinking about how the entire course of my life had changed in the last twelve hours.

I knew that John didn't think we were through. I knew that John thought I was angry - maybe he understood why, maybe he didn't - but that if he gave me a little time, I would cool down and then we would talk it all out. I knew that John didn't know just how angry I was, and how hurt I was. And not for one moment would John think that I would be with another man - even Chris. Especially Chris?

I saw everything with much more clarity than I had the night before, when I had been throwing pillows around. I was done hiding in the background for John, waiting for the right time when I could make my appearance and be viewed as an acceptable mate for him. And I was through putting my life on hold.

I had spent so many years basing my entire life around him - either being with him or trying to survive without him, or trying to find some balance in between the two. In my state of enhanced clarity, I knew that I loved him as much as I ever had, and I knew that he loved me. He wanted to spend his life with me, I wanted to spend my life with him. Even in the midst of my anger and hurt, that hadn't changed. But I was no longer going to try to fit into the Uncle Teddy mold for the perfect Kennedy wife. That was not me.

I was going to be a figure skater. I was still the best in the world at what I did, and I got to do it with the two best partners in the sport. I wasn't going to give that up to pursue a degree that I would never use.

But it wasn't all about me, either. If John and I did talk again, and I did get the chance to tell him all of this, he also needed to know that I would support him regardless of what career he wanted to go into. If he felt the calling into public service, I would support him in that. But he would have to decide if he was willing to sacrifice a trophy wife in exchange for, well...me.

I took a quick shower, got dressed, and then grabbed my car keys and my skates and headed to the rink, excited to begin the next chapter of my life, and anxious to see if John would make an appearance.

28. SOUVENIR

Two nights ago, present day, George and I met at a little diner in Los Angeles for dinner. We go there together quite often when we are both in the area, mostly because no one ever seems to catch us there. As we sat there eating fattening, greasy food, he asked me how the book was coming along, and I had to confess that I was stuck.

It has been five weeks since I wrote the last chapter. Words and stories had been flowing freely, then suddenly, I didn't want to go forward.

I was trying to explain that to George, and he was asking me which specific incidents were stumping me. I listed them for him, and of course I didn't have to explain further, since he was there with me every step of the way, but he didn't understand the problem.

"George, from 1988 to about 1991, I didn't have a clue what I was doing with my life. There were some pretty tough times in there. Don't you remember?"

"Yes, of course I remember, but I also remember that I had never been as proud of you as I was during those years."

I laughed. "I was a mess!"

He looked at me with a quizzical expression on his face. "Hmm. I just don't remember it that way at all. As far as I'm concerned, Abby, those were the years that shaped us. We're who we are today because of those years. I mean, c'mon, I did *Return of the Killer Tomatoes* in that time frame.

Best years of our life, babe!"

We continued to talk about those years and all of the painful experiences, and as we did, I began to see his point. Each time he pointed out that "if _____ hadn't happened, then _____ wouldn't have happened either," I saw it more and more his way. But I still didn't have any idea how to write about it. Then George had an idea.

After dinner, we left separately and went to his house, George on his Vespa, me in my Volvo, avoiding paparazzi at every turn. We are pretty good at that when we really want to be. And when we got to his house, we went in and George set about the task of looking for whatever he was looking for. He pulled out a shoebox - at least I thought it was a shoebox - but as I looked closer, I realized it was too big.

I moved closer. "Is that a skates box?"

"You know what this is!" I sat down on the floor next to him. "This is my Abby Box!"

I stared at him ignorantly. "Your what?"

"My Abby Box. Don't you remember? My birthday after we met, my seventeenth, we'd only known each other about a month and you didn't know it was my birthday until the day of. You drove to Augusta to have dinner with my family, but I had just invited you to dinner, and I never mentioned it was my birthday. When my mom brought out the cake, you felt so bad that you didn't have a gift for me, even though I told you it was no big deal -"

I cut him off, excitedly picking up the story that I suddenly remembered so vividly. "So I ran out to my car to see what I could round up, and all I could find was the box that my new skates had come in!"

He smiled that beaming Clooney grin. "Yep. And you said that it was my Abby Box, and that it was empty then, but it wouldn't be for long, because I was supposed to fill it with every memento and important scrap from our friendship."

The Abby Box was overflowing. There were papers and photos and memories galore. My eyes filled with tears. "I can't believe you kept that. It's been more than thirty years!"

We looked through the box together and laughed more than anything else. Our prom photos are in there, various notes and letters through the years, a review of *Out of Africa*, wedding photos, programs from award ceremonies we attended together...you name it. The Abby Box held our history. But he was looking for something in particular.

"Here it is!" He pulled out an envelope - his address was Los Angeles, my return address was Simsbury, Connecticut.

"What in the world is that?"

"It's a letter that you wrote right in the midst of it all. 1988. Remember? I was off filming *Red Surf* -"

"Ha," I snorted laughter. "I forgot about *Red Surf!*"

George shot me a look. "I've tried to forget. So I was off filming *Red Surf*, and I didn't know about anything. I missed about three of the biggest months of your life, remember?"

I didn't remember until then. "That's so crazy. I could have sworn you were around for everything."

He shook the envelope at me. "That's because of letters. This was the first one during that time. You wrote this to me, and I thought it was significant enough to put in the Abby Box. Now, I think you should put it in your book. It's all in here, every bit of it. You wouldn't have to try to figure out how to say it all, because you've already said it. And I think you'll realize that you weren't as lost as you remember that you were."

So, because my best friend suggested it, here is the original letter in its entirety. The only explanation necessary is a little bit of help to decipher the George and Abby Code. The need for secrecy in certain cases was all-consuming, so we had nicknames for each person, and looking back they weren't all that clever at all. George was Tim, using his middle name, Timothy; I was Kate, using my middle name, Katherine; John was Eddie, randomly, just because his identity was the most difficult and important to protect; Sergei was Grink, which was just what George called him anyway; Chris was CBB, short for Cute Blonde Boy; and of course Isabelle was Yoko.

September 24, 1988

    Dear Tim,

    I miss you. I wish you were here. I'm lost without you. I miss you. But I hope you are having a wonderful time, enjoying the beach. The beach sounds nice. It's starting to get pretty chilly around here. I miss the summer already.

    My, oh my, you have missed a lot. I was kind of just holding off telling you some things, because they seem like the kinds of things which should be told in person, but the latest series of events made me think I should just go ahead and tell you. And I thought about calling you, but that somehow seemed worse than not telling you at all. Where to begin? Okay, we'll go back to July. Eddie agreed to introduce Uncle Dearest at the DNC. No big deal in general, I guess, but he was a hit. You may have seen it. All the talk the next day, etc. Still might not have been a big deal, except it lit a fire in him. He was praising Uncle and even said to the world that he didn't know if he was going into politics or not. I was not pleased.

    Long story, and I can tell you more details later, but...CBB came to my place to check on me. He saw Eddie's performance, and knew exactly how I would take it. One thing led to another, very quickly, and...yep. Me and CBB. (I know that if you were here and I was telling you that in person you would say, "It's about time.") He spent the night, we - ahem - had a very nice time, then it was kind of business as usual the next day. Except, not. I felt really close to him. And there was no weirdness. It was really great and special and made us closer than ever.

    Okay, so two days later, we're at the rink, CBB is working with Grink and me on a new routine, and in comes Eddie, who I hadn't talked to since right after the speech. I think CBB was torn between slinking off and getting out of the way and staying with me to make sure I was okay. Awkward as hell. But you would have been proud. He stuck around. And then there was poor Grink, who of course didn't know anything that was going on. He greeted Eddie, while CBB stayed close but acted like he was busy doing things. Most uncomfortable moment ever.

    As far as I was concerned, Eddie and I were through. You wouldn't even believe how mad and hurt I was on DNC night. Felt super betrayed. And I was just tired of it. Tired of not feeling like I was good enough. CBB had made me feel like the most important person in the world - pretty major contrast. Don't get me wrong - I'm not revisiting CBB feelings. We talked. Neither one of us thinks we should go back. But I was feeling like if one can treat me one way, it's not okay for the other to disregard my feelings altogether. I was never made to feel like I wasn't good enough for CBB, that's all I'm saying.

So anyway, I had been dreading the Eddie confrontation. I didn't know when it would be, but I knew it had to happen sometime, and I had been preparing myself. I really thought I was ready for it. I love him, but I just don't see how we can be together, and I was going to tell him that. And then he just showed up. And I just felt weak when I saw him, because I do just love him so damn much, you know? (And he hadn't shaved, and you know how defenseless I am around sexy, scruffy men.) I was so frustrated with myself when I realized I was happy to see him. I was _so mad_ at myself. But I still knew we had to be through. That didn't change. I just knew it was going to be harder than I thought.

And I chickened out. I didn't tell him. I should have told him right then, but I couldn't. I just couldn't stand to hurt him, but something had to be done. He knew I was angry, but he didn't realize that we were done. I agreed to meet with him the next night so we could talk. After he left, CBB and I decided we needed to tell Grink everything, since there was just no telling what would come about in the next few days. So we told him that Eddie and I had been secretly together for a while, and the history with Uncle Dearest so he knew _why_ it was such a big secret, and we told him about the DNC and we told him about CBB and me. Not just the one night, but a shortened version of the whole history. It actually felt really good to tell him everything, but I think he was pretty overwhelmed! (By the way, he said to tell you he owes you some lettuce??? I have no idea what that means, but he assured me you would.)

Next day, I met with Eddie as we had arranged and I told him everything. He was hurt, of course, but the worst part was he blamed himself. I had blamed him too, of course, but once he blamed himself it was really hard to keep blaming him. I told him I love him - always will - but I have to move on with my life and he needs to move on with his. For real this time. He argued, I cried, and I finally asked him to leave. There were a few pretty rough days after that, but I was so glad that Grink was in on everything - he was so sweet and caring and really helped me a lot. CBB did too, but Yoko was around *(as always), so it was good to have Grink.*

A week later, Eddie showed up again at my place. And he just broke my heart. He said he had done a lot of thinking and it was so sad to him that my first time hadn't been with him. He said he wasn't saying it in any negative way against me, he just completely blamed himself. He said there had never been a scenario in his mind when it wouldn't be him and me, and he had taken that - and me - for granted, and he was sorry. And I was shattered again. I'd built myself up to be strong and independent, but when all is said and done, I'm in love with him and I want to be with him for the rest of my life. So I told him we could work on it, but I told him I was going to keep skating and I wasn't going back to school, and if he wanted to go into politics it didn't matter to me, but I was tired of hiding. Either he was with me, regardless of what anyone thought, or he wasn't with me at all. He said he was with me. But he was still worried about Uncle Dearest - not that he cared what he thought, just that he still didn't know what he would do - so he wanted to talk to his mother first, and get her advice on how to proceed. She was in India or somewhere for eight weeks. We agreed to lay low until she got back, and then talk with her and get it all figured out. So we just spent time rebuilding the trust. Again! But it was good.

And then about six weeks later, I fell when I was practicing with Grink. You know I don't fall much, but there was something really weird about this fall. It was a double loop throw - which we've done 5,000 times - and there was nothing wrong with his throw, but my legs just couldn't figure out how to land. Grink rushed over of course, and I thought I was fine, but then I felt lightheaded and just kind of weird, so he took me to the emergency room. They got me in a room and he called Eddie and CBB to let them know I was there, and that we didn't know what was going on. CBB was right there in Simsbury, Eddie was in Manhattan, but they both said they were on their way.

CBB got there, unfortunately with Yoko, about fifteen minutes later, right after I visited with a doctor. I was pregnant, but something wasn't right. Grink was with me when the doctor was in there, so he knew what was going on, and thank God he acted quickly and offered to take Yoko to get some coffee so CBB and I could talk. Maybe Yoko was crossing her fingers that I was dying and she was okay with letting CBB be alone with me for a minute to say goodbye, because she actually went with Grink.

So, I told CBB. It's unreal how, even though we knew that having a baby would mess with our lives in more ways than you can imagine (end my career, end my relationship, end his relationship, ruin our reputations, etc.), we wanted that baby. Just instantly. We created a life together, you know?

He stayed with me as long as he could, then he had to go get rid of Yoko, so he dropped her off to shop with a promise to meet her for dinner. By the time he made it back, I'd found out that the baby was gone. He was strong for me, but we were both so sad. Actually, we still are. We didn't know it was happening until it was over, so it doesn't seem like it should be as sad as it is, does it?

Eddie showed up a little bit later, and he walked in - I was crying, CBB was sitting in the hospital bed, holding me - and I don't think he knew what to react to first. But he ignored CBB and he asked me what had happened, and I told him. I didn't know if he would storm out or punch CBB...I didn't know what to expect. But what he did was ask CBB if he could be alone with me for a minute. CBB stood up to walk out and Eddie stopped him and said to him, "I don't know what to say," and then he put his hand out to shake CBB's hand. And CBB shook it and said, "Thank you." And I know it doesn't change a thing and I know they still despise each other, but I was so overwhelmed by the decency of those two men I love.

Eddie and I talked, and he was comforting me, and I asked him how he could do that - even though the baby wasn't there, that didn't change the fact that I had been pregnant by another man. But he said that didn't matter, and if he'd forgiven me for sleeping with CBB - something that was in my control - and been prepared to be with me anyway, why should something that wasn't in my control - apart from being with CBB in the first place - change anything?

But I told him it changed everything. I couldn't hold him back any longer. If he entered politics, which is what he wants to do in his heart of hearts, someone somewhere would dig up the dirt, sooner or later. And I could quit skating, I could get any number of fancy degrees and I could even convert to Catholicism if I wanted to. I could justify skating with a Brit, and I could even justify skating with a Soviet - it was a peace movement, right? But I could never erase this pregnancy from the history books. What's more, I never want to. Those few minutes of waiting with CBB to hear the fate of our child, while traumatic and stressful and something I never want to experience again, were enough to make me crave a normal life. A life with less drama. A life without politics. A life in which I don't feel like I constantly owe someone an apology for being who I am.

So he's gone. I didn't break down when he left, but I do miss him. I guess I probably always will. And I do love him. But he - like my Brit, and like my Soviet, and like the baby I wasn't meant to have - is now part of my history that I grow more and more proud of every single day.

I miss you. I miss you. I miss you.

Love,

Kate

29. NO MAN'S LAND

George was right. Reading that letter did send me back to 1988 in a way that my memories alone hadn't been able. The miscarriage had been painful, and saying goodbye to John, for what really felt at the time like the final time, had been painful. I had remembered the pain, but I hadn't remembered the hope and optimism until I read the letter - a letter which I had forgotten all about, but George treasured as an artifact from a defining moment in our lives.

Now, all I can think about when I remember that time is how many of the wonderful things in my life that occurred after that point would never have come about if I hadn't experienced the pain. Of course, at the time that wasn't what I saw. At the time, I saw the pain but I forced myself to be strong and optimistic. What was the alternative? Crumbling up and dying? Well, I was tempted at times, but in the end that just wasn't my style.

Maybe my letter to George conveyed that I was in better shape than I actually was, but I think there was an element of self-fulfilling prophecy to it all. I probably held my chin a little higher in that letter than I did in the privacy of my bedroom, alone at night. But I had to. We all do that, right? We want our friends - even our closest, most trusted friends - to believe that we're going to be just fine, even before we believe it ourselves.

I knew that saying goodbye to John was the right thing to do, but I sure did miss him. It was so tempting to pick up the phone and call him, just to see how he was, but I didn't. And he didn't call me either, though I know it must have been every bit as tempting for him. In September, when *People* Magazine named him the Sexiest Man Alive, I wanted so badly to joke with him about it, because that's what I would have done if the magazine had hit newsstands a few months earlier. I would have made fun of it, all the while agreeing with their choice, of course. Instead, I laughed at George's jokes about the ridiculousness of being Sexiest Man Alive, so many of which I got to turn around on him years later - twice!

And then there was Chris. That day in the hospital changed us. As I said in the letter to George, in so many ways it brought us closer than ever, but it also instantly and irreversibly made us grow up. We had been playing with fire for far too long, trying to channel our attraction to each other so that we could be explosive on the ice, and it had worked for a very long time. But in the days after my miscarriage, we were forced to take a very long, hard look at the very real consequences which had resulted.

The end of my relationship with John was not one of the consequences. Chris and I knew that, and even John knew that. John and I had run our course for that period of our lives, and we both needed to move onto other things. But there had been a time when moving onto other things for me would have meant one thing and one thing only: moving onto Chris. We both thought more than felt that running back to each other was no longer the way to go. It was safe, and it was something we both wanted, but it didn't feel like the time for safe. It felt like the time to explore life without the safety net of each other.

But we thought we would keep skating together. We wanted to explore life without the safety nets, and yet we weren't ready to go without seeing each other every day and sharing our lives, and of course, though we didn't immediately realize it, that meant we weren't really trying it without the nets at all. It took the emotions bubbling to the surface once more to know that we had to do more than say we weren't going to look at the fire in order to avoid getting burned.

After the miscarriage, I had to take some time off to let my body heal, and while I knew it was a necessity, I wasn't happy about it. I went to the rink almost every day and watched Chris work with the Duchesnays, or I tried to distract Sergei while he trained, but I was so bored. I wanted so badly to be on the ice, and one day I sat there after everyone was gone and just stared at the ice and cried. I was feeling restless and helpless and weak, and alone. I had spent almost every day for ten years in someone's arms - Chris, John, Sergei, even Bob for a short time - and I didn't feel like I knew how to survive without the physical contact. It had been five weeks. I had one week to go, and I didn't know if I would make it.

And then over the scratchy P.A. system, I heard Chris say, "Ladies and gentlemen, making their triumphant return to the ice representing the United States of America and Great Britain -"

"And Soviet Union!" Sergei came across faintly from the back of the announcer's booth.

I smiled and stood up to look at the two of them high in the rafters.

"Yes," Chris resumed, "representing the United States of America, Great Britain, and the Soviet Union - you may know her as a gold medalist in ice dancing, a gold medalist in pairs, a failed has-been on the junior singles circuit, or a Hollywood one-hit wonder, but rest assured you know her! And you know him as simply the greatest skater ever on the ice -"

"In ice dancing! Only ice dancing!" Sergei interrupted again.

"In ice dancing!" I could hear Chris trying not to laugh at Sergei. Meanwhile, my heart was about to burst listening to the two of them doing whatever silly thing they were doing. "Regardless of how you know them," Chris continued, trying to be serious once more, "you love them, ladies and gentlemen. Or you're at least tired of that incessant drumbeat from *Bolero* which now seems to be played every single time anyone on television mentions figure skating."

Sergei started humming *Bolero* in the background

and the tears of laughter started streaming down my face.

"So, without further ado, making their triumphant return to the ice and performing the only song from Billy Joel's *The Stranger* which they haven't previously performed –"

Sergei interrupted once more and sang some of the words, in very broken English, of "Scenes From An Italian Restaurant," making light of the sing-along aspect which had begun to be a tradition, not only when we skated to that number, but also when Billy Joel performed it in concert.

Chris chuckled, "Not today my friend!" Sergei hilariously said "Aww..." in very disappointed fashion. "Not today! So without any further ado, Abigail Phelps and Christopher Dean!"

I applauded and continued laughing, not sure what they had up their sleeves, but thoroughly enjoying the show. Chris emerged from the booth and smiled at me. He hurriedly made his way down to where I was, just off the ice. When he reached me, he bent down and removed his blade guards.

I smiled at him. "Do I get a private show from the legendary Christopher Dean?"

"Nah," he smiled as he reached over and tucked a loose strand of hair behind my ears. "He's no good without his partner."

He picked me up in his arms and carried me to the center of the ice, then he looked up to the booth where Sergei remained, and Sergei started the music. Billy Joel's "She's Always A Woman" began to play.

With only the three of us in the building, and Sergei out of sight, Chris carried me around the ice, carefully and protectively, yet artistically. I was completely undone. I had so much that I wanted to say to him, and yet I couldn't bring myself to ruin the perfection of the moment by interrupting it with words. I just held onto him, and savored being in his arms. Though my feet never touched the ice, I felt as if I were skating with Chris again, and I was so grateful for that gift.

I have no doubt that it all began as a fun and sweet

idea to try and cheer me up and get me back on the ice, even if I was only being carried. And they succeeded. They had me laughing and wondering what I had ever done to deserve the partnership and friendship of those two men. But as Chris carried me around the ice, and we looked into each other's eyes, both of us wanting to speak but knowing there weren't words to properly convey anything we were feeling, it all bubbled to the surface once more.

Tears began streaming down my cheeks, because I knew that this time, Chris and I wouldn't embrace the longing we felt for each other. There would be no realization that the pieces had fallen into place for us, after two thousand years, and it was finally our time to be together. We could have gone that direction. It would have been easy to do, but we both knew that wasn't what was going to happen. And that was heartbreaking. We could have chosen, alternatively, to maintain the status quo, to keep dancing around the fire, pretending it wasn't there. But it *was* there. We had tried to extinguish it and it had come back stronger than ever. It always did. By the time the song ended and Chris set me down on the edge of the ice, we both knew the time had come to walk away from the flame.

Sergei, who had previously been so oblivious to much of the drama that took place off of the ice, sensed that the moment had turned more serious. He turned off the music and shut down the spotlights, then he walked to where Chris and I stood in silence. He said nothing, he simply kissed me on the top of my head, patted Chris on the shoulder, and left.

I finally spoke. "Thank you for that."

"No, thank you. I've been going kind of crazy not being out there."

I smiled. "I know the feeling." I knew what was coming. We both did. "If we walk away, Chris..."

"Now, Abigail..."

"If we walk away, Chris, what will you do?"

He sighed. "I'll work with Paul and Isabelle. I'll choreograph for you and Sergei..." He stopped himself, knowing that he was still dancing around the fire, just a step back from where he had been. He cleared his throat in an attempt to clear away the threatening emotions. "I will skate with lots of women, sleep with lots of women, and just basically forget that you ever existed."

I smiled at him. "No you won't."

He caressed my cheek with his fingers. "No. I won't." He pulled me to him. "What about you? Won't you be bored being half of only one legendary pair? You may have to take on a Japanese fellow or something."

I laughed and pulled away to look at him. "Actually, I haven't told Sergei, but I'm thinking of retiring."

Chris looked shocked. "Since when?"

"Right now, actually. I love skating with Sergei, and I will miss it, but you know as well as I do that my heart was never really in this one. I did it for him, and it served its purpose. Nothing like going out at the top of my game, right?"

"Right," Chris nodded sadly. "Let me just say, as a spectator and lover of this sport, it'll be sad to see you go. You will go down in the history books as the best there ever was."

I shook my head. "I will go down in the history books as the lucky stiff who found herself blessed with the two greatest men this sport has ever seen."

"That too." We smiled, and then Chris pulled me to him again. "Why does this feel more devastating than the last time we said goodbye to each other?"

"A lot has happened since then, but I don't think it is more devastating this time. This time, we're just making the best choice for the both of us. We're parting on our terms as the closest of friends, and we're not left to wonder what might have been, because we know. But we have no idea what we might do and who we might become separately. It's just time to find out."

He sighed again. "I know."

We discussed doing one last performance together, but I couldn't skate for another week, and then it would take some time for me to build up physical strength again after my hiatus. And we both knew there was a very real possibility that if we waited that long, we would decide to wait a little longer, and a little longer...

I announced my retirement from the sport the following week. It was done without fanfare, but it still drew a ridiculous amount of attention. I had already said goodbye to Chris and Sergei, and Chris flew to London and Sergei flew to Moscow before the announcement to try and keep media coverage at a minimum as they returned home. I didn't hold a press conference or give any interviews. I just issued the following statement:

It is with sadness and yet a great deal of excitement for the next chapter of my life that I announce my retirement from figure skating. My skating partnerships with Christopher Dean and Sergei Grinkov have been officially dissolved. Ten years ago, Chris and I were asked to participate in an experiment for the International Skating Union in which we would be partnered with a skater from a separate ISU nation. Until that time, we had each worked hard in our disciplines and managed to achieve only mediocrity. However, the first moment we stepped on the ice together, something extraordinary happened. We were born to skate together, and we never took that for granted. To have found the partner I was meant to have once was unbelievably fortunate, but several years later it happened again when a teenager named Sergei Grinkov showed up at my door in the Olympic Village in Sarajevo, and that was nothing short of a miracle.

I'm proud of all that I accomplished with both of these men. Did our partnerships promote peace and solidarity between competing nations? I hope so. I do know that the kindness and support I received from both of my adopted countries, as well as the United States of America of which I am most proud to be a citizen, was overwhelming and humbling, and I thank you all. And to those of you who may have had concerns that by representing another nation at the Olympics and in other competitions I was disloyal to the United States, please know that in my heart I have represented America with pride every single time my blades have ever touched the ice. Though I have not always felt this way, I know now that representing my country isn't about which national anthem plays as I stand on the podium. I represented the United States by working hard, doing my best at all times, and publicly showcasing the freedom that we are blessed with as Americans. I am extremely proud of that, but more than anything I am proud that the two men who entered my life as apprehensive strangers have become two of the people I love most in this world. Their dedication, talent, creativity, and most of all, friendship left me in awe every day, and though I will no longer be working with them, I know that you never really say goodbye when someone has shaped your life so profoundly.

Thank you for your support and well-wishes through the years. Thank you for watching, thank you for cheering, and thank you for singing along.

So then, the question was "What Now?" I told myself, and everyone I talked to, that I wasn't in a big hurry to answer that question, but of course in reality I was going crazy within a week. Sergei began as a trainer for the Moscow Skating Club, which wasn't quite the career let-down that it would have been for Chris or me if we had done the same at our hometown skating clubs. The Moscow Skating Club produces new champions like my home state of Kentucky produces champion thoroughbreds. He was a top trainer at one of the top champion-producing skating organizations in the world. We talked regularly by phone, which was sometimes a challenge since we weren't able to rely on our tried and true method of communicating with the assistance of facial expressions and hand gestures. But his English was decent by that time, and my Russian was slightly below decent, and we made it work.

When I wasn't talking to Sergei, I was just left to miss those who weren't in my life any longer, so about two weeks after announcing my retirement, I left Simsbury. It was a place I had come to know as home but which had outgrown me, and I it. I moved to Los Angeles. George and I got an apartment together, which suited us both tremendously. He was out of town for long periods of time, filming random bad movies and destined-to-fail television pilots, but he was working, which was more than I could say for myself.

I was determined not to mope, but after a few days of just enjoying time with George and a few days of sightseeing, I was bored out of my mind and always on the verge of calling Chris and saying I had made a terrible mistake.

One Tuesday evening, George walked in the living room as I watched *thirtysomething* on TV. On one side of the couch next to me was a bag of potato chips and on the other side, a pile of used tissues. I was bawling my eyes out.

"What? What now?" George was patient and loving, but also tired of my crying over nothing.

"*thirtysomething!*" I cried. Now, if you never saw the television show *thirtysomething*, you need to know that it was quite often a tearjerker. But not that particular episode. "That's us, George! The prime of our lives...gone! And I'm going to be forty soon."

George moved the chips and sat beside me, grabbing a clean tissue to wipe my tears. "When?"

"Someday."

"In thirteen years!" he laughed.

"But it's there. It's just sitting there like this big dead end."

"Abby, you have to find something to do. What do you want to do?" He grabbed a bag and started disposing of the mess all around me.

"I want to skate," I cried.

"Besides skate. What do you want to do that isn't skating, and that doesn't involve Chris or Sergei or John, or really anyone besides you? What do you want to do, Abby? Something as far away as you can get from everything that you have done so far in your life."

I thought for a moment. "I've always liked to write. Nothing major, just letters and musings and such."

"Great!" George saw an open window and he was determined to make the most of it. "Well, now is your time. What do you want to write? Poetry? A novel?"

I sniffed. "I like conversations."

"Okay then, a script! Let's get you to work on a script! You're going to write a movie, Abby Phelps. And I will make you a promise right here and now. If it isn't any good and when you're done you would like nothing more than to see it fail and die a horrible death, well, I know how to make that happen. I will star in your film. Deal?"

He got me laughing, and he got me working. I sat

down and started writing a script, though I had no idea how. *Out of Africa* was the only film script I had even seen before. But George was right. I needed something to do, and it needed to be completely different from anything I had known prior.

Of course, it's hard to write about something you know nothing about, so what I wrote about was men and women being friends. More specifically, I wrote a script which asked the question, "Can men and women be friends or will sex always get in the way?" And if sex does get in the way, can the friendship survive? Can you be friends with someone you want to have sex with?

It was the story of Chris and Abby. It was the story of George and Abby. It was the story of John and Abby. And it was the story of Sergei and Abby. But by the time it was complete and made it to the screen, it was the story of Harry and Sally.

[FROM THE DESK OF DR. ALEC B. REDMOND And now she's the great playwright and screenwriter, Nora Ephron. I am intrigued by the conversation with George which is reminiscent of a conversation she and I once had, which I included earlier. I am not certain that I know what to make of that, except that apparently, at least in once scene, in the fictional account of Abigail's life, I am played by George Clooney. Brilliant casting. I approve.]

30. BIG SHOT

I buried myself in the writing of my screenplay, and for the most part it was therapeutic. I wrote things that had actually been said, but I wrote them a little funnier. I also wrote things that I wished had been said. When I started, I didn't really know that it would be as centered around sex as it ended up being. It was going to be about the friendship between a man and a woman, and that was pretty much it, but I quickly realized that the audience, even if the audience was just me, would be rooting for the male and female leads to get together in the end. So then it was going to be about a man and a woman and their friendship, which leads to love. Well, that seemed kind of predictable. It was George who led me to my breakthrough.

I had been whining about my writer's block for the better part of an hour. George read everything I had written, which amounted to enough words for a very dull, hour-long film.

"There's some good stuff here." He flipped through the pages, which were crinkled from my numerous attempts to throw them in the garbage can.

"Yeah? Like what?" I asked in disbelief.

"I like the part when she is upset and she says she's going to be forty and he points out that that's years away."

"George!" I buried my head in my arms on the table, so frustrated with him and the entire writing process. "You like that part because you said it!"

He laughed. "Okay, okay. Let's get serious here. Okay, so that part's good, but what if he's comforting her and they kind of have a 'moment' sort of thing?"

"What do you mean?" I asked, not having a clue what he was talking about.

"You know." He looked at me like it was so obvious and he just didn't understand why I didn't know what he was talking about. He sighed. "He kisses her. And then they..."

I gasped. "No! They're just friends at this point!"

"You're such a prude!" he laughed. "If you want anyone to actually have any interest in this thing, I'm sorry Abby but they're going to have to have sex!"

"But that's *our* scene, George! That just feels wrong." I had settled on "wrong," but "incestuous," "unrealistic," and "icky" had also come to mind.

"I know," he laughed. "But you and I are the exception. I mean, that's not to say that men and women can't just be friends, but I think it takes a special dynamic. I'm going to tell you something that I've never told you before..." I took a deep breath as I waited to hear what he would say. I didn't think there was anything that George and I hadn't said to each other. "You're gorgeous, Abby. In all honesty, I think you are one of the most beautiful women in the entire world. But the thought of sex with you makes me physically ill."

I busted out laughing. "I feel the same way about you! Well, no. That's not really true. If we're being honest, I don't even think you're really all that attractive."

He started laughing along with me. "Coming from you that's a compliment. Because we're the exception. But here's the thing: give me a moment like that, where I'm comforting any other woman who I find attractive, and it probably would have led to sex. Just being honest."

"But then what?" I just didn't see how it could work. I was bombarded with memories of having sex with Chris, and memories of not having sex with John and wishing I had, but certain that it only would have made things more complicated. "They have sex and then, boom, everything's perfect? It doesn't work that way, George."

George stopped laughing. "You're right. It doesn't. And that's your story."

And he was right, of course. The path of Harry and Sally's story completely changed that day, and it went from being just another boy-meets-girl-and-falls-in-love story to a frank comedy about the very real impact that sex and sexual attraction have on a friendship. I might as well have had *Bolero* playing during the opening credits.

I finished the script in about five weeks and was left with a very strong sense of satisfaction, but also restlessness. I was proud of it, and thought it was entertaining and heartwarming, but I didn't know what I was supposed to do next. As it turns out, I didn't have to wait very long to find out.

In early 1988, during the time when John and I were together, but not, I was set up on a blind date with Tom Hanks. John was publicly "dating" Christina Haag and I was just sitting around waiting for the time when he and I would be together. George's girlfriend, Kelly Preston, who knew nothing about my John situation, was determined to set me up on a date. Frankly, I think she didn't like that her boyfriend's best friend was a somewhat attractive, single woman, though she needn't have worried about George and me, obviously.

Kelly had just filmed *Twins* with Arnold Schwarzenegger and Danny DeVito, and prior to that Danny DeVito had filmed *Throw Momma From The Train* with Billy Crystal. Somehow, Kelly worked through all of these Hollywood A-listers to get me a date. It would be humiliating if I allowed myself to think about all of the conversations they must have had about my love life, or lack thereof. Regardless, Kelly turned out to be a pretty fantastic matchmaker, not that it went the way she had hoped...

Billy Crystal referred his friend Tom Hanks, who was in the process of becoming the huge star we all know. He had already filmed several successful movies - perhaps most notably *Splash* with my old friend Daryl Hannah (Hollywood is such a small world) - but with *Big* in 1988, Tom began to morph into the critical, awards, and blockbuster phenomenon that he remains to this day.

Tom and I went to dinner, he talked about his divorce, and I talked about the Olympics. It was the most boring date ever. Neither one of us wanted to be there. Tom's friends were forcing him to get back out there on the dating scene, and he was only doing it to shut them up. I, of course, was committed to someone else, but not allowed to tell anyone that, so I couldn't get out of it either.

Within months, Tom was married to Rita Wilson and the next time I saw him, he was a much happier guy. We bumped into each other at the lighting of the Rockefeller Plaza Christmas tree. They had me on site for the television special, skating with some kids at the Rockefeller Ice Rink, and Tom was there with Robert Loggia, re-creating their already-classic performance of "Chopsticks" on the giant F.A.O. Schwartz piano.

I really don't think he even remembered who I was until I said, "Remember? Probably the most dull blind date ever?"

Tom introduced me to Rita, and the three of us got along very well. We ended up getting together for dinner in L.A. the following week, and we quickly became great friends. One thing led to another and in the course of dinnertime discussion, I started talking about *When Harry Met Sally...*, as I had decided to call it. Tom wanted to read it, so I sent the script to him, and he was very interested. But he was also one of the most in-demand actors in Hollywood, and he was booked solid.

He sent the script to his friend Billy Crystal with a note, "You sent Abby Phelps to me in the first place. I'm sending her back. Trust me - you'll enjoy your time with her script more than she and I enjoyed our date. Read this. You're welcome."

He read it, and a week later I was back in New York meeting with Billy and Rob Reiner, who was interested in directing. The two of them had worked together on *The Princess Bride* and were actively seeking another project to work on together. I agreed to sell them the rights to the script for next to nothing in exchange for casting approval. The money wasn't very important to me - it never has been.

I still had more than enough money rolling in from endorsements. What mattered was protecting the script which was so personal to me.

Very early on, they wanted me to consider playing Sally, but I really wasn't interested at first. Like I've said, I had no desire to be an actor. I was perfectly content being a Hollywood one-hit wonder, as Chris had called me. Besides, I didn't know if I even knew how to do comedy. I had written it, but acting in it was a completely different thing.

One day in the Castle Rock production office, Rob and I were working on a script revision when Billy walked in with that day's *New York Daily News*. On the cover: a very fit and shirtless John Kennedy Jr. rollerblading through Central Park with an equally fit and attractive Daryl Hannah.

"Daryl Hannah!" Billy said, throwing the paper onto the table in front of us.

Rob picked it up. "She's got the comedy chops, we know that."

"And she's going to be a big, big name around town now if she really is dating Junior." Billy looked at me. "What do you think? Do you want me to call her people? Have we found our Sally?"

I swallowed the jealousy and disgust in the back of my throat. "Actually guys, what if I did give it a shot? Is it worth a screen test at least?"

Billy and I read the "days of the week underpants" scene, adlibbing most of it and cracking each other up, and most importantly, cracking Rob up, and Harry and Sally were born. All because I couldn't stand the idea of Daryl Hannah walking away with anything else of mine.

«««§»»»

By the time filming wrapped on *When Harry Met Sally...*, I had definitely been bitten by the acting bug, although, again, I wasn't doing all that much acting since so much of the film was loosely based on various relationships in my life. (Present Day Side Note: George said I should create a drinking game in which you watch *When Harry Met Sally...* and drink a shot each time you see a reference to something that occurred in my real life - something you didn't know about before you read this book. Try it if you like, but prepare to get very drunk.) I loved romantic comedy. I had found my niche.

I went back to L.A., already in talks to work on another project with Rob Reiner. But before *When Harry Met Sally...* even premiered, I began working instead on a project with Rob's ex-brother-in-law, Garry Marshall. *Pretty Woman* was a stretch for me, and the love scenes with Richard Gere took me way out of my comfort zone, even more than Sally's "I'll have what she's having" moment, but I loved getting lost in the characters. I loved staying busy and not having much time to think about how much I missed skating, and my guys.

Speaking of my guys, it was around the time I started filming *Pretty Woman* that George got married to Talia Balsam. He and Kelly had split up a few months earlier and, if it hadn't been for Max, the pot-bellied pig who suddenly lived with us in our apartment, you wouldn't have known that the Kelly Preston years had ever taken place. George was instantly back on the dating scene, and one of the first names he mentioned to me was Talia Balsam, but I didn't really get the impression that he was any more serious about Talia than he was about any of the others. And then they took off for Vegas in a Winnebago one weekend, and the next time I talked to him, they were married.

Usually, George's girlfriends tried to get close to me. They knew how tight he and I were and they may have even gotten the impression that I would use my influence to get rid of the ones I didn't like, but I never did that. There have been a few through the years who I have gotten along with very well, and then a few who tolerated me, and I tolerated them. Talia didn't fit into either of those categories. I always got the impression that she felt that she had won, so it didn't matter what I thought. Of course, I don't know what she thought she had won. George's women have never seemed to accept the fact that I am not a competitor for his affections.

George moved out of our apartment, and

thankfully took Max with him, and promised me that nothing would change between us just because he was married. He may have believed that, but of course I didn't. I knew that the new Mrs. Clooney would never tolerate it. We still talked on the phone often, but we saw each other less and less.

Strangely, I was okay with it. I missed getting to see him all the time, but it somehow just felt like part of growing up. Besides, I was extremely busy.

With the release and success of *Pretty Woman*, I became a bona fide movie star. Most of the praise I had received for *When Harry Met Sally...* had been for writing, including an Oscar nomination, but with *Pretty Woman* I received my second Academy Award nomination for Best Actress, six years after my debut in *Out of Africa*. I lost again, this time to Kathy Bates for *Misery*, but I did win a Golden Globe for Best Actress in a Musical or Comedy. I didn't have George there with me to laugh at it all, and I didn't prepare a melodramatic speech that I knew I would never have to recite. Instead, I thanked the producers, and Garry Marshall, and the cast. It was dreadfully dull and safe, but very grown-up.

I was very much in demand, and had my pick of movies that I could have filmed. Tom Hanks and I wanted to work together, and he begged me to do a baseball movie called *A League of Their Own*, directed by Penny Marshall. I had worked with Penny's brother and her ex-husband, so I joked that it only seemed right to work with the entire Marshall/Reiner Hollywood triumvirate. I was very close to signing on, and then life took a slightly different path.

I remember very clearly the contents of my mailbox that day: my electric bill, a Spiegel catalogue, a reminder that I was due for a dental cleaning, and an invitation to the wedding of Isabelle Duchesnay and Christopher Dean. I was instantly furious, not that he was getting married - though the emotions regarding that fact came soon enough - but because he hadn't told me personally.

I had not spoken to him in more than two years, but I marched into my house and dialed the last phone number I had for him. Unbelievably, he answered the phone after the second ring.

"Hello?"

"How dare you just send me an invitation like I'm anyone else?" I was so irrationally angry.

"Abigail?" He was clearly completely shocked to hear from me.

"You were there that day, Chris. That day at the BBC, the stupid April Fools' joke. Didn't that teach you anything?" I broke down and began to cry. "How can you just throw this at me without any warning?"

He sighed. "I didn't. I was going to call you. I didn't know invitations were going out."

Of course. Yoko. "Oh." I wiped my nose and tried to compose myself. "Sorry."

"No, I'm sorry."

We sat there on the phone, in silence, for several seconds. I felt like a fool.

"Well," I tried to regain my last shred of integrity, "congratulations."

He laughed an empty laugh. "Thanks. And congratulations on all of the movie success. You made one hell of a hooker, let me tell you!"

Damn it. I missed him so much. "Thanks."

"So, look, I've got to run, but I really would love if you could make it. It's in Paris, so that could be a nice getaway, and Sergei's a groomsman, and I'm sure he'd love to see you. And bring George and get drunk and have fun_"

"George is married."

"Really? Hmm. Well, bring whoever you want, but please come." He paused. "But if you don't want to, I understand."

I took a deep breath and thought for a moment about how much I sometimes hated being an adult. "Of course I'll be there, Chris."

«« § »»

I decided to pass on *A League of Their Own* because the news of Chris's impending nuptials had gotten me in the mood for writing again. I was wondering if I was ever

243

going to find love - love with someone I could actually be with, anyway. I had an idea for a script loosely based on the Cary Grant and Deborah Kerr classic *An Affair To Remember*, but with a modern take.

I wrote it with Tom Hanks in mind. Well, I wrote it with Christopher Dean in mind, but for Tom Hanks to act in. I finished a rough draft of *Sleepless In Seattle* right before Chris's wedding, and sent it to Tom to look over while I was in France.

I arrived at the rehearsal dinner, which Chris had insisted I go to - though I obviously was not a member of the wedding party - and didn't see anyone I knew. I didn't take a date because I couldn't think of anyone who would be sympathetic enough of my rollercoaster emotions apart from George, and Talia would never have allowed it. My hope was to immediately connect with Sergei and spend the entire wedding weekend with him, but I did keep in the back of my mind the thought that he may not be as pathetic as I, and he may arrive with a date.

There were swarms of busy French people everywhere I looked, but finally I saw Isabelle's brother, Paul. I'd never had a problem with Paul, so I hurried over to him for guidance as to what I should be doing. I also took the opportunity to ask where Sergei was, and he informed me that his flight was delayed and he wouldn't be arriving until the next day.

And then I saw him. Cool and casual, and the bastard actually had the audacity to wear the shirt that he had been wearing the night of the 1988 Democratic National Convention. I flushed at the memory and wondered if he had done it on purpose, then I mentally chastised myself for the thought. *Snap out of it, Abby. It isn't all about you. He's allowed to wear whatever shirt he wants.*

He spotted me and smiled, and then walked away from people who were demanding his attention and made a beeline to where I was standing, soaking in the sight of him like I had been wandering in the desert for years and finally I had reached water.

"You're late."

I laughed. "You wouldn't know what to do if I was

ever on time."

"True." He pulled me to him, and I couldn't help but hope that Isabelle wasn't watching, and yet somehow, irresponsibly, hope that she was. "It is good to see you."

He smelled the same and he felt the same, and I was filled with regret. "It's good to see you, too."

He steered me away from Paul and everyone else. "So, isn't this quite the occasion? My soon-to-be in-laws are driving me insane already, Sergei is delayed and I'm just hoping he makes it before the wedding, and Isabelle is determined it's all doomed because some blackbird flew into the church earlier, or some such nonsense. I cannot tell you how happy I am to see you, a port in the storm."

"What can I do to help?" I was determined to be a good friend to him and not get lost in the regret and the longing and what might have been.

"Just don't leave my side!" He pulled me close and laughed.

Well, that wasn't going to help.

31. TEMPTATION

As requested, I stuck right by Chris's side as he mixed and mingled with the hundred or so people at the dinner. He greeted everyone and played the perfect host, but I could tell he didn't know half the people in the room.

Finally, I couldn't take it any longer. "Who are all of these people?"

"Hell if I know. Some of them are Isabelle's family of course, and my mum is around here somewhere. Other than that..." He looked at me and comically shrugged his shoulders.

He took care of a bit of my confusion by explaining that it wasn't really the rehearsal dinner like I thought of a rehearsal dinner. In other words, all of the people whom the groom had never met before didn't necessarily have a role to play in the wedding. The dinner was basically a big party - since so many people had come from out of town, or out of the country, or continent, they were making a whole weekend of it. That was on Friday. Saturday was the actual rehearsal, as well as a brunch, and Sunday was the wedding.

We squeezed in as much conversation as we could when we weren't being bombarded by people. Obviously, many of them were greeting Chris, but I think just as many went out of their way to meet me. And yes, more than one or two greeted us with a quickly hummed few bars of *Bolero.*

We made our way to a little secluded balcony. "Are

people ever going to stop singing when they see us?" I asked him.

He laughed. "I hope not. It's nice, I think."

"I guess so," I smiled. "Actually, I guess I've kind of missed it. They greet me completely differently when I'm not with you."

"Oh yeah?"

"Yeah. It's usually either 'Big mistake. Huge!' from *Pretty Woman* or, more often, *When Harry Met Sally*'s 'I'll have what she's having.'"

He took a gulp of his champagne. "So, what you're saying is you would rather be identified as one of the lovers of *Bolero*, throwing yourself into a volcano, than as Sally having an orgasm in a diner?"

I pretended to think for a moment and took a casual sip of my champagne, knowing Chris well enough to know that the entire purpose of that sentence, and for even throwing the word "orgasm" into the mix, was to shock me and make me blush. But he forgot: I was the woman who had written and performed that scene. I wasn't quite the innocent girl he had once known, and that was all his fault, of course.

"Actually, they aren't all that different, except as one half of the *Bolero* lovers, I never had to fake anything."

He inhaled sharply in surprise and champagne went simultaneously down his throat and up his nose, and he started coughing loudly. All I could do was laugh.

Once he finally gained his composure, he said in a strained voice, "That wasn't funny. This is real champagne. Those bubbles hurt!"

I just laughed harder and offered a very insincere apology.

We stood there in silence for a few moments after that. I was staring out in one direction at the lights of Paris until he pointed behind me. "You're looking the wrong way."

I turned around and gasped. There, in plain view in all its lit-up glory was the Eiffel Tower. "Oh, wow, I didn't even notice. Isn't that funny?" I rested my forearms on the ledge of the balcony and leaned over, as if trying to get as close to the tower as I could.

"Yeah," he squeezed in next to me and duplicated my posture, leaning on the ledge. "It's not that the rest of the lights of Paris aren't beautiful and fantastic and just right, in so many ways, because they are. But they can't help but dull in comparison to that. It doesn't matter how many times I've seen it or how well I know it, I can never seem to get enough. I don't know that I understand its power over me, actually."

We weren't talking about the Eiffel Tower anymore. He knew it and I knew it, and it was time for a decision to be made. He had left it up to me. We were approaching dangerous ground, and it was up to me to take us in a safer direction and pretend that we really were talking about the lights of Paris rather than the attraction which still existed between us. I probably should have played it safe but like I said, I was no longer the innocent girl he had once known.

As close as our bodies were on that tiny balcony, I found a way to scoot myself even closer to him, and I was rewarded with another sharp intake of breath - this time without the comical results. Neither one of us was laughing anymore.

I moved my hand to the right a few inches until it found his, and even then I could have just held his hand like I had for so many hours over so many years and we could have let the moment pass, but I didn't want to let it pass. My fingers didn't latch onto his, instead they danced with his, caressing and enjoying the feel of his skin brushing against mine. We both continued to look out at Paris, and anyone who may have walked up behind us would have suspected nothing. All the while our fingers continued their sensual, forbidden dance.

His hand made its way further up my arm, and I could barely breathe. I whispered to him, with a mischievous smile, "You wore that shirt on purpose, didn't you?"

He chuckled, and responded in a hushed tone which matched my own. "Maybe that's it. Maybe it has nothing to do with you and me, you just have a thing for copper-colored shirts or something."

"That can't be it, because as nice as the shirt is, I always seem to be very focused on getting rid of it."

He let out his breath and muttered, barely audibly, "Why can't I ever get enough of you?" And then, more deliberately but still quietly, he asked, "Where are you staying?"

I answered without hesitation, thinking of nothing and no one except Chris, not caring in the least what the consequences would be. "L' Hotel de Sers, room 443."

He turned and looked at me for the first time, and I met his gaze as he smiled. "Race you there."

I blushed, and I even giggled a little bit, and though I was disappointed that the vixen had momentarily faded and the naïve young girl had returned, Chris didn't seem to mind. "Abigail, this is so wrong." Then he urgently took my face in his hands and kissed me.

I never wanted his lips to leave mine, but I forced myself to pull away, and I handed him a key to my hotel room. As I placed it in his hand, I said only, "Hurry." Then I turned around, quickly fluffed my hair, and walked back into the crowd. I was halfway across the crowded room when I saw Chris enter from the balcony and begin making his way to a separate exit. And then, our old friend Bad Timing decided to make an appearance.

"Ladies and gentlemen," a Frenchman called out in English, in a booming voice, "please welcome the bride, Miss Isabelle Duchesnay!" The crowd applauded as Isabelle entered through the very door through which Chris had very nearly made his escape. "And there is her groom to greet her!"

Chris searched the crowd for me, his face full of apology and disappointment, and when his eyes met mine, I smiled, shrugged my shoulders, and began clapping with the rest of the crowd. As devastated as I was, I also knew there was nothing more I could do at that moment than play along. His eyes didn't leave me, and Isabelle quickly noticed that she did not have his attention. She followed his gaze, and the smile fell off of her face when she saw me. It was replaced with an icy stare.

She turned back to Chris and whispered something to him, then she pulled him to the balcony - our balcony. I tried to see what was going on, but of course I didn't want to be spotted spying. I got caught talking for a few moments to some random stranger who asked me if I was a friend of the bride or the groom. I stayed there, pretending to care about the conversation, partially because it was refreshing that he had no idea who I was, but mostly because I had a clear view of the balcony.

Isabelle was doing most of the talking, but Chris was handing it back to her as well. There were lots of hands up in the air and Chris kept trying to walk out on her, and she would pull him back. No one seemed to notice, apart from me, of course.

"Are you a figure skater, too?" Random Stranger was asking just as Isabelle entered the room again, followed by a defeated-looking Chris. She was making a beeline towards me, and I knew what was about to happen.

"Excuse me," I said to Random Stranger, and I met Isabelle in the middle of the room. "I did RSVP, Isabelle. You knew I was coming. Actually, I think you are the one who sent the invitation, right?" I looked at Chris, who looked like he would rather be anywhere else in the world, and I immediately changed course. I couldn't do that to him. "But it's okay. I understand that you have never been my biggest fan, and the feeling is mutual, so I will go. I wish you nothing but the best, congratulations, you'll make a beautiful bride...all of that."

Isabelle looked satisfied that I was leaving but somewhat disappointed that I had taken away her opportunity to do the dirty work. "It's time for you to move on, Abigail. The days of Christopher always being on the sidelines, waiting for you, are over." She leaned in closer to me, and with the noise of the crowd, I knew Chris couldn't hear her when she said, "You lose, Abigail. Go home."

I hated that woman and I wanted her fiancé, but still I don't know what came over me. As calm and as cool as could be - in other words, in a way that was so unlike me - I said, loud enough for both of them to hear, knowing that only Chris would understand, "You remember Sergei's flight number, don't you? The number I just told you a few minutes ago?"

His eyes met mine once more, and without hesitation, he repeated my room number. "443."

Without another word, I turned and walked out into the cool Paris night, hoping I hadn't just seen Chris for the last time.

I took a taxi to my hotel room and rode the elevator to the fourth floor, everything that I had said and done finally soaking in. I have to admit, I was slightly horrified, but strangely I didn't regret it. My only regret was that I wouldn't be able to be there for Chris on his wedding day as I had planned, though there was a part of me thanking my lucky stars that I wouldn't have to bear witness to his union with that woman.

As I walked into my room, I knew that I wouldn't be seeing him that night, or for the rest of the weekend. There was no way she was going to let him out of her sight. He would be kept busy with friends and relatives and strangers, and he would have time to think, as I would, and he would come to the conclusion that Isabelle arriving when she did was the best thing that could have possibly happened, keeping us from making the biggest mistake we could have made.

I lectured myself as I took a shower. What kind of woman had I become that I was okay with seducing a man on the weekend of his wedding, at his wedding party? Was I just that desperate for sex? I had gone on a few dates in the few years since saying goodbye to Chris and moving to California, but I hadn't had sex. There just hadn't been anyone who interested me enough. Chris had ruined me for other men, I guess. I wasn't even interested in being with a man if that level of passion and intensity wasn't there. And of course it never was.

By the time I slipped into my nightgown, I was absolutely ashamed and humiliated by my behavior, but I think only because I was imagining how Chris must have been feeling about it all, a couple of hours later. I knew that he had probably cooled off and was being incredibly romantic and sensitive to Isabelle out of a sense of guilt and acknowledgement of what could have been lost.

I had just finished brushing my teeth when he knocked on the door. I knew instantly that it had to be Chris, and I had no doubt as to the reason he was there. He wanted to clear the air and not leave any awkwardness between us. Before I even made it to the door and looked through the peephole to confirm it was him, I was so grateful that he was there. I couldn't stand the idea of losing him from my life once more.

I opened the door and he was standing there with a hand-held stereo, a bottle of champagne, and two glasses. "Sorry about Yoko."

I immediately cracked up with laughter, hearing him refer to her that way. "It's okay. Whether or not I like it, this is her wedding, and if she doesn't want me there, I shouldn't be there. Come in, come in." He walked in and I shut the door behind him. "She didn't, umm...she didn't know, did she?"

"Oh no. She didn't have a clue. She just noticed that my attention wasn't 100% focused on her, and that wouldn't do, I suppose." I could tell he was angry with her, and I was too, though of course he and I were the ones who were so in the wrong.

I wanted to lighten the mood and get on with the part of the evening where Chris and I ensured that our friendship was still solid and would survive this latest bit of drama. "So, what's with the boom box, you hipster you?"

He smiled a smile of pure adolescent delight. "I made you a mix tape."

"Ha! You what?" Every time I thought I had Christopher Dean all figured out...

"Yes. You see," he walked to an outlet and plugged in the stereo, "knowing you were going to be at the wedding, and therefore at the reception, I realized that I had a very rare opportunity and I fully intended to make the most of it. But since you've been cordially uninvited, I had to make other arrangements." He turned to me. "You and I have never danced together."

I cleared my throat. "Hmm... See, I'm not sure if

you remember, but we actually used to be partners in a sport called ice dancing. Some people thought we were quite good at it..."

He smiled at me but was not deterred. "I mean, on a non-slippery surface, wearing shoes, not blades. Just regular old dancing."

I thought for a moment. "Is that really possible? Have we really never danced together?"

"Not even once," he shook his head.

"So you thought your wedding reception was as good a time as any to give it a go, and you made a mix tape for the occasion?"

"Yes," he said succinctly, as if it all made perfect sense. And somehow it did.

"Well, then," I reached down and moved a small coffee table out of the way. "Let's see what kind of damage we can do."

He pushed play on the cassette player, and the opening of *Bolero* began. I started laughing as he got down into the opening position, on his knees. I pushed him over, and he started laughing too. "Okay, just kidding. Let's get serious." He stood up and forwarded the tape to the next song, and things got very serious very quickly.

My breath caught in my throat. "I thought this song was retired forever," I said as I listened to the opening melody of "Vienna."

"Who said that? I never said that." He smiled innocently as he put his hand on my waist and pulled me to him.

We discovered very quickly that we weren't as graceful without our skates, but that just made it even more fun. He twirled me around the room, and we talked and we laughed about things that had once been so painful. The passage of time had done that magical thing that only it can do - it had softened all of the edges of the past.

Somehow, each time we went through hell and back together, Chris and I, we came out on the other side more bonded together and caring more about each other than we'd ever thought possible. This time was no exception. I held onto him, so grateful that after the

253

disaster of the evening, after very nearly ruining his relationship with the woman he was marrying in thirty-four hours, after very nearly ending the friendship which had survived so much, against all odds, over the last thirteen years, we were there, together, and we had survived another storm.

But then, irrationally and irresponsibly, and in a way that was almost beyond our control, we stopped dancing and he kissed me again - this time softly and gently. And it could have stopped there. It could have been a farewell to that part of our lives, a tender send-off to something which had meant so much to us both. But unlike on the balcony, he didn't leave it up to me, not that I would have done anything differently. And I realized then that Chris had not been having the thoughts of guilt and regret that I had imagined him to be having.

Without saying a word, he walked away and turned off the music. Then he dimmed the lights before walking to the door and locking it. Then, never taking his eyes off of mine, he walked back to me, kissed me again, took my hand in his, and we walked hand-in-hand to the bed, where we spent the next twelve hours, making up for lost time and storing up for the uncertain future.

32. SHAMELESS

We dozed intermittently throughout the night, but we probably got a total of only four or five hours of sleep. Each time we awoke, we talked - not about serious things, not about the consequences of our actions or how Chris was going to respond to Isabelle's inevitable questioning regarding his whereabouts all night. We talked about random things. Memories we shared, television shows, books, breakfast cereal. And we laughed. We were happy and carefree, though we had no right to be. And each time, after we talked and laughed, we were in each other's arms again, and then we would sleep. We repeated this pattern all night long and through much of the morning.

When I finally awoke for the day, it was 10:00 in the morning. Chris was no longer in bed beside me, but I knew he was still there. I smiled as I climbed out of bed, knowing that he was going to be wearing the infamous copper-colored dress shirt which was clearly my Kryptonite. I remembered the morning after our first time, walking into my kitchen in Simsbury and seeing him in that shirt, which had been so neatly pressed and tucked into his jeans the night before. The morning after, it was wrinkled and untucked, and one less button was buttoned at the top, and he couldn't have possibly looked any sexier than he had in that moment.

I was expecting to see him all cool and casual again, but the sight when I exited the bedroom wasn't relaxed at all. He was wearing the shirt, but it was completely unbuttoned, his khakis were on but not zipped or buttoned yet, and he had one sock on and was struggling with the other. He had just gotten out of the shower and his hair was still dripping wet. He was muttering all sorts of curse words under his breath and looking around the room, searching for something.

It was pretty funny to see the usually unflappable Mr. Dean that out of sorts, and somehow still very sexy.

"Good morning," I greeted him.

He jumped a bit. He hadn't heard me enter. "Hey, do you have a shirt that I could wear? A t-shirt or anything?"

"Chris, I don't think my shirts would fit you. Besides, I mostly brought fancy stuff. I thought I was going to a wedding." I smiled and walked over to stand behind the chair he was sitting in while he worked on his socks. I put my hands out to run my fingers through his wet hair, but he stood up just before I touched him.

Okay. I was starting to think that this morning after wasn't going to go as well as the last one had.

"Do you remember where I took off my shoes?" He was lifting the skirting on the bed with one hand and attempting to button his shirt with the other.

I giggled at his attempt - he had missed at least two buttons. "Here, let me." I walked over to him and unbuttoned the mess he had made, and though my original intent had been to then re-button for him, I really didn't want to. I held onto each side of his open shirt and looked up at him, silently begging him to kiss me.

But he didn't even look at me. He kept looking around the room for his shoes, and when he spotted them by the front door, he pulled away. "There they are." He rushed over to them and started putting them on, leaning against the door.

Tears welled up in my eyes and I begged them not to fall, though the thought occurred to me that he probably wouldn't notice if they did.

He unplugged the stereo and wrapped the cord around the handle. "Sergei should be getting here in a couple of hours. Do you want me to send him your way after the rehearsal?"

I quickly wiped away one tear that had managed to escape. "Sure. Thanks."

He walked to the door and unlocked the latch. I thought he was going to leave without even saying goodbye, but as an apparent afterthought he turned back and rushed over to me, kissed me on the cheek and said, "Sorry I have to run."

And for the very first time, I felt like the other woman. I felt like his mistress, nothing more, and I hated myself. The stupid tears fell and I couldn't face him, so I ran into the bedroom, shut the door and locked it.

He was about five seconds behind me, knocking on the door. "What's wrong? Let me in."

How could I have been so stupid? Don't get me wrong, I don't think I had any unrealistic expectations about what was happening between us. I knew he was still going to marry Isabelle in twenty-four hours, and I knew that we would each move on with our lives, but I had really thought that the last twelve hours had meant as much to him as they had to me. Yes, the sex was fantastic, as we both knew it would be, but it somehow, in the end, wasn't supposed to have been about sex. The music, and the dancing, and the tenderness...had it really all been about one last torrid fling before he took a vow of fidelity?

"Abigail, open the door. I have to go, but I would really like to know that you are okay before I do."

I threw my wad of tissues at the door, like *that* would show him. "Don't worry about me," I said through my sobs. "I'm fine."

He sighed, "You don't sound fine. Please tell me what's wrong. Please."

I kept crying. "I'm just so stupid. And once again I was playing around with big girl, grown-up emotions and circumstances that I had no right to mess with." I didn't even know what I was saying. I wanted him to go. I wanted him to stay. I just wanted him, and I wanted him to want me.

I could picture him on the other side of the door - running his hand through his hair, looking at his watch, beginning to lose his patience with me and very much on the verge of just walking out, as he had always done when he was frustrated with me. I knew that was probably best, because I couldn't picture myself getting composed enough to face him anytime real soon.

"You do know that I have no idea what you're talking about, don't you? I'm a man, Abigail. I'm afraid you may have to spell it out for me."

I spoke quietly and hesitantly. "You just kissed me on the cheek and said, 'Sorry I have to run.'"

That hadn't cleared it up for him at all. "Well, I *am* sorry I have to run."

I took a quick moment to mentally lecture myself and tell myself to grow up, and put Chris's needs before my own. Then I took a deep breath and walked to the door, unlocked it, and turned the knob. He was leaning against the frame of the door, but he stood up straight and crossed his arms as I removed the wooden barrier between us. "I'm sorry, Chris. It's probably just the lack of sleep making me emotional." I deliberately looked at the clock on the wall for effect. "Oh, look at the time. I'm sorry. You need to get going."

He didn't budge. "Are you going to tell me the truth?"

I blew my nose. "About what?"

And then he officially got frustrated with me, and started running his hand through his hair. "Don't do this, Abigail. Don't ruin our goodbye."

Well, that set me off and I lost my composure. "Excuse me? Don't ruin our goodbye? Didn't you already do that by doing all you could to get away from me as quickly as possible? You did everything but promise to call me next time you're in town on business, Chris!"

He stared at me for several seconds without reacting or saying a word. And then, "That's what you think? That I think of you as my mistress or something?"

"Well, technically speaking, isn't that what I am?"

He growled at me. He was angry. I didn't expect that. "Really, Abigail? After thirteen years of pouring my heart out to you and all we have been through together, you still don't get it, do you?"

Chris and I had never had any problem having a good shouting match when the occasion arose, but it had been a very long time since we had. And in that moment, I felt something different from every other time we had fought. I knew that I was going to see this argument through to the end, but I also didn't want to fight with him. And that was the difference. I had always enjoyed our fights, strangely, and I think he had too. They amused us, and they had always represented the passion between us. This fight was different, already. I knew that there was no way we both walked out of this fight without someone being damaged, and I was willing to do whatever I had to do to make sure it wasn't him.

And that realization resulted in another. *Damn it*, I thought to myself as I realized I was still in love with him. He was the one I wanted to be with, not for the night, but for the rest of my life. Our bad timing had reached a new low.

I forced myself to stifle everything I was feeling and everything I wanted to say to him. I knew him. I knew that if I frustrated him enough, he would walk away. He would go to his brunch, his rehearsal, and his wedding. His honeymoon. And then he would call me in a few weeks and we would start rebuilding our friendship. Again.

"Look, Chris…" I wanted to tell him I loved him. "Like you said so long ago, let's call a spade a spade." I wanted to beg him not to marry Isabelle. "The sex is great, but it is what it is. At the end of the day, it was just sex, and like I said, I think I'm just exhausted. Let's not make a big deal out of this." I wanted to beg him to marry me instead.

He stared at me in disbelief. "Just sex?" he muttered, bewildered and hurt. "You don't really feel that way."

"I care about you. You know that." He looked at me like he wasn't buying it - I had taken my disinterest too far and had to reel it back in. I smiled. "I mean, you're one of the most important people in the world to me. You always have been and you always will be. And I will always be grateful for this time that we had together. But now," I looked at the clock again, "will you please go? You may actually miss your own wedding rehearsal."

He still didn't budge. "I don't believe you."

"Well, just look at the clock yourself, then..."

"You know what I mean." He closed the gap between us and firmly grabbed my arms and pulled me to him. "Don't act like last night didn't mean...everything."

And I could continue the facade no longer. Tears rolled down my cheeks again. "Why not? You acted like it meant nothing."

He groaned, and he kept his grip on my arms. "I'm so tired of it, Abigail." He spoke through gritted teeth. "I'm so tired of you being everything. When you aren't in my life, I'm better by the world's standards. I function, which is something I can't seem to do when you're around. But it's empty. Completely empty. Every emotion I feel and every action I take is half-hearted at best. All I do is function. I don't laugh. I don't live. I don't love. And I'm tired of it, Abigail. I have tried to purge you from my heart time and again, and it's useless. My heart only exists to love you."

And within seconds, all attempts at composure on both sides were eradicated, and we collapsed to the floor in a flurry of hands and lips and torn clothes.

««§»»

"Well, I think you're officially late," I whispered to him a half-hour later as we lay on the floor, covered only in a sheet we had pulled off the bed.

He pulled me closer to him and kissed me. "I don't care."

I put my head on his chest and looked up at him. "This is bad, Chris. Really bad. Right about now, Yoko is probably forming a search party to look for you."

He put his hand in my hair and played with my curls, something he hadn't done since the café in Vienna. "I don't care."

I laughed. "But you *will* care. You will care when she somehow finds out where I'm staying and she puts two and two together and shows up at my door, and she sees you wearing the same shirt you were wearing last night, only now it's missing a few buttons. Then you'll care."

He sighed. "Yes. Then I will care."

"So, come on. We have to get up."

He grumbled like a little boy who didn't want to go to school but he got up, and another twenty minutes later - after he convinced me that we both had to shower anyway, so we may as well save time and water - we were finally getting dressed.

I decided to go down to the lobby and offer any man roughly Chris's size as much money as I had to in order to get him a shirt, and it worked. I actually rounded him up a very nice light blue dress shirt and a dark blue tie, and with his slightly wrinkled but otherwise fine khakis and tan leather shoes, he looked ready for brunch. And it only cost me a few bucks and an autograph.

As he prepared to leave, things were much different than they had been an hour earlier. He kissed me endlessly, and he held me and he wiped away my tears.

"Chris," I whispered, "I'm going to ask you something, and I want you to just tell me the truth. I know you are getting married tomorrow. I know that you do love Isabelle. I know that this can't happen again. But, I just have to ask."

"Of course. Ask me anything you want."

I took a deep breath. "I'm not asking you to, but if I did ask you to not marry Isabelle, and I asked you to marry me instead, honestly, what would you say? I know that's a rotten thing to even think about, but for some reason I just have to know -"

He cut me off with a kiss. "Honestly?" I nodded. "Well, I think I would say, 'Don't move from this spot. I'll be right back.' And I would go have a very difficult conversation, and then I would come right back here and carry you back to bed."

"Really?" Why did I have to ask? I broke down crying again and he held me tightly. We both knew I wouldn't ask that of him, but I knew his answer was sincere. I had to force myself to view it as an answer to a question rather than an offer.

"Actually, no," he said after several seconds of

silence. "Close but not exactly. I would take you with me. I think maybe I've finally learned my lesson on that one. If I left you here, there's no telling who would sneak their way in while I was gone. I'm pretty sure I wouldn't ever let you out of my sight again." He smiled, trying to keep it light, but I understood every single unspoken emotion. And though it was an awkward subject to broach, I thought of something he needed to know. I needed him to know that in all of our years apart, no one had ever meant to me what he did.

"You're still the only man I've ever been with," I said softly.

Love and sadness overtook his face at the same time. "I wish I could be the only one forever," he whispered.

I was overwhelmed by how much I wished that too. "You and I will survive this," I said resolutely. "I know that there is absolutely nothing in the world that can tear us apart. And maybe we can't have it all, for whatever stupid reason that seems to be the case, but we'll find a way to have enough."

Chris smiled a sad smile. "Hey, we survived Kennedy, and a volcano, and a miscarriage, and the Cold War!" We laughed together at the memories of our ridiculous past. "What's a little thing like my marriage?"

"Exactly."

We stared at each other, knowing we had more to say, but also knowing that there was nothing that could be said which wasn't already known.

Well, maybe there was one thing. I had never put it into words before - at least not to him. "I love you, Chris. I am so desperately in love with you, and I'm sorry it took me so long to figure it out."

"Timing." Chris bit his lip to control the emotion. He pulled me to him for one last kiss, and then with his lips nearly touching mine and his eyes never leaving mine for a moment, he said, "You are the great love of my life, Abigail Phelps. Never forget that."

And then the man I loved left me to make amends with the woman who would soon be his wife.

Here's a sneak peek at

SCENES FROM
HIGHLAND FALLS,

Book Two in the Abigail Phelps Series

AVAILABLE NOW!

And don't forget:
The greatest advertisement is word of mouth.
Please consider leaving a review on Amazon and
any other site where you see fit.

Join the Abigail Phelps Fan Page on Facebook:
www.facebook.com/abigailphelpsseries

Join the Bethany Turner Fan Page on Facebook:
www.facebook.com/seebethanywrite

Follow Bethany Turner on Twitter:
@BTLiteraryStuff

Abigail Phelps Series site: www.abbyphelps.com

Bethany Turner site: www.seebethanywrite.com

Thank you for being a part of Abby's world.

TURN AROUND

There was no point in wondering what I could have done differently. There were a million things, and I was fully aware of them all. I could have asked him to stay, then or any other time in our history when I had let him walk out of my life. I put my shoes on and grabbed my purse eight different times, ready to run out the door and stop him from marrying her. But each time, I stopped. What we had said was true: Chris and I would be fine. He would still be in my life.

I know that in the movies the guy always marries the right girl. If I were writing the script for *Chris and Abby*, that's how it would have gone. Just like in all of the best romantic comedies, and the worst ones too, I would have run to brunch and crashed the party. No, more dramatically, I would have thought about it all night long, crying and remembering all of the good times. A girlfriend would have come to the hotel room and convinced me that I couldn't let Chris - my partner, in so many ways the other half of me - marry the cold, bitter French woman. And I would have shown up at the wedding (maybe while they stood at the altar, but probably before the wedding while Chris put the finishing touches on his tie, just before the wedding planner knocked on the door and said it was time) and I would have told him all the things I should have been telling him for thirteen years. I would have told him that I wanted him, and only him, and if he still decided to marry Isabelle, I would understand, but I just had to try. And he would have taken me in his arms and kissed me, and because the movie is called *Chris and Abby*, we would have had sex right there on the floor, and that would have been the end. Sure, dozens upon dozens of wedding gifts would have been awkwardly abandoned, and a couple hundred people would have flown to Paris for nothing, and the cold, bitter French woman would have had her heart broken, but you never see that part.

In real life, for some reason, that part is all you can think about. A man doesn't just abandon his fiancée at the altar. At least the kind of man worth having doesn't. And Christopher Dean was a man worth having.

I didn't want to be alone, primarily because I didn't trust myself to stay put, but I didn't know anyone in the entire country who wasn't at the brunch. I picked up the phone and made an international call to Los Angeles.

Talia Balsam picked up after the first ring, and I was taken off-guard. I had sort of momentarily forgotten that my best friend's wife existed.

"Um, hi Talia. This is Abby. Abby Phelps. Is George available by chance?"

She sounded disinterested, as she had every time I had ever spoken with her. "No, he's not."

I needed to talk to George. My voice started wavering. "Talia, please, I just need to talk to him."

"Sorry, Abby, he's really not here. He's filming a pilot." She paused for a moment. "Are you okay?"

"Will you please tell him I called? No, actually, never mind. I'm traveling so he wouldn't have any way of getting in touch with me anyway." I didn't know who else I could call. "He's really not there, right? You're not just saying that?"

She sighed, "Abby, I don't have a problem with you and George being friends. Really I don't. I just don't happen to like you very much personally, but I'm not going to stand in the way of your friendship."

I couldn't help but smile. "Well, that actually makes me feel a little better. I'm not crazy about you either."

She laughed. "I know. I'll let him know you called. Take care, Abby."

I held the phone in my hand, wondering who else I could call. I mean, there were people I could have called, but my emotional breakdown on this one wasn't going to be pretty. It wasn't the time for the faint of heart.

I briefly considered calling John, though I knew there would be nothing positive or healthy to come from it, but thankfully I was interrupted by a knock on the door. The screenwriter in me quickly realized that I hadn't considered that scenario. He could come running back to me. I ran to the door and threw it open, butterflies in my stomach, not allowing myself to fully imagine the Happily Ever After which kept trying to take over my stream of consciousness.

It was a very good thing that I had already been lecturing myself that this wasn't a romantic comedy: this was real life. Had I been counting on the romantic reunion as the credits rolled, I would have been sorely disappointed. Instead, I was thrilled to see Sergei standing in the doorway.

He opened his arms to me, but the expression on his face wasn't one of joyful reunion, it was one of comfort and sharing in my sorrow. Chris had told him. I snuggled into my friend and the emotional breakdown began. He let me cry until the tears ran dry.

I knew that the wedding rehearsal was in progress at that very moment, but I didn't have to ask what Sergei was doing there. My mind went back in time to just after Hyannis Port, when George suddenly appeared before my eyes, as arranged by the man who loved me so much, even then. I could have no doubt that Chris had worked his magic once more.

"How is he?" I asked Sergei. He had seen him since I had, and I desperately needed a progress report.

We sat on the floor, propped up on pillows against the wall in one little corner of the hotel suite.

Sergei sighed, "He is sad just like you are sad."

I think in that moment, I realized for the first time just how much I had matured, because there was nothing inside of me that was happy to know he missed me enough to be sad. I didn't want him to be sad. If I was sad, that was okay. I wanted him to be happy - that was what mattered. And yet I knew that he would be thinking of me when he kissed his bride, and that just wasn't how it was supposed to be.

I know I had matured, but even more than that, I think I loved maturely for the first time. I had never felt such unconditional, selfless love as I felt for Chris, and I knew that his love for me was just as true, just as strong, just as selfless. He had been anxiously awaiting his friend Sergei's arrival. The rest of his groomsmen and ushers consisted of Isabelle's brother Paul, Isabelle's cousin Lloyd whom he had met once, and two Duchesnay family friends whom he had never met at all. Sergei was his choice, the person he was going to lean on throughout the wedding festivities. And he had sent him to me.

I got up on my knees next to Sergei. "Sergei, you have to go back to him. Tell him that I am sad, but strong, and I am leaving Paris this afternoon. And tell him that I hope he has a wonderful day tomorrow and I will be thinking of him. Please."

"You are leaving Paris?" I was amazed at how much his English had improved, but his Russian dialect was still very strong of course.

"I think so. There's no reason to stay."

"Yes there is reason to stay! We are to visit with each other." He looked hurt. I had totally forgotten that he and I were planning three days in Paris together after Chris left for his honeymoon.

I looked at Sergei and was filled with such affection. He was no longer the teenage boy I had taken to the Statue of Liberty, neither of us understanding a word the other said. He was a twenty-four-year-old man, and though I still felt very naturally protective of him, I knew that our friendship would be different now. It was time to start viewing him less like a little brother and more like a peer. He knew the general story of Chris and me, but it was time to really let him in and not guard him from all of the more adult subject matters Chris and I had always kept from him in the past.

"Well, okay, I'll stay. But I've got to check into

another room." I stood up and put my hands down to help him stand as well.

He looked around the room as he stood. "Why? This room is very nice."

"Yeah, it's nice, but Chris and I had sex everywhere!"

He looked shocked, but only momentarily, and then he very comically looked down at the floor where he had just been sitting, with a look of mock disgust on his face. We both started laughing and I knew I was right. Sergei wasn't a kid anymore.

Bethany Turner was born and raised in Kentucky, but now lives in Colorado with her husband and two sons. She studied theatre at the University of Kentucky before going on to a career in bank management, which eventually gave way to writing. She finally knows what she wants to be when she grows up. Visit www.seebethanywrite.com.

Made in the USA
Lexington, KY
15 October 2015